Lineberger Memorial
Library

Lutheran Theological Southern Seminary   Columbia, S. C.

All We Know of Heaven

All We Know
of Heaven

❖ ❖ ❖

Rémy Rougeau

Houghton Mifflin Company

Boston · New York

2001

For information about permission to reproduce selections
from this book, write to Permissions, Houghton Mifflin Company,
215 Park Avenue South, New York, New York 10003.

Visit our Web site: www.houghtonmifflinbooks.com.

Library of Congress Cataloging-in-Publication Data
Rougeau, Rémy.
All we know of heaven / Rémy Rougeau.
p.   cm.
ISBN 0-618-09499-7
1. Monastic and religious life—Fiction.
2. Cistercians—Fiction. 3. Young men—Fiction.
4. Manitoba—Fiction. 5. Monks—Fiction. I. Title.
PS3568.O882 A45 2001
813'.6—dc21   00-066977

The chapters "Signs and Wonders" and "Cello" first appeared,
in slightly different form, in the North Dakota Quarterly
and the Atlantic Monthly, respectively. Material that was later incorporated
into this book was first published, in other forms, in Image: A Journal
of the Arts & Religion (a story entitled "Saints of the Desert") and
the New Quarterly (a story entitled "Monsieur Flaubert"). Grateful
acknowledgment is made to these publications.

Printed in the United States of America

QUM 10 9 8 7 6 5 4 3 2 1

*For the Cistercian monks in Manitoba with whom
the author lived and worked for six years*

*And for the Benedictine monks with whom
he lives and works today*

Acknowledgments

The author wishes to acknowledge with gratitude the help and inspiration he received from Brother Alban Petesch, Brother Aaron Jensen, and Jane Catherine Voglewede.

The author also wishes to acknowledge and thank Jessica Treadway and Andre Dubus III for the aid and encouragement they so generously provided. Thanks are due, also, to Leslie Lawrence, Ralph Lombreglia, James Carroll and Alexandra Marshall for reviewing sections of this book and coaching the author in the craft of writing, and to fellow students at Emerson College with whom the author shared workshops.

Finally, the author is deeply grateful to his agent, Richard Parks, and to his editor, Eamon Dolan.

All We Know of Heaven

1

Signs and Wonders

The lady sitting next to Paul Seneschal asked if he was an American. He shook his head, then looked down at his shirt and back at the woman. Why, Paul wondered, did she think him an American when he was dressed like anyone else on the train? Was it something about his face? She smoothed brittle hair at the nape of her neck and Paul could see that her hands were stained with dime-sized spots.

"Spiro Agnew resigned," she said. "That's the only reason I inquire." She pursed her lips.

"Who's he?" Paul asked, scratching his ear lobe. The lady leaned toward him.

"You're not very old, are you?" she said.

"Nineteen."

She allowed herself a puckered smile. "Shame on you. You're old enough to be interested in news developments. Agnew was the vice president of the USA, but his misbehavior brought him down. Others will follow, we can hope. Where are you headed?"

"Winnipeg."

"So am I," she said. "I've lived there all my life, on King Edward Street."

Paul was short. A mop of black hair nearly covered his ears.

With the lady's gaze fixed firmly upon him, his large brown eyes wandered from the window to the lady and back again.

"You don't look nineteen," she said. "More like fourteen. Do you have relatives in Winnipeg?"

"No."

"I see. Well then, certainly you don't live by yourself. Perhaps you're off to college?"

"I'm from St. Jean-Baptiste," he said, "forty minutes south of here."

Paul shifted in his seat. His watch was slow, but he knew the train was due in soon. From the window an early October landscape rolled by. Endless flat land was dressed in yellow and orange. Trees lifted their gray branches into the air. Rows of ripe sunflowers hung their black heads mournfully beside fields of stubble. The lady cleared her throat. When Paul looked at her she was rearranging the contents of her purse.

"You speak French, then?" she asked.

He nodded, but she was not looking at him.

"Of course, you're not obliged to *answer* me," she said. "I'm just an old lady, and I assure you that old ladies are accustomed to being ignored."

Paul kept his eyes on her but hardly knew what to say. She wadded a Kleenex and jammed it into a corner of the purse.

"You're shy," she said. "But you'll learn to get over that and keep up a healthy conversation."

"I want to become a monk," he said.

"Excuse me?"

"A monk. At the Cistercian abbey in St. Norbert, south of Winnipeg."

The lady blinked. "Oh," she said. "Why would anyone do that?"

"To find meaning in life," Paul responded.

"Oh dear," she said, and became mute.

At the Winnipeg station, people rushed about while a loud-speaker announced arrivals in English and French. Paul carried his satchel to a yellow cab and crawled into the back seat. He waited while the driver finished a cigarette.

"Where to?" the driver asked.

"St. Norbert. The Cistercian abbey."

"The cistern what?" the driver asked, flicking his live cigarette butt onto the pavement. Paul had been through this before.

"Take 42," he said, "and beyond the Perimeter about two miles you'll see a street sign on the right that reads RUE DES TRAPPISTES. Go down that road to the gate."

The man drove off with a clean screech of his wheels. Not a word was exchanged as he sped along city avenues. When they passed the University of Manitoba the car radio squawked, but the man did not answer it. Soon, the cab was south of the city perimeter near the Red River, where high-rises no longer obstructed the view, businesses vanished, and houses moved back from the street, making room for front yards. All the while, the taxi meter brought up higher numbers with a brisk little whir. Paul opened his wallet. Before long, they were heading into open farm country along a gravel road while Paul counted bills. The cabdriver hit his brakes and stopped in a cloud of dust. Before them a wrought-iron gate blocked the road, and large letters formed an arch above it that read SIC TRANSIT GLORIA MUNDI. A white house stood to the left of the gate, and Paul saw nothing beyond it but tall elm trees in yellow foliage. An iron fence ran to the left and to the right, protecting both the house and the old elms from the road. The cabdriver turned to his passenger.

"What is this? A cemetery?" he asked.

Paul shook his head and counted out bills of various colors.

"Don't look like a soul around here," the driver said. The place did look abandoned. Paul got out of the cab, and a minute later found himself alone in a cloud of dust that followed, like a long tail, the disappearing cab. He pulled his jacket collar up. Elm leaves fell through the air and a smell of rotten pumpkin came from inside the gate. He picked up his satchel and went to push a black doorbell at the entrance to the house.

Several minutes passed before a stout monk appeared. His head was shaved. A black scapular fell from his shoulders to his knees over a white robe that was discolored with use around the hip pockets. Under the skin of his nose, a network of tiny veins ran like circuits.

"Ah *oui*," he said, and turned without another word. He walked down a dark hall and Paul followed him inside, asking a question in precise French.

"Will I have the same room as last time, Brother Henri?"

"*Oui*," the monk said as he opened the door of a small chamber. No sooner had Paul placed the satchel inside the room than a clear pitch met his ear, ringing brightly. He recognized it as the sound of a metal clapper against a bell.

"Ah," the monk said as he hammered the face of his wristwatch. "Come, come." He waved impatiently for Paul to follow. They left the house from a second door, this time within the enclosure of the gate, and walked up a road through the trees.

The monk put his hood up over his head. "This time, you are coming to join?" he whispered. He spoke French without formal pronouns, and Paul was freshly amused by the clipped pronunciation.

"No," he answered. "But very soon, I hope."

"Then, for Vespers, is necessary you still sit outside the cloister by yourself, upstairs. Tomorrow, novice master come visit you at breakfast."

Beyond the trees, a large building became visible; from its fieldstone foundation blond brick rose high into the air and formed a series of arched clerestory windows. The church had a solid, heavy appearance. The bell tower, anchored in the middle of the structure, was capped by a large silver dome, and the tolling that came from it grew louder as they drew near. Paul had to cover his ears.

The monk pushed a heavy door and led the way up a narrow stairwell to the balcony. As they reached the top of the stairs, the bell stopped, its echo died away, and Paul could hear Brother Henri's labored breathing. Beyond the loft railing, what Paul could see of the vaulted nave reminded him of a high forest canopy.

"Thank you," he whispered. The monk nodded and left. The church was silent, and Paul sat for a while, looking about. A sweet smoke hung in the air like the remnant of a cedar fire, and rosy evening light warmed the windows, tinting the blank white walls. The glass was bright. Running his hand along the wooden bench, he noticed dust.

Because Paul knew what to expect, he got up and moved to the railing; below, forty monks stood in silent attention, facing away from him like the ceramic guards of an emperor's tomb. He smiled. A lean voice from the choir began to sing in fluid notes.

"Deus, in adiutórium meum inténde."

The choir of monks responded in Latin, and the church was awash in unhurried melody from the Middle Ages. Paul wondered if music was the thing that brought him to the abbey. Liturgy in his hometown church was not smooth and solemn. His parish priest spoke the Mass, and it plodded forward like a courtroom proceeding. But here, Latin chant and incense made of the worship something mysterious and pure. He closed his eyes and listened.

That night, he woke to the ringing of the church bell. Without looking at the clock, Paul knew it was half past three. The monks were at Vigils. He did not rise and dress, but neither could he fall back to sleep; he had forgotten about the scratchy bedsheets. The house carried a vague smell of ammonia: that he had forgotten, too. Nonetheless, he felt content. Quiet hours of the morning seemed clean at the abbey, free of radio jingles and the smell of burnt toast.

He slept again and woke to the buzz of his alarm clock and dressed quickly. The sun had not yet risen. Off he went through the trees to morning prayers, and then to eat breakfast in the church basement, outside the cloister of the monks.

Five men sat at a table eating pancakes in a cellar room. Paul had seen two of them before. All were guests at the abbey, men who drifted about the country and stopped there for food and a place to sleep. Some of them worked for their keep, doing odd jobs for the monks, then traveled on. A short, toothless man wore a cap at the table. Three others had oily clothes on, and the breakfast table smelled of diesel fuel. All of them ate in silence, syrup dripping from their mouths. The toothless man pointed at the pitcher of milk and wiped his mouth on his sleeve; when it was passed, he poured a glass, drank quickly, then rose and left the room. Paul took a plate of food.

After the men finished and left, the basement was quiet except for groans from a coffeepot connected to a wall socket. Paul finished his pancakes. He was about to leave when the door opened and a thin monk entered the room. He was the same height as Paul. This was Father Yves-Marie, the novice master.

"Good to see you again," Yves-Marie said in French. He smiled with pleasant energy. His head was shaved, just like Brother Henri's, and his pink, scrubbed face bore no lines or wrinkles that might indicate how old he was. His forehead was narrow. Rimless spectacles magnified his irises. And with a small nose, his head seemed only a pair of eyes.

Paul was full of questions. "How is Brother Eli?" he asked.

Yves-Marie scratched his head. "How do you know Eli?" he

asked. "The infirmary is inside the enclosure, and few of us have permission to speak with guests."

Paul smiled. "Last time I visited, Eli was pushing a wheelbarrow near the gatehouse, and he got angry when I spoke to him."

"That's encouraging," Yves-Marie said. "He himself is usually talking when he's not supposed to. What happened then? Did you respect his need for silence?"

Paul shook his head. "No, that wasn't it. He was angry because I spoke in English. Even after I switched to French, he shook his fist at me. I was really frightened for a moment. But he looked far too old to be pushing a wheelbarrow, and too old to hurt me."

"Yes, he is," Yves-Marie answered. "And he's doing poorly, I'm sad to report. He won't be pushing wheelbarrows. Not for a while, at least. Did it disturb you, that a monk should raise a fist?"

Paul smiled. "Part of what attracts me to this place," he said, "is that everyone seems so interesting. Take Brother Henri at the gatehouse. He's not pious. He's not boring at all. And there's something very attractive about him."

They continued to talk while Father Yves-Marie led Paul through the church basement and out into the morning sunlight. "Henri has been a monk for many years," he said. "Like us all, he has seen many trials. If you wish to be a monk, you must prepare yourself for a life that is not always peaceful."

They walked from the abbey down a gravel road. Trees shaded them on either side. To the right, beyond the rows of elm, fields of sweet corn had been harvested and all that remained were dry stalks with their paper leaves rustling in a light breeze. The dairy barn stood at the end of the road, an eight-minute walk from the abbey, and Paul could hear the cows bellowing inside the barn, creating an echo.

"What kind of work would I do here," Paul asked, "if I came to join you?"

"Everything that we do," Yves-Marie answered. "We have the dairy, where several monks work. We also have beef cattle, chickens, and hogs on two thousand acres of LaSalle river bottom, some of which is cultivated every year. Then, of course, there are the vegetable gardens, the orchard, bees, and cheese making, not to mention the housekeeping and cooking. You'd be given various assignments until you'd found your place."

Paul was springing alongside the calm monk. "I think I want to bake bread," he said. "I want to work in the bakery."

"All in good time," Yves-Marie said.

Walking in front of the massive dairy, they avoided puddles in the gravel road. Across from them stood an old horse barn; hundreds of chickens were housed there instead of horses, and Paul could hear clucking and fussing, a chorus of nervous voices on the edge of disturbance. Further on was a forge, a pig barn and a granary. They headed off toward the pig barn, then took a different road back to the abbey.

"Father Yves-Marie, do you think the Abbot will allow me to enter the abbey if I ask him?"

"I don't know," he answered. "You're very young. We prefer that candidates wait until they are at least twenty-one."

As they strolled past a potato field, Paul saw two monks using sign language; they looked like deaf-mutes consulting each other about the cost of vegetables. Yves-Marie did not seem to notice. He was looking up at the sky.

"What do your parents think of your wanting to live here?" he asked.

"My parents don't understand anything," Paul said. "I told my father about the sign language you use, to speak as little as possible at the abbey, and he told Mother that the monks take a vow of silence. That's not true, of course. You've already explained that to me. And when Mother asked me what a monk does, I made the mistake of telling her that they meet in the church eight times a day for prayer. I tried to tell her about the farm, too, but by then she wasn't listening. My parents think this life is unbalanced, too holy for normal people."

They crossed the road at the end of the potato field and stopped. From there, Paul could see the church at a new angle, and the monastery behind it. The two were of a piece. The monks' quarters rose upon the same fieldstone foundation, built of the same brick and sharing the same arched windows. Three stories high, the monastery was crowned with a series of dormer windows set upon a mansard roof. The architecture plainly showed that the life of monks was inseparable from what went on inside the church, back and forth, their quotidian affairs melting into liturgy.

Before moving on, Yves-Marie and Paul waited for an old monk to pass on the road. He walked toward the withered garden of late autumn with twelve pigs following him like dogs.

Paul lived as a guest among the Cistercians for a week and almost did not want to return home. School was scheduled to start, however, and on a Greyhound bus he returned to St. Jean-Baptiste. He walked into the house and felt as though he had returned from a foreign country: the television seemed a very odd contraption. A newscaster spoke of a ban on oil exports to the United States, imposed by Arab nations after the outbreak of an Arab-Israeli war. After that, he heard nothing else in French or English except Nixon Nixon Nixon. His mother switched off the television set and shrugged.

"Dull," she said. "The news, it bores me."

She spoke with a cigarette in her mouth. Smoke curled about her head as she returned to cleaning and painting her nails. Madame Seneschal was fat. She was also the mayor of her little town by the almost unanimous vote of its 288 citizens. "And I don't want to hear about monks," she said. "Finish your school first."

"I'm tired of school."

Madame Seneschal took the cigarette out of her mouth and looked at him. "Do you remember Lizotte from down the street? He consulted God about you," she said.

"Lizotte?"

"René Lizotte, the husband of Marie on the corner with the big tree in the yard, the one they call charismatic. You know him. He speaks to God in a tongue only God can understand. He asked me about you and I told him about the monks. Lizotte became excited and said he will ask for a *fleece* for you. 'A fleece?' I asked. He tried to explain to me. A sign from God, I think he means."

"A sign? Why do I need a sign?"

The cigarette was in her mouth again and she painted her nails with deft little strokes. "He thinks you need a sign," she said. "I told him, 'Good. Let's have a sign.' I need a sign — the right sign — because me, I know God wants me to have grandchildren. And grandchildren won't happen with no monk in the family."

Early the next morning, Paul climbed into the family's Oldsmobile Delta and drove south with his father. They followed the Red River to the United States border and into Minnesota. Here and there they saw combines harvesting fields of sunflowers. The cool air smelled of burning sugar from beet-processing plants farther downriver.

Omer Seneschal was small. Wisps of brown hair grew above his ears, and his eyes were large and sad. He spoke French with an English accent and English with a French accent. Besides renting one thousand acres of farmland, he made a living as a crop insurance man.

"Why not go to a Winnipeg school next year?" he asked. "Then we'll see you more often."

Paul kept his eyes on the road. "It's a better university in Minnesota," he said, but truthfully he wanted to quit school altogether. School was boring. At one time he had been excited about university studies, but economics and sociology classes taught by professors who seemed bored with their own subject damped his enthusiasm. And dormitory life was dissolute. He shared a room with a beer drinker who brought a different woman to the room each week. Paul had wanted to drop out of the university, but Madame Seneschal insisted he return for another semester.

"What do you think about the monks?" Paul asked his father. A grain truck pulled out onto the highway and rolled down the opposite lane toward them. The driver lifted a finger from the wheel. Omer waved.

"What? You mean those monks you visit? Are you serious about them? Monks are a bunch of beggars. They go from door to door, asking for money. What kind of life is that?"

"No," Paul said. "You have it all wrong, Pop. It's the opposite. They never leave the grounds. They farm for a living and give money to charity."

"Farm?"

"Yes," Paul said, feeling some pride. "They work hard. They have dairy and beef cattle, chickens, pigs, and grain crops."

Omer scratched his head and looked toward his son with sad eyes. "You can do that in St. Jean-Baptiste," he said. "You can farm *my* land if you want. Besides, if it's priesthood you're after, why not become a Jesuit? That'd be nice. A Jesuit. But a monk? What would I tell the neighbors? The boy is a *monk?* That sounds bizarre. Besides, your mother, she doesn't like the idea and she will blame me if you go."

Catholicism for Paul's parents meant fulfilling obligations. They attended Mass each Sunday. They were seen as modestly devout. He knew that Lucie, his mother, fully expected him to leave St. Jean-Baptiste one day, but she did not expect religion to carry him off. And Omer, with all his sleeping through Sunday sermons, had no sympathy for a boy who wanted to find meaning in life. Monks confused Omer. So did writers and philosophers. If Paul had wanted to be a poet, his father would have scratched his head just the same.

"Me," Omer said, "the only thing I know about monks is from *The Lives of the Saints* that Momma read me as a boy. I thought they begged. But you say they run a farm. Okay. Only thing is, you need a sign from God, don't you? In the book, a voice from heaven came to those people, telling them to do something special. You can't become a monk without a sign from God, can you?" Omer and his son remained silent the rest of the way to school.

Paul's roommate listened to a single song over and over — Roberta Flack's "The First Time Ever I Saw Your Face" — and stayed up all night smoking cigarettes while staring out the window. Bradley Eisschrank mumbled but did not engage in conversation, and generally seemed confused about his class schedule. He was fond of breath mints, or so Paul thought until empty packages of NoDoz filled the wastebasket.

School, for Paul, was no easier the second year. He found himself in classrooms with eighty students and more. Teachers were familiar only with lists of names, while teaching assistants graded students' papers. Paul did well enough, but by December he was eager for a holiday.

He took the Greyhound bus north. St. Jean-Baptiste was frozen in its corner of Manitoba with only an illusion of warmth radiating from Christmas lights everywhere. Madame Seneschal had Omer string a thousand blinking lights onto a sleigh with reindeer that ran across the eaves of the house.

"They look like mules," Omer complained while observing the display from a distance. "I never seen reindeer without antlers. And what's that thing they're pulling? A buckboard? Santa had a sleigh, not a buckboard. But I can't tell your mother anything."

As mayor, Madame Seneschal organized a pre-Christmas dinner for the town. She moved with ease among dozens of ladies cooking meat pies in the kitchen of the parish hall. They gossiped as their mothers had done in the days before television. Hungry husbands descended on the hall. Santa himself appeared with a tree and spoke to the children, and afterward Paul spent the afternoon washing dishes. He was cooling off on the icy back stoop of the church when he saw René Lizotte.

"Praise Jesus!"

Lizotte said this all the time. He was round and soft inside his orange parka. People shied away from him because he tended to hug anyone within reach.

"There you are! Paul Seneschal back from school. Paul, my man, you seen your fleece I asked for yet? I been praying for you."

For a moment Paul had to think what a fleece was: Gideon, the lamb's fleece in the Bible. A sign from God. He shook his head.

In the cold air, Lizotte's breath escaped from his nostrils like teapot steam. He came to sit down and Paul had to edge over to an unwarmed area of the stoop. He attempted to dodge Lizotte's hug but suddenly found his head wedged within a big arm's grip.

"God will send you a sign," Lizotte said.

"For what?"

"About the monks," Lizotte answered. "Whether or not God wants you to go off and join the monks. Your mother don't like the idea, I know, but praise Jesus! Wonderful! How special to be a monk."

Paul found it hard to breathe and squirmed out from under Lizotte's arm. "Why do I need a sign?" he asked. "And besides, how would I know if something is a sign from God?"

Lizotte slapped Paul on the back. "You'll know, son. Take me. I been troubled in my heart about what to do for others. Can't be selfish with Jesus. And it all come to me in a sign. I was in my pickup, driving along one day, and I seen a billboard. There it was. It said, KEEP IT BASIC: DRIVE A DODGE."

"Oh, you mean *that* kind of sign," Paul said. "I didn't know a billboard could be a sign from heaven."

Lizotte's mouth hung for a moment. "But that's the beauty of it," he said. "God's message can come from anywheres. Even advertising. Me, I just left out the Dodge part and took the rest to heart. Got home and mailed off a big check to Save the Children's Fund. Marie wasn't any too happy. That money was earmarked for a new freezer."

Lizotte stood and dusted snow from the seat of his trousers. "Turned out, though, we had enough money to get that freezer anyways. God is good with those that give. Praise Jesus, and you have yourself a good Christmas, young man."

That evening, Paul watched three hours of television, waiting for an advertisement to leap out at him, until his father wanted the TV for a hockey game. Paul was left with a vague itch. Toothpaste, cracker, potato chip, and pudding commercials caused him to stand motionless before the open refrigerator. His mother looked at him as she spoke on the phone. With a wave, she gestured for him to close the door, then covered the phone with her hand.

"What's the matter with you, eh?" she whispered. "Go outside and get some air."

He put his parka on and went out the door. The night air was brisk. Not for the first time he walked all the way to the edge of town and kept walking. He headed down a country road, hardly able to see his way on a moonless night. Away from the few street lamps and many Christmas lights of St. Jean-Baptiste, he could see the Milky Way stretched from one horizon to the other as if it were a gauze blanket protecting the earth. From a distant yard a dog barked. The ground was covered in a thin layer of snow, and as he moved through it, Paul could hear a light, sugary whisk at his boots.

He had few thoughts. Still full of the sights and sounds of television, his mind was listless in anticipation of bed and pillow, where soon he would experience the dreamy unraveling of the day's images.

Something caught his eye. The headlights of a car? No. It was a single bright light too high for the road. Paul glanced up and saw a firecracker: perhaps something shooting from a Roman candle. But he was outside of town. Who would be lighting firecrackers on a country road? The ball of fire curved gracefully toward the west, its long flaming tail licking the black sky, as if God had tossed something to earth for him to catch. The specter seemed to glide just over a grove of trees, missing it by inches, and Paul heard a vaporous hiss like water thrown upon coals. The object headed down toward the field in front of him. His pulse raced in his ears.

For an instant he imagined the meteor hitting the earth with a tremendous thud, throwing up dirt enough to bury him and the little town of St. Jean-Baptiste, but it landed without a sound not three hundred yards away. Paul could not walk any farther. He rubbed his eyes and looked again. The object had simply disappeared, and he froze as if he had just seen a flying saucer. Not knowing whether to investigate or run back to town, he stood in the middle of the road with a slack jaw and large blinking eyes.

Only when the cold sank into him did he begin to walk again, to warm himself. He went into the field but could hardly see his way. He searched until he grew stiff with cold, then went home to bed.

At first light of day, Paul returned to the field, where stubble poked through the snow like giant whiskers. Though he looked carefully, in exactly the area he thought he saw the flaming ball hit the ground, he found no evidence and his eagerness slowly turned to doubt. He kept searching, wondering all the while if he had really seen a meteor.

A pickup truck turned down the gravel road, and Paul stooped low in an effort to disappear. Embarrassment filled him. He could hear old Norrissey or Benoît Lanctôt asking his mother, the mayor, whether her son had taken a sudden interest in snow as topsoil moisture, or was he just plain lost out there in that field? But the truck raced by without slowing and disappeared, leaving Paul to continue his inspection.

At last he found a small scar along the ground, as if someone had raked a spot the size of a grave; the snow around it was pitted with ash. If this was the result of the impact, that fireball, he thought, must have been as insubstantial as a paper lantern, fallen from a Chinese theater in the sky. He shook his head.

The ground was frozen. He could not dig. Over and over again he examined the spot but found only a small stone the size of a golf ball, glassy, smooth, and black. The object looked so unlike anything else on the ground he was surprised he had not seen it straightaway.

Paul walked back to town with his prize. He examined the rock carefully, speculating on whether or not it was actually a meteor. Perhaps the stone had orbited in deep space for a million years, then fell from heaven at his feet. If such were the case, then of the several billion people on earth, Paul was privileged — chosen, as it were — to witness the descent and to collect the little stone.

He arrived home to a house full of relatives. Cousins sat around the living room television watching *Kojak* while, through the open door to the garage, the voices of his father and uncles could be heard: "Fuel intake." "No. The head bolt heater." Madame Seneschal was in the kitchen on the phone, even while participating in the conversation of five aunts standing around her. Paul thought he would suffocate. He could not turn around without running into someone.

Aunt B cornered him near the pantry and asked about studies at the university and how he intended to make use of his expensive education once he finished. "You young people are spoilt," she said. "I made a good living with only a fifth-grade education." He surprised her by letting slip that he was not going back to school. Her eyes widened. "You're what?" He was amazed by his own announcement, but he thought about his sign from heaven. He had his assurances. It was God's will. He could apply to the Cistercian abbey now and the doors would open, even though he was not yet twenty-one.

Aunt B excused herself and hurried off to the kitchen. The aunts buzzed. Moments later Aunt Q found Paul in his bedroom and came in, uninvited, to scrutinize him. She wore false eyelashes. "B says you're not going back to that Minnesota school." She waited for an explanation, but none came. She pressed on. "Did you get a girl pregnant?"

"No," Paul said.

"Then what did you do? Flunk your classes?"

"I want to become a monk."

Her eyelashes fluttered. "I suppose you think that's funny," she snapped. "Young people these days, they're full of sarcastic remarks." But Paul's face was as solemn as a priest's. *"Mon Dieu,"* she said. "You're serious! Jesus, Mary, and Joseph!" She was off to the kitchen.

When the news reached Madame Seneschal, her voice rose above the other ladies' and the entire household became agitated like a beehive with an angry queen. After their heated conversation she marched directly to Paul's bedroom and stood in the doorway with her hands on her hips.

"What?" she yelled. "You want to spoil Christmas for everyone? I thought you had the monk business flushed out of you."

Though he trembled, Paul could take back none of the words he had spoken to Aunt Q. As he clutched the black rock, he remained convinced about the nature of his vocation. He could not explain his complicated feelings to his mother, but a Scriptural line rose up inside his head: *Arise, let us open our eyes to the light that comes from God.* Madame Seneschal sucked in air.

"You say nothing!" she yelled. "You sit there with that serious face and say nothing. Have you already taken a vow of silence?"

For days they did not speak. Madame Seneschal sat near the tree on Christmas Eve as if by a casket. "I will never have any grandchildren," she said. When Paul ignored her grief, she yelled at him.

"Don't come crawling back to me," she said, "when you find you made a mistake. All these years of sacrificing for a child that locks himself away in a monastery. You break your mother's heart!"

Two days after Christmas, Paul sent his baptismal and confirmation records to the Cistercian monks, and he asked his parish priest, Father Pitt Colombe, to mail a recommendation to the Abbot, Dom Jacques Bouvray. Father Colombe wrote immediately. He showed the letter to Paul; it recommended the Seneschal boy as a good Mass server, "a solid young Catholic, a good fellow, and quiet." After the letter was sent off, there was nothing Paul could do but wait and hope that permission to enter religious life would be granted him.

Meanwhile, Omer carried himself about the house with a flat mouth and sad eyes, exactly as if he had the flu. "As far as things go nowadays," he kept saying with an air of resignation, "at least the boy will be out of harm's way. He'll be kept safe with the monks."

"*C'est en masse!*" Madame Seneschal screamed. "You don't remember that we will be childless!"

On a freezing Thursday in January, a one-page onionskin message arrived from the Cistercian abbey. Father Yves-Marie Morice informed Paul that they were expecting him. The weak typewritten characters jutted over and under the line: "The Reverend Father gives his consent. You may come."

Madame Seneschal snatched the letter out of Paul's hands. She swore, after reading it, that she would play no part in delivering her son to the monks, that he could find his own way there, that she would never visit him or write him, and that as far as she was concerned, she had no son.

The next day she was packing his underwear while Omer gassed up the car. Paul walked nervously back and forth in front of her.

"Mother, I can take the Greyhound bus."

She pulled a handkerchief out of her sleeve and blew her nose. "No son of mine will stand out in the snow on Highway 75 and wait for the bus."

"I can catch the train in Morris."

"What?" she said. "Do you think you're an orphan?"

Madame Seneschal put out an enormous lunch; no one spoke at the table. When the dishes had been cleared away, they set off for the abbey. Omer drove, straining his neck up over the dashboard, and he and Madame spoke as if Paul were not in the back seat.

"One of my sisters," Madame said, "she is a nun. Agnès. Ten girls in the family and my mother pointed at Agnès and said, 'You. Go be a nun.' She obeyed. Those were the days when children obeyed their parents. Agnès packed a little brown suitcase and went off to the Bon Secours. That's the way it was with French families. Always had to be one given back to God. The parents picked which one. They had authority. Just like when they approved or disapproved spouses for the other children."

"Bullshit," Omer said. "Your mother hates me."

"This is true," Madame replied. "But she I don't blame. A good reason she didn't point to me for the convent. And you know what I'm talking about. We had our little bun in the oven by that time. She was forced into letting me marry you."

Paul yawned. He had heard the story before. Whenever the wedding of his parents came up, he entered into it as a nameless piece of dough, the cookie on the way, the bun in the oven, the surprise cake, the accidental dumpling. He wondered which had really come first: the desire to get married and the dough as a scheme, or the dough as an accident and the marriage as a scheme. He dared not ask. In any case, his parents seemed happy enough, happy as his uncles and aunts, happy as any couple in St. Jean-Baptiste. What part had God's will in their marriage, he wondered.

"And this business about Agnès," Omer said, "that's bullshit too. Agnès joined the convent to get away from your mother."

"What's that?"

"Agnès does not belong in the convent."

"What are you saying? She's been there for twenty years."

They argued with each other for the next forty minutes, going back and forth on family issues, even while Omer turned onto the rue des Trappistes, both of them talking and neither of them listening. They kept this up until they reached the abbey gate it-self; the look of it made them pause.

"What's this?" Madame Seneschal asked. "A graveyard?"

Paul said nothing. He rubbed his palms against his trousers, then felt for the stone in his pocket. His mother turned and looked at him.

"*Ma pitoune*, you'll be buried alive!" she said, and burst into tears.

Omer rocked his head from side to side and threw up his hands. "Your sister in the Bon Secours, she's not buried alive. *Mon Dieu*, she eats better than we do. She has yearly vacations, and she went to France last summer!"

"This is not the Bon Secours," Madame said. "There's a big fence!"

As they argued, Paul opened the door and crawled out of the car with his satchel in hand, then knocked on the driver's window. Omer rolled down the glass. Paul cleared his throat.

"I'll go in alone," he said.

The suggestion hung in the air like the cloud of vapor from his mouth. Madame Seneschal pressed her face into a handker-chief and her frame shook. Omer nodded to Paul.

"Maybe you'll work it out of your system, son. Then you can come home. Don't be ashamed to come back when you've had enough. You call and I'll come to pick you up."

Paul turned away because Omer looked so unhappy. Before his father could say anything more, he walked to the gatehouse and pushed the doorbell. He waited. So did his parents.

Minutes seemed to pass. Frigid air needled his nose and ears even while sweat accumulated under his arms and began slowly to trickle down his sides to his belt. The place was so quiet he could hear the faint ticking of his wristwatch. He lifted his hand to push the bell a second time when the door opened and the stout figure of Brother Henri appeared.

"Oui," Henri said, and with a finger he invited Paul into the house. To his parents he waved a last good-bye and went inside. Before he closed the door, he heard the motor of the Oldsmobile start and the car move slowly away with the crunch of gravel under its tires.

A vague odor of ammonia still hung in the gatehouse, along with an old-wood scent like bay leaf. The atmosphere was severe, owing to spare furnishing, none of it turned or stuffed, and to curtainless windows. Discolored shades protected the walls from sunlight.

"It's cold in here," Paul said. Instantly, Brother Henri lifted a finger to his lips.

"Shhhhhhhhhh."

Paul remembered that the peculiar ambiance was due also to the silence of the house: it was devoid of speaking voices and the noise of television and radio, and no traffic stirred outside. Paul had not heard such quiet since his last visit to St. Norbert.

In the days following, Paul became intimate with the steady tick of a clock in the downstairs parlor, along with a twisting creak in the floor near his bedroom and two squeaky steps on the stairwell. Brother Henri, although hardly ever seen, lived in the room next to his, and three transient lodgers were staying somewhere in the house; Paul was aware of them only because of the rush and bump of water pipes, and because of their sullen appearances at meals.

Although Paul was already familiar with the schedule for prayers in the church and meals in the abbey basement, Brother Henri came to collect him punctually, in a silent form of solicitude. The only monk allowed to speak with Paul, now that he was a postulant, was Father Yves-Marie, who visited each day at four o'clock in the afternoon. For almost an hour he spoke on matters pertaining to Cistercian life. Monastic comportment was discussed. Yves-Marie showed Paul the complicated books that the monks used in choir. Books were given him to read, all about seeking God. Paul was being prepared for his formal entrance into the community, when he would move from the gatehouse into the abbey dormitory. Yves-Marie's eyes moved behind thick spectacles like fish in a bowl. One day he saw the black stone on Paul's dresser table and poked at it.

"What is this?" he asked. "Melted plastic?"

"No, Father. It's a rock." Paul held his breath as the priest took the stone from the dresser and rolled it in his palm. He seemed fascinated.

"How extraordinary," he said. "My rosary is attracted to it." Indeed, the rosary Yves-Marie carried in his right hand quivered each time it was brought near the rock in his left. "It's magnetic. How clever!"

From a pocket Yves-Marie brought forth several safety pins and a paper clip: these stuck to the stone as if it were a ball of tar. Paul was astonished but said nothing. Pretending to have known all along about its properties, he was even more convinced that the stone was a propitious object. Nevertheless, he was afraid to tell Yves-Marie that it was a meteorite because Yves-Marie would then ask how he knew such a thing and Paul would not say. The stone's story was his sweet secret.

The priest returned the object to the dresser top and spoke seriously. "Tomorrow," he said, "you will attend chapter for the first time and be introduced to the community as a postulant."

The chapter room was situated next to the church so that monks could easily proceed, according to rank, from one place to the other. Twice a week the Abbot formally addressed his community, delivering a sermon and then offering information on practical matters. Because the Abbot listened to the news — the only one allowed to hear it — on an old RCA-Victor 110K in his office, his chapter room comments ranged from Gerald Ford's inauguration to the price of milk in Manitoba.

The Abbot, Dom Jacques Bouvray, was short and plump, and he moved with the dignity of a pope. On his head he wore a black skullcap. The only other details that distinguished him in dress from the other monks were a wooden pectoral cross hanging from his neck and a silver ring with a bright blue stone on his left hand. He spoke French in a clear, precise manner, like the voice of authority on Radio France Internationale. The Abbot addressed the community from a raised throne while the monks sat facing one another across the room on benches along the walls. The day Paul was introduced, the sermon was about distractions.

"God is a great mystery," Dom Jacques began, "and a mystery cannot be adequately perceived or felt unless distractions are left behind. We monks, in order to appreciate our place in the world and the mystery of God's love for us, leave aside the distractions of the secular world. We forget every other concern and live monastic life in all its simplicity, that we may be attentive."

Two old monks dropped their heads and began to snore. Paul was awed, nevertheless, by the experience of sitting among forty ascetic-looking men hearing their abbot speak.

"Because we remain dissatisfied with anything but the truth," Dom Jacques continued, "we leave behind concepts of human origin. Superstition, for instance. Long ago our ancestors worshiped thunder, trees, and stones. But they gave these things up in favor of the true worship of God. We, too, leave behind superstition and magic. We root out whatever is not of God and abandon it."

The Abbot continued in this vein for some time, creating in Paul's mind images of Neanderthals cowering at the sound of thunder, bowing down to large rocks. Then he remembered his little magnetic stone. Suddenly he was confused; he wondered anew if it had actually come from the heavens as a sign.

When the Abbot finished his sermon, he introduced Paul. "Seneschal is one of us," the Abbot said, which meant — Paul was not sure — a Canadian, a French Canadian, or a Roman Catholic.

"Paul is requesting admission to our community," the Abbot continued. "He will move into the dormitory tomorrow. Keep him in your prayers and give him your good example."

With that, the Abbot stood and the community rose with him to enter the church for prayer. Paul felt a tug within him, whether to respect the black stone as a divine omen or despise it as superstition; he felt an urge to clutch it to his breast and an equal urge to throw it in the river. Suppose the great event that seemed to have confirmed his vocation to the abbey — the fireball in the sky — was simply his own interpretation of a natural occurrence! Perhaps God had said nothing to him?

The next day Paul moved into the dormitory. The world inside the abbey seemed at first aloof to him; though he now lived side by side with forty other men, they moved about like ghosts. Because talking and whispering were discouraged almost everywhere inside the building, the abbey seemed uninhabited at times. Only the occasional sound of footsteps or the squeak of a door reminded him that he was never alone.

"Your shoes are too loud," Father Yves-Marie said during their daily meeting, which had moved from the gatehouse to his office. He sat and faced Paul across a small wooden desk painted black. "Hard soles are noisy on linoleum and wood. Wear these," and he pushed a pair of well-worn shoes across the desktop. Paul looked at them as if they were dead fish.

"These shoes are ancient," he said.

"Yes, they are. They belonged to Father Marc Bureau, and he has been dead fifteen years. The shoes might be a size too big, but one must take what one gets in religious life."

Paul slipped the shoes on; they were roomy.

"When do I get a habit?" he asked.

"Not for another six months," Yves-Marie answered. "You will wear your secular clothes until you become a novice. And you may as well know now that your name will be changed."

"My name changed? Why?"

Through his thick spectacles Father Yves-Marie's eyes seemed too large. "We already have a Brother Paul," he said. "Paul Sicard works in the barn and he is not much older than you are. Around here, since we go largely by the first name, duplication is avoided as a policy."

"What will my new name be?"

"That is entirely up to the Abbot," Yves-Marie said. "You must learn to accept all that comes to you as a monk."

The prospect of a new name did not appeal to Paul. He imagined receiving an ugly name, like Cyril or Gall: something to test his humility, and go on testing it for years. A bigger issue weighed upon him, however, in the stone. He wanted to consult Yves-Marie about signs and wonders without actually giving him details and telling him what he meant.

"Father, do you wear a medal?"

"You mean a blessed medal to protect me from danger? No. I wear nothing like that."

"Why not?" Paul asked. "Do you consider such a thing superstitious?"

After deliberation that would have been suitable in a court of law, Father Yves-Marie spoke carefully. "Catholic tradition attributes no intrinsic power to medals. They act only as symbols to remind us of faith and religious duties. Why do you ask? Because of the Abbot's comments in chapter about superstition?"

Paul wiggled his toes inside his shoes. "I'm confused," he said, "because sometimes the line between superstition and religion seems terribly thin to me. I want to know what I should keep and what I should throw out."

Father Yves-Marie looked at his watch, then pushed back his chair and stood. "Around here," he said, "we don't believe in magic, if that answers your question."

He put an apron over his habit and led Paul to the door. "Our time is up. I must scrub the floor in the refectory and you must go to the church to dust the choir stalls. We will continue this conversation another day."

Paul's work as a postulant included shoveling snow, washing dishes, dusting furniture in both the church and the scriptorium, washing floors in the basement, cleaning bathrooms in the infirmary, and, as Manitoba days lengthened through March and April, setting up bedding plants in the greenhouse with Yves-Marie.

Paul learned sign language. It was explained to him that signs had been used for centuries among monks, particularly Cistercians, who were sensitive to the need for silence in a way of life that was at once highly communal in its demands and contemplative in its aims.

"Our signs have nothing in common with the language of the deaf," Yves-Marie explained. "Monks use rudimentary hand gestures to curtail noise around the abbey buildings and to communicate within places where speaking is entirely prohibited, such as the abbey church and the cloister."

Paul asked where the signs originated.

"Nearly all of our signs come from French abbeys," Yves-Marie said, "where they have been used, in some cases, for hundreds of years. The point, obviously, is not to facilitate communication but to make interaction between monks brief and to the point. You may use signs whenever you feel the need, but you may not speak to anyone except the Abbot. You can talk to him anytime and anywhere, unless he prohibits it. No one is to speak or use signs after the last prayer in the evening until after Mass in the morning. We call this period the Grand Silence."

Kissing the fingers of one hand, he explained, meant "thank you." Striking fists together, one on top the other, meant "work" or "get to work." Blowing on a raised forefinger meant both "fire" and "electricity." Scratching at the top of the nose, between the eyes, meant "you're late." In all, there were probably one hundred signs, Yves-Marie explained, and they could be combined in clever ways to communicate effectively while keeping the silence.

"For instance, one need not shout across the yard," he said. "In broad daylight, a sign can be seen farther than most voices carry." He smiled. "On the other hand, if you should see me about to step in front of the dairy truck, please yell as loudly as you can. I don't want to be killed. Or if you should notice that the barn is on fire, don't start blowing on your finger. Yell in your biggest voice, for heaven's sake."

Yves-Marie spoke only in his office, during their daily scheduled meetings. Otherwise, the two exchanged not a word. In the hallway, they greeted each other with a nod. When they worked side by side, Paul heard only the ticking of a clock, the clank of steam pipes, or, when he was shoveling snow, the atmospheric swoosh of a jet overhead.

Silence took some getting used to. Paul strained to hear, expecting words from people when words would not come. The monks seemed thoroughly at ease without talk. But Paul, with his lack of experience, believed that silence was indicative of some kind of bottled tension, and only after several weeks inside the cloister did he realize that the tension was in his own head.

At length he grew accustomed to the quiet, much as a person on holiday allows himself to forget about the news.

For the better part of six months, the robed figures that lived in the abbey remained nameless. The custom did not exist for a monk to introduce himself. Thus, learning a name became something of a skill: Paul had to memorize the person's place at table, and later steal away, into the refectory, to read the nametag atop the blue-checked napkin. Or, more difficult, he had to notice where a person hung his white choir robe, memorize the number above the hook, then read the list of names and numbers in the vestry. Paul asked Father Yves-Marie why none of the tombstones in the graveyard had names on them. He explained that the stones had been whitewashed, and no one bothered to paint the names back on.

"There's a list somewhere," he said. "I'm sure the list has it straight, who's buried where. Most of us remember." Curious society, Paul thought, where names meant so little.

The snow began to melt, and at the beginning of May, when winter finally released its grip upon the Canadian prairie, Father Yves-Marie asked Paul to write a formal petition to enter the novitiate.

"What do I say?" Paul asked.

"Tell us why you wish to become a monk."

In the following days Paul rubbed his chin until it chafed. He was no writer. And only a philosopher, he thought, could adequately explain why people search for meaning in life. He thought perhaps he should mention the meteorite. On the other hand, would a meteorite be helpful information? He was not sure: at times he thought it was important, but at other times he could picture forty monks in the chapter room laughing at hooey about shooting stars. He decided to keep his secret.

"What have other monks written?" he asked Yves-Marie.

"Any variety of things," the priest answered, "which proves that God builds upon whatever material we offer. Give God a stick and it will turn into an apple tree. I don't think it matters much what you say, Paul. Just speak from your heart."

Paul wandered about with paper and pencil in hand, but nothing got written. For days he tossed back and forth in his head the reasons he might use for being a monk. He thought about the meteorite again.

He put some words together on paper about what he saw in the sky that night. He expressed himself with a certain amount of poise, but he was unsatisfied with the results; it read like a testimonial. He tore up the pages. Starting again, he attempted to sound more down-to-earth.

"Monastic life," he wrote, "is good for those that need order in their lives." In the best words he could summon, he went on.

You monks are quiet. There's no yelling or laughing. Nobody says "good morning" or "how are you?" I'm really not used to that. I'm used to noise. I kind of miss my radio station. But I'm getting used to having no interruptions, though. Yesterday, during meditation in church, we were all there not making a peep, and a meadowlark perched on the windowsill. Remember? That window was open to catch the breeze. And the meadowlark started singing, right during meditation, I guess because he couldn't hear that only a few inches away from him were forty men. I thought that was neat. That bird just kept singing and singing. It was even kind of loud. But pretty. And when that bird was good and finished with his business, he flew away. By coincidence, almost as soon as he flew away, we started to sing Vespers. Just like the bird. It was really neat. It sort of all made sense to me then. Anyway, I'm not sure what being a monk means for sure, or if I'm really supposed to be here, but I'm looking for meaning in my life. I don't want an ordinary life. And you all seem to know what you're doing, without talking about it. I'm thinking to myself more and more that I made a good choice coming here. I like order in my life, too. And I want to learn about faith from monks who have a lot of experience under their belts. Please let me become a novice.

This petition was signed and presented in June. Paul made no mention of the stone; the black thing seemed more like a fetish to him every day. He wanted to throw it away, and even carried it to the banks of the river that ran through the abbey property. But he could not raise his hand and let go of it. He wondered if, without a sign from heaven, he could believe that God still loved him, that God made efforts to communicate with him, that God even existed.

The chapter approved Paul's petition immediately. He was summoned to the Abbot's office.

Lilacs bloomed that day. When he knocked at the Abbot's oak door, a heavy sweet scent brought to his mind memories of church services in St. Jean-Baptiste: little girls in white dresses for their first communion, and banks of flowers closing out the air with perfume, like being stuck in an elevator with an old lady. Paul entered the office and sat down in a chair in front of the desk.

"*Benedicite,*" he said. He had been coached on the proper greeting by Yves-Marie.

"*Dominus.*"

"My parents will be unhappy if they can't call me Paul," he said. "What name will you give me?"

The Abbot looked comfortable at his desk. His smile revealed a small space between his two front teeth, and his left eyelid seemed heavier than the right. "Your parents may call you anything they like," he said, "but here, we can't have two Brother Pauls. I'll make it as painless as possible. What is your middle name?"

"Joseph."

The Abbot frowned. "No. We have one of those, too. Father Joseph Castinié is in the infirmary. He is eighty years old, but he could live another ten years." He opened a book of Christian names. "You deserve a good monk-saint as a patron, to help you through the years ahead. Let's see. How about Cyril?"

Paul coughed as if a moth had flown down his throat. The Abbot looked up from the book. "Or Hugo, perhaps? Maybe Gall? We don't have a Gall."

They continued to speak about the name change, but because Paul had no suggestions — only firm opinions about what he did *not* want — the Abbot sent him away with reassurances that something nice would be found.

The day before vesture, Paul sat in a small room in the basement where the clipper and scissors were kept. Already nervous about his head being shaved, he was relieved to learn that the shearing would be done unceremoniously, in the privacy of the barber room, and not before the entire community. Yves-Marie told him that even in the old days when the monastic corona was worn — the finger-wide band of hair around the head that looked like a furry sweatband — the shaving was done in the barber room. No one knew exactly why the corona was worn; it was apparently a sort of branding device from the Middle Ages. It was discontinued in the mid-1960s, when shaving the entire head became the custom.

A large mirror hung on the wall behind the barber chair. Standing at the door, Paul could see that his thick black hair was much too long, covering his eyes and falling to his shirt collar: six months of growth. Although shaving would relieve him of fuss with a comb, he had no idea what his skull might look like. Was it an odd shape, with bumps and moles?

The door popped open and in walked Brother Paul Sicard, a young monk with ill-focused eyes that seemed full of mischief. He had rosy cheeks, and lips so well shaped and deep in color that they looked painted on. Slapping the barber chair with one hand, he smiled. Paul Seneschal became nervous. The monk curled his right forefinger and drew it back and forth over his head, brushing the stubble that grew there, a sign for "shave," but Paul hesitated to climb into the seat. The monk plugged the clipper into the wall socket and turned it on, producing a noise similar to a giant insect, and when Paul still did not move, the monk stretched the electric cord and went at him where he stood, next to the wall. Vibrations eased through his skull to his teeth. After a few strokes, Paul's head felt strangely cool. He was stunned. The monk finished quickly, put the clipper away, and stood back. He studied Paul and made a tossing gesture with his hands that meant "so-so." Then, just for a moment, he leaned close to Paul.

"Don't blame me for your name change," he whispered. "I was Joseph when I came here, and they already had Joseph Castinié, so they named me Paul." He knocked on his head while crossing his eyes, then waved and left the room.

Alone again, Paul stared into the mirror. All that was left on his head was a dense shadow, and the way his ears stuck out, he wondered why he had not noticed before that they were large. They were Omer's ears. Black hair clung like wool to Paul's shirt and trousers.

The next morning, monks gathered in the chapter room. Sunlight penetrated high windows and yellowed the walls with a thick, warm light. Paul Seneschal was called forward.

"What do you seek?" Dom Jacques Bouvray asked in a solemn tone.

Paul had memorized the necessary formula: "To live here with the brothers and learn your rule of life, to live in prayerful penance and obedience, to follow Christ crucified in poverty and chastity."

"May God bring to perfection the good begun in you."

The Abbot sprinkled a woolen habit with holy water. Father Yves-Marie, the novice master, and Brother Paul Sicard, his assistant, dressed the new novice. They placed a white tunic and a white scapular over his street clothes. When they had finished, Dom Jacques continued.

"Paul, you were brought here six months ago by your parents to begin monastic life among us as a postulant. This date, recorded in our books, was January 17, the feast of Saint Anthony of the Desert, founder of Christian monasticism. For that reason, I have chosen the name Antoine for you. Because we do not celebrate birthdays in the abbey, your feast day shall be the same day as his from now on. May Saint Antoine be your intercessor in heaven, and may you learn holiness and wisdom from the witness your patron has given you. Study his life as it has been written down, and pray to this great saint."

Paul felt like a citizen of a new country. The monks rose and sang the *Te Deum,* then went off to morning work. After they had gone, Brother Antoine followed Yves-Marie down the hall to their daily conference. They nearly ran into Brother Paul Sicard as he hurried by. "Good saint," he signed by placing a palm on his chest, rubbing up and down, then folding his hands in prayer while looking up at the ceiling. "Father of monks is good," he signed before rushing out the door and toward the dairy barn.

Antoine continued down the hall waddling awkwardly; his accustomed gait was no good anymore since the hem of his habit gathered between his ankles. He and Yves-Marie entered the office and Antoine shut the door.

"I've never worn a dress," he said.

"It's not a dress. It's a *habit,* Brother Antoine." Yves-Marie sat down at his desk. The novice remained standing and raised the habit to his knees.

"I can't believe it," he said. "How long will it take for me to get used to being called Brother Antoine?" He suddenly thought of his mother and father. Only monks had been allowed at the ceremony. Would his parents approve of the name? He thought of René Lizotte and Father Pitt Colombe and the role each had played in his decision. He even remembered Bradley Eisschrank. Was he still at school? And the old lady on the train who announced the resignation of Spiro Agnew. Where was she now? What had happened in her life? The vast milling of individuals and their free will, both good and bad, drew and pushed the world about. Antoine's parents had met seemingly by accident. He was conceived seemingly by accident. Most things happened seemingly by accident. Yet this push and tumble was but a single side of the interplay. What people saw was the flatly real tugging with something else. What they saw played with the unseen. Earth spun in a vast expanse of heaven, and we knew only the half of it. But Brother Antoine felt good. He had been given a special sign from God. He had his stone.

"Father Yves-Marie, what brought *you* to the abbey?"

The priest was blowing his nose into a handkerchief. "That's not the least bit important," he said, stuffing the handkerchief away. His eyes were active behind the thick lenses, as if blowing his nose made them wobble. "Something incidental brought each of us here. Matters little how we begin the journey. Sit down."

Antoine took a chair and rubbed his hands together. When he spoke again, his voice was trembling. "My father thinks that an extraordinary vocation needs an extraordinary sign of confirmation."

"Just like the saints, eh? Brother Antoine, that's hagiography."

"Pardon me?"

"That's stuff written after the fact. Your father need not be- lieve everything he reads."

"But if something extraordinary *did* happen, what do I make of it?" Antoine paused for a moment. "I'm not sure," he said, "but I think God gave me a sign."

Father Yves-Marie sighed and put his elbow on top of the desk. He balanced his jaw on his knuckles and gave Antoine a tired look. "An apparition? Don't tell me. You've spoken to the Virgin Mary?"

"Oh no. Nothing like that," he said. "I saw a meteor one night, just outside the town of St. Jean-Baptiste." His hands began to shake and he hid them away. "Just when I needed something from God to confirm my decision to come here, out of the heav- ens a sign came, and the meteor landed practically at my feet. I'm almost certain I collected the right object. It's that magnetic stone you saw on my dresser top."

Yves-Marie remained silent for a while. His eyes seemed to quiver in their effort to focus upon Antoine's forehead. "That's nice," he said at last. "I'm glad you haven't had an apparition. I haven't the strength for an apparition."

This answer was not reassuring to Antoine, and he began to move in his chair, fussing with his habit. "What do you mean? Is it real, then? Did God speak to me? May I keep the stone as a sign that everything will be all right? Am I chosen?"

Sunlight came through the window to create a book-sized patch on the desk, and a fine layer of dust became visible where no dust had been seen before.

"Brother Antoine," the priest said, "of course you're chosen. Yes, God loves you. Doesn't God love us all? Listen, I don't pre- tend to know everything, and heaven knows I've had few com- passes to steer by in my own life. I'd like one myself. But do you really *need* a sign? Isn't *everything* a sign? Isn't the whole universe amazing just as it is?"

Briefly, Antoine's eyes met Yves-Marie's, then he looked down, nervous and quizzical. He did not understand anything special about being chosen if everyone was chosen. Nor did he understand how a stone could be amazing if the whole universe was amazing.

Yves-Marie took off his glasses and rubbed his eyes. "You may keep the stone," he said, "for as long as you need it."

Brother Antoine looked down at his habit while searching the unfamiliar hip pockets. He located an opening at the top of the pocket lining where he could reach his trousers. He brought forth the black stone. Carefully he placed it on the top of the desk, near the growing patch of light.

"You keep it," he said.

Both of them studied the object, a curious black lump looking something like obsidian, not terribly interesting in itself, although when Antoine saw it on top of the gray soil and snow of the field it had looked foreign and somehow ominous. Even on the dresser top in the gatehouse, the stone had radiated a kind of power. But now, here, it looked like an ordinary pebble, perhaps from a brook. Antoine pushed it toward Yves-Marie. As he did so, Yves-Marie brought out his rosary and placed it nearby.

The beads closest to the stone itched and moved slightly: they were like Mexican jumping beans until Yves-Marie edged them closer with a finger and they latched on to the stone, pulling their companions with them. The priest lifted a hand to his mouth and began to laugh.

"I'm sorry," he said. "I can't help myself, it's so amusing. If I keep the stone, I'll be playing with it all day. I think you'd better take it back."

"But Father . . ."

"Oh, what harm is there in having it?" Yves-Marie said. "Count it as one of God's everyday miracles. Let it remind you of all things wonderful in the world."

"Yes, Father," Antoine replied. He dutifully watched as the priest played with the magnetic stone and the rosary. Words from the Bible popped into Antoine's head: "No one comes to me unless the God who sent me draws him." He had no clue as to what this meant, except that a magnet seemed to be described. The words would baffle him for years to come, their meaning near as a warm breath, yet far away. The stone would baffle him, too. He kept it, and on starry nights he'd take it from his habit pocket because he believed God spoke to him. Other nights, when clouds rolled before the moon like silk parachutes, he couldn't believe in a god at all.

2

Passing Eli

The house bell made a rapid clanging, and Brother Antoine looked at his watch. The ancient electric alarm system sounded five minutes' warning before every scheduled prayer period in choir. But even while he made a mental note of where he had stopped, putting the dust rag into a box and rolling down his habit sleeves, Antoine realized that Vespers was still three hours away. The bell could mean only one thing: the monks were being called to Brother Eli's room.

Perched high on a ladder, Father Véran held a metal bookend in his teeth and waved Antoine on with a finger because his arms were full. He would follow later.

Antoine walked out of the scriptorium into a bright, butter-yellow hallway. Through a windowpane, the limp leaves of an American elm seemed to pray for a breeze: it was July. He flexed his arm. Immediately he gritted his teeth and closed his eyes. The pulled muscle still hurt; he was incapable of even holding a book for very long. The injury had taken place while he was stacking hay on the farm, square bales weighing sixty pounds and more.

Most of the monks were in the hayloft at that moment. Four were in their twenties, as was Antoine; the rest were thirty-five and older, which meant they were limited, as far as he was concerned, and he was sorry he could not assist. As for Brother Eli Baudrillard, he was very old and rapidly sinking toward death.

Harvest was no time to be dying. So that no monk should die alone, the infirmarian rang the house bell any time a sick man appeared to be slipping into his last agony. But it was summer. Few could put aside the pressures of work to attend him. Hay had to be put up. Vegetables needed picking. Canning had to be done. Honey was ready for extraction and apples hung plentiful on trees. In addition, all the usual chores awaited. The scriptorium had not been cleaned in weeks, and as soon as Antoine was finished dusting it, he was expected to scrub toilets with his good arm.

Eli was dying, nevertheless, and those left in the house put down their work to attend him. Only after the old monk rolled his eyes and released his final breath would the toll begin: one tilt of the big bell *Saint-Joseph* for every year Eli had lived, and those outside would stop their work, no matter if stacking hay or milking cows, checking brood frames from the beehives or picking beans. Each would pause for Eli's passing while overtones of the bell would reverberate for several seconds, rattling the many loose panes in the church tower.

Antoine made his way through hallways toward the infirmary. He had never before witnessed a death and was not eager to see one. The act of passing, to him, seemed a private thing, in the same category as bowel trouble or childbirth. Why people should have to witness such an embarrassing moment was beyond him, convinced as he was that if it were he giving up the ghost, he would rather do it alone in the woods. People might find him later, covered with the beautiful leaves of autumn.

Eli would not have that luxury. Until recently, he had taken care of himself, walking slowly from one place to another. The stroke came in late spring, and in a few short weeks he rapidly faded to a bedridden and incontinent old man with few lucid moments. When his mind was clear, he complained bitterly about his condition.

Antoine knew relatively little about Eli. The old monk had been one of the first he encountered, and the sight of the stooped man pushing a wheelbarrow was still vivid. Antoine spoke to him that day in English and Eli became enraged, shaking a fist. After that, Antoine had regularly cleaned bathrooms in the infirmary for the six months he was a postulant and the year already spent as a novice. But Eli seldom acknowledged him. He seemed in no way eager to communicate. Antoine had noticed that, before the stroke, when anyone got too close to Eli, the old man knitted his brow and took a swing with his cane. He disliked people.

The infirmary smelled moldy. Eli's door was open and only four monks kept vigil around the bed: Father Jude Sanders, the infirmarian, old Fathers Cyprien Crey and Marie-Nizier Delorme, who lived in the infirmary anyway, and Brother Sauveur Conil, a young monk who had been excused from the barn because of his hay fever. From the bed, Eli took short, quick gasps for air. His eyes rolled and his mouth moved. He seemed vaguely disappointed, as if his pillow were not quite right or the sheets clung uncomfortably to his skin. Father Jude, a tall, fair man with freckles, began the rosary while Antoine and Sauveur knelt on the floor. Marie-Nizier had installed himself in an old stuffed chair like a dog, and Cyprien sat on the edge of a maple sideboard because he could no longer go down on his knees.

As Antoine said his rosary, he was distracted by Eli's face. Each time the dying man drew in air his nostrils flared like a moose testing the breeze. Antoine remembered the last time the bell *Saint-Joseph* had tolled. It was on a wet September morning the year before. The bell tipped and released its low, reverberating metal voice, and several monks, sunk in mud up to their shins, looked at wristwatches. Antoine was among them in the potato field. He wondered if Father Jean-Marie had made a mistake. But Jean-Marie was never wrong with the bell, and *Saint-Joseph* tipped again after the full long length of an *Ave.* Everyone understood. The bell was not being rung, it was being tolled. Someone had died, and each sound from the bell represented a year of his life.

Anxious to learn what had happened, the monks walked from the field. They kept track of the tolls as they went. "Nine: *Ave María, grátia plena: Dóminus tecum: benedícta tu in muliéribus . . .* Ten: *Ave María, grátia plena: Dóminus tecum . . .*" Antoine reviewed the possibilities in his head, all of them old monks: Father Louis Rondel, the retired cobbler, eighty-two; Father Joseph Castinié, a retired parish priest who had joined late in life, eighty-eight; Brother Gabriel Eremasi, who had once worked on the Orient Express and now kept pigs, ninety-three; and, of course, Brother Eli.

The bell tolled for none of these; it stopped at twenty-eight. Antoine waited outside the Abbot's office with the others, but Dom Jacques Bouvray was not there. He was in the cow barn. An ambulance arrived, and the community learned that Brother Paul Sicard had been crushed by a bull.

This news sent Antoine to the LaSalle River, where, he hoped, the sight of lazy brown water spinning through reeds might calm him. But after five minutes in an agitated state, he had to walk again, and eventually he found his way to the church. Even there, he could not calm himself.

He knew Paul. Paul was his friend. Once a month for a year, he had trimmed Antoine's hair. Natural clown that he was, Paul made Antoine smile and then laugh and break the silence. Crossing his eyes, for instance, Paul took a bunch of hair once and managed to paste it above his lip, looking for all the world like a bald Charlie Chaplin. "Oh, oh, oh!" Paul said, when Antoine began to laugh. "Now you've broken the rule and you must do penance."

"But you're talking," Antoine said. "Words are not allowed."

"Oh, my! You've used words now, too. That's double the penance."

Antoine groaned. "What about you?"

"Oh, I don't have to follow the rules," Paul answered, switching on the razor. "I'm in charge. I'm the barber."

Paul Sicard was too young to die, Antoine said to himself as he tried to sit comfortably in his oak choir stall. He knew that Paul had been teasing the Holstein bull for weeks; he had seen Paul by the fence waving a handkerchief to irritate Julius. The bull lowered his head and raked dirt with a hoof. Paul laughed. Soon, even the sight of Paul sent the bull trotting back and forth on his side of the wire, eager to do damage, while long strands of saliva ran from his vast pink mouth.

Sitting in the quiet church, Antoine reviewed what must have happened. The Abbot said Julius plowed through the wire fence. So while Antoine and the others had been working in the potato field, Julius charged, snapping the fence wires, and tossed Paul Sicard into the air. Antoine pictured the awful scene: the young monk coming down on the bull's back, then sliding off. From the coroner the monks later learned that Paul had been killed by the weight of a hoof on his chest, perhaps after the bull lost interest, an inadvertent step backward while chewing a mouthful of field parsley, crushing the unconscious monk.

When the corpse was returned from the funeral parlor, the bell *Saint-Joseph* tolled again, but Antoine could not bring himself to look at a dead man. Throughout the funeral he kept closing his eyes, banishing the unpleasant from his mind.

Julius was not put down. The animal was too valuable to destroy. Even now, while Antoine knelt at Eli's bedside saying the rosary, the bull was in the east pasture, doing his business with a cow.

Each time Antoine moved a bead through his fingers he felt a sharp pain in his forearm, and the hardwood floor pressed into his knees. Yet old Brother Eli continued to breathe with flaring nostrils, unaware of those around him, perhaps sleeping.

"He was always a cripple," Marie-Nizier said from his stuffed chair, right in the middle of the rosary. "I should know. I've been here longer than anyone."

Father Jude said something about silence, but Marie-Nizier did not hear it. He was stone deaf, and mumbled to himself often.

"Eli came here sixty-two years ago," Marie-Nizier said in French, "and even back then, he wasn't what you'd call healthy. I was already a novice. The superior at the time thought the monastic fasts would kill Eli. He looked like a skinned fox, so scrawny that his clothing hung on him. And he had that clubfoot besides. But the superior kept him, I think because the war was on, you see, and all the healthy young men had been shipped off to Europe. The superior had to take what he could get."

"Shhhhhh," Jude said, but Marie-Nizier ignored him and the rosary came to a halt.

"Of course his clubfoot wasn't really a clubfoot," Marie-Nizier went on, speaking to the window. "When he was five years old, he fell through the rotten floorboards of his family shack. They lived somewhere out in the country near Ste. Agathe. My mother knew the family."

Eli moaned without opening his eyes and Jude mopped his forehead with a damp cloth. Antoine wondered, kneeling on the floor, if the old monk could hear Marie-Nizier prattle on.

"They say he'd been jumping up and down on the rotten floor

of that shack, playing some kind of hopscotch game, and the wood gave way. Eli was stuck until his father came back from begging, or whatever he did. God knows. Anyway, the family couldn't afford a doctor, so the father refused to bring the boy in for any medical attention. And that foot swelled to enormous size."

Father Marie-Nizier had a nervous habit of grinding his dentures, and when he was not sleeping or mumbling to himself, he emitted a small, persistent squeak by pressing his upper and lower plates together.

"The swelling eventually went down," he continued. "And those broken bones knitted together as they were. His foot remained bent, just like a clubfoot, and did not grow like the other. Eli hobbled for the rest of his life."

It was true, Antoine thought to himself: Eli did hobble. The monks seemed accustomed to Eli's pace, as accustomed as they were to the sound of the bell, but his slow limp annoyed Antoine during the dreaded *statio*. Every community activity was done in rank, according to the length of time one had spent in monastic life. In rank, the monks stood in choir, sat in refectory, walked down the hall. *Statio* meant that the Abbot went first, followed by the prior, the sub-prior, and the novice master. Fathers Cyprien and Marie-Nizier, who had been at the abbey the longest, came after the superiors. Brother Eli — when not confined to bed — walked next in line, dragging his bad foot. The rest of the community was bottlenecked behind him. Eli did not care. The superiors, Cyprien, and Marie-Nizier left everyone else far behind. And Eli took his time.

Antoine heard a snore from Marie-Nizier. Apparently he had talked himself to sleep, and his head was flopping against the back of the chair so that his nose pointed up at the ceiling. With his mouth hanging open he looked like a baby bird expecting a worm. Antoine shifted his weight to prevent his left foot from going to sleep. On the sickbed, Eli looked dead but his chest continued to rise and fall as if it were connected to a mechanical spring. Father Jude went on with the rosary aloud and beads slipped through his fingers.

Eli's horrible youth must have embittered him, Antoine reasoned. Eli was famous for his uneven temper. But neither did Eli ask for special considerations. He ate what was given him. He wore a patched habit. He never complained about his health. When he was not sick, he did his work reliably.

Brother Sauveur barked a sneeze, loud enough that Antoine thought surely the old monk would wake, but his eyes did not even flutter. Then, as the group began yet another decade of the rosary, the wind went out of Eli. His chest collapsed, and everyone except Marie-Nizier — who was still asleep — fell silent and leaned forward. Jude felt for a pulse. He bent down to put his freckled ear against Eli's chest.

Antoine heaved a sigh of relief and had started up from his knees when suddenly the old man coughed. After taking a vast gulp of air, Eli began to breathe again as regularly as before. Antoine rolled his eyes and stayed down on the floor.

By this time his left foot had lost all sense of feeling. He wanted to get up and walk around for a while, but the others continued the rosary in a drone. What were they waiting for anyway? wondered Antoine. Everyone passes on, saint or sinner. Were they expecting a final gesture of some sort, a whispered word that might explain an entire life of grumpy dedication? The man's energy was gone. There would likely be no last fizz and pop from him.

Eli's eyes opened while his lips stretched and a sound came from his throat. His tongue shaped a word, but his loose dentures prevented its articulation.

"What?" Father Jude asked, leaning close to the bed. The rosary stopped again. Eli continued to move his lips as air whistled through his teeth. Jude became impatient.

"I can't hear you," he shouted. "Speak up."

Eli's breathing was coarse. He mumbled incomprehensible words, and Jude made him repeat them.

"Soixante-deux?" Jude asked. *"Soixante-deux* what?"

The room was silent. Through the open window Antoine heard the distant clank and scuttle of a bale elevator. Marie-Nizier woke up, wiped his nose with his hand, and looked toward Eli with fresh interest as Jude began shouting a list of possibilities into Eli's ear.

"Sixty-two dollars? Sixty-two rosaries? Sixty-two minutes? Sixty-two days? Sixty-two years?"

"Oui," Eli responded.

"Sixty-two years? Of what?"

Jude waited, and when he received no answer, he turned to the others and lifted his shoulders. I have no idea, he seemed to say.

Antoine was now completely exasperated. His left foot tingled and his arm felt sore and he wondered what last-minute piece of business prevented Eli from moving on to his eternal reward.

Jude turned back to the bed. "You can let go now, Brother. It's not important. Leave it behind. You can die in peace."

With energy that surprised them all, Eli lifted his feeble arm and slapped at Father Jude. Brother Sauveur backed away from the bed. A rattled breath came from the old monk, and he gazed around the room without seeming to recognize anyone. Suddenly, Sauveur's face lit up.

"He means he's been a monk for sixty-two years," he said, "and he's proud of this accomplishment!" Sauveur lifted his hands and smiled broadly.

Eli rolled his eyes. "Ignoramus," he moaned.

All the while, old Father Cyprien had been observing the action from his place at the maple sideboard. He made signs across the room to deaf Father Marie-Nizier, who looked at him expectantly. "Second wind," Cyprien signed. "Two whole nights we spend here. Now this. He's snapping out of it."

Marie-Nizier signed back, making eager little sounds in his throat. "No. He is dying. I get dying brother's room," his hands said. "Abbot says I get dying brother's room."

Near the sickbed, Father Jude stood at arm's length and yelled at Eli, "Do you want to confess? Is that what you want? Confession? I can tell the others to leave the room and you can confess to me."

Antoine liked this idea so much he got up off the floor and prepared to leave. His left foot felt as if sand were flowing through it, but he was only too happy to be up, and he awaited the order that would release him. Eli's breathing changed, but he said nothing. He made no indication that he wanted confession.

The breathing was clearly different now: a gargling intake, then a wheezy release. Jude turned and pointed at Antoine.

"You," he said. "Go to the barn and fetch the Abbot. Brother Eli has something to say."

Antoine's shoulders relaxed and he smiled. He hobbled through the doorway and down the hall. Relief came over him once he escaped the stale atmosphere of the infirmary, and feeling began to return to his leg as he walked down a set of creaking stairs. Minutes later, he left the building and entered bright sunshine and heat.

The farm was a quarter mile away, and Antoine walked beneath the canopy of elm trees that sheltered the road. To his right was a cornfield. A monk was there, ripping ears from plants as high as his chest. To Antoine's left was a field of potatoes, and beyond their mounded leafy rows he noticed taller stalks of parsnips and rutabagas. Crows chattered in the trees by the cheese house. Sparrows alighted on the gravel ahead of him, their plumage nearly invisible among the gray stones, and flew when he drew near.

The sun's warmth cheered Antoine. Moisture collected under his collar and around the roots of his stubby hair, but he did not care. Being free of the house made him feel good. Circulation returned to his leg. He stretched muscles and began to run. Anyone seeing him might have thought the young monk was running for help, but Antoine's mind had already wandered far from Eli. He was glad for his own health and imagined that he might have been a good athlete, had he not come to the abbey.

In the hayloft above the dairy barn, eight monks stacked alfalfa bales. Another four stood on the bed of a 1967 Ford F700 tandem grain truck feeding bales into the elevator. Antoine caught the attention of one of them and brought two fingers to his forehead: "Abbot," the sign meant. The monk on the truck bed turned and signed up to the loft, and several minutes later the Abbot appeared at the dairy barn door, mopping his forehead with a handkerchief.

"*Benedicite*, Reverend Father," Antoine said.

"*Dominus, Dominus, Dominus,*" Dom Jacques answered. Sweat dripped from his face and dry pieces of alfalfa clung to his shoulders. He wore overalls that made his short, full frame seem bundled together with denim. "What is it? How is Brother Eli?" he asked, puffing. "Is he dead? Then why haven't we heard the tower bell? Where is Brother Jean-Marie?" He wiped the back of his neck and his face.

"Pardon me, Reverend Father, but Father Jude sent me down to ask if you would come to the infirmary. Brother Eli has something to say. Apparently it's only for your ears."

The Abbot leaned against the barn wall. The air was heavy with the tealike smell of alfalfa, and green flakes drifted all around them. The Abbot heaved a sigh.

"*Mon Dieu,*" he said. "We have so much work to do. All right, all right, all right. Give me a minute to catch my breath." He looked at his watch and ran a hand over his scalp while Antoine closed his eyes toward the sun and smiled. Not yet overheated like the Abbot, Antoine was comfortable, and he thought that the most wonderful thing would be to sun himself for the rest of the afternoon. Without opening his eyes, he spoke.

"I was dusting in the scriptorium, Reverend Father. Would you like me to return to my work now? Or must I go back to Eli's room?"

"Walk with me to the abbey," the Abbot said.

They started out slowly, as the Abbot was still recovering his energy. A small breeze ran through the corn rows and circulated dusty air. Antoine smelled only cheerful things: mellow sap from cornstalks, a faint sweet scent of roses, a sudden waft of cow manure. In the cornfield he noticed how rippling leaves protected the many bloated cobs, all of them wrapped tightly in green. Farther away he saw a shimmer of heat warping a distant field. The Abbot blew his nose into a red handkerchief.

"How's your arm?" he asked. "We could use another pair of hands in the barn."

"Still quite sore, Reverend Father."

"Ah, yes. Rain is expected tonight, you see, and we must move those bales out of the weather," he said. "This devilish heat! How is Brother Eli? Is he comfortable?"

"He's about the same, Reverend Father."

"Since I've become abbot, I've buried seventeen monks. Amazing to think. Seventeen. And only four new people have professed vows in that time."

Antoine had no response to this. He glanced up at the canopy of elms that shaded the road. Sunlight formed a patchwork through the leaves like a living quilt. At his feet, grasshoppers popped from the grass in every direction.

"I've watched many people die," the Abbot continued. "It amazes me, the body's resilience. But we're like machines and eventually we just plain wear out. Our gears grind down and we stop. I'll stop. You'll stop. Worn down like that old gas-powered bale elevator, jammed on us twice today. Someday it will break down altogether."

"Yes, Reverend Father."

Antoine wanted the Abbot to hush up. The topic was depressing. The scent of flowers in the air had become funereal, and he did not want to think about death. A bright beetle landed on his sleeve and Antoine thought to catch it, but it reared its hind legs, opened its armor, and flew away with a buzz.

"Why do we have to stand around that bed and watch Brother Eli die?" he asked. "If I were in his place, I'd be embarrassed. I wouldn't want all those people in my room. Suppose I had an accident in my bed? Why don't people just leave Eli alone? Or why not ship him off to a nursing home where they can look after him better than we can?"

"Eli is a member of our family," the Abbot said.

"But he never liked people. I've seen him swing his cane. He *wants* to be left alone. I say let him die in peace."

The Abbot walked a little faster. "Our custom," he said, "is to support one another with our hands as well as our hearts. It's not Christian simply to leave a brother to die alone. We want to wish him farewell."

Antoine frowned. "I suppose that means I have to go back up there, to that stinky old room."

They reached the west entrance of the abbey. Antoine held the door for the Abbot, who walked in and went directly to the infirmary without washing his face or taking a cool drink. Antoine followed him. They passed Father Véran carrying a load of books in the hallway. When the Abbot had passed, Véran looked at Antoine with raised eyebrows, then sheepishly put the books down and followed. They climbed steps, went through the infirmary hallway, and entered Brother Eli's room; now it had a rotten smell to it. Father Cyprien had moved his chair into the room, and he and Marie-Nizier were snoring like two uncoordinated musicians. Brother Sauveur was staring out the window in a daze. Eli seemed not to have changed at all, lying on his pillow with his eyes closed and his mouth wide open. Air went in and out of his nostrils in an anemic pant.

"Where is the infirmarian?" the Abbot asked. "Where is Father Jude?"

Brother Sauveur took his eyes away from the window, scratched his head, and said, "I don't know. Is he gone? He was just here." He glanced about the room as if he had never seen it before.

Alfalfa still clung to the Abbot's overalls and sweetened the air. He approached the bed. With a look of concern, he spoke softly.

"What is it, Eli?" he asked. "What's on your mind? Do you wish to make a confession?"

Fathers Cyprien and Marie-Nizier woke up. Eli took a great gulp of air and opened his eyes to gaze at his superior. He moved his mouth. Father Jude entered the room with a bedpan and froze near the doorway when it was clear what was happening.

"For sixty-two years . . ." Eli said.

The Abbot waited. No one moved. A fat bumblebee flew in wide circles near the ceiling. Antoine wondered if it had entered the room with the Abbot. Except for the buzzing of the insect, no sound could be heard but a disturbing rasp from Eli's throat. With his ashen hand, he snatched at the Abbot's sleeve, then pointed at Father Marie-Nizier.

"For sixty-two years," he repeated, lifting his head. "I had to . . . stand next to that man." Eli coughed. "I had to listen to that idiot grind his damn horse teeth everywhere, in choir, in the refectory, in the cloister." He choked again and coughed. "Sixty-two years I had to sit next to him in *statio* and suffer! Does he care? He's deaf as a post."

Eli let go of the Abbot's sleeve, and his eyes rolled back in his head. A strand of saliva ran from his mouth. His head dropped back onto the linen pillow, but his breathing remained shallow and rapid.

Dom Jacques Bouvray remained motionless as if waiting for some small signal from the old monk to redeem the situation. Marie-Nizier reached into his pocket and pulled out his rosary beads with an expression of boredom; it was obvious he had not heard Eli's complaint. Cyprien sat motionless. Sauveur, Véran, and Antoine stood in silent astonishment.

The Abbot turned to Father Marie-Nizier and signed, "Go to your room."

"Eh?" Marie-Nizier said, pulling at his ear.

The Abbot moved his hands more emphatically. "Go to your room," he signed again, "you are finished here." The others made no effort to move while Marie-Nizier shrugged and pushed himself to the edge of the stuffed chair. He rocked back and forth twice and came to his feet using a cane.

"I knew I'd outlive him," Marie-Nizier said loudly. "But I never thought it would take this long." For a moment he studied the wheezing figure of Eli, then turned and shuffled out.

No one knew what to do. Jude stood near the doorway red-faced and still holding the bedpan. Sauveur and Cyprien were left in the middle of the room, blinking. Antoine put his hands in his pockets, removed them, and put them back again. The Abbot had turned his attention toward the window. Through the insect screen, a large cloud with a violet underbelly billowed up on the horizon. The air seemed cooler.

"I must get back to the barn," the Abbot said. "Please stay with Brother Eli."

He left the infirmary, and with him went the fresh green alfalfa smell. The bumblebee had come to rest against the window screen as if absorbed in attention over something outside. The only sound was Eli's shallow panting. Antoine wanted to flee. Death, he thought, was contagious. Through the window he saw the Abbot walking back toward the barn, and panic seized him. His throat began to close as he backed toward the door. Jude started the rosary again, and the repetitive incantation seemed to shrink the room. Antoine turned and walked out. He ran down the creaky stairs and out the west entrance, sprinting fifty yards down the road to the Abbot.

"*Benedicite,* Reverend Father," he said breathlessly. He stopped and put his hands on his knees. The Abbot turned to look at him.

"What is it, Antoine?"

A cool wind rushed through the corn rows and raised the leaves of the elms overhead in a swoosh that sounded brittle as paper. The air was fresh as an ocean breeze.

"I can work," Antoine said in a high, uncontrolled voice. "Please don't make me go back to that room. I don't want to be in that smelly infirmary with monks who hold grudges for sixty years." He had tears in his eyes.

The Abbot turned away from Antoine. He seemed to look about the yard for clues. Several crows tumbled through the air like black rags on the wind. Dust rose from the field and suddenly lifted the hem of Antoine's habit to his knees.

"Who are we to judge?" the Abbot shouted over sudden applause from the leaves. "Who are any of us to judge what Eli has suffered? He's dying. The mind fixes upon strange things in that agony."

The two of them pressed on toward the barn. Although the cloud was still far away, its large skirt fanned out and rushed ahead with the wind. Bits of twigs and leaves whirled around them even on the lee side of the barn. The Abbot pushed open the wooden door. They entered a dark space. In various high places the barn whistled, but its entryway was calm. Monks had stopped their work up in the loft, and through small windows Antoine could see the cows hurrying in for shelter. Each, he knew, would take its accustomed stall.

The Abbot spoke again. "Listen," he said, resting his hand against the wall. "Brother Eli Baudrillard must make peace with his own conscience. Besides, words are only words. Most of us don't mean exactly what we say. We don't know how to put the truth into sentences. It's too difficult. That's one reason why monks try to live a life of silence." He paused for a moment. "A monk's life must be judged by all its parts, not just the end."

Antoine wiped his eyes with his hand.

"I know," he said. "But it seems to me they ought to be sad, and not fighting with each other, Eli and Marie-Nizier, like mean-spirited old . . ."

"Coots?" the Abbot said with a smile. He raised a hand to cover his mouth. His cheeks flushed and his left eye closed altogether. Then his expression became serious again and he listened carefully in a sudden silence.

A pelting sound came from the loft as if someone had dumped apples down the stairs. The noise turned into a rushing vibration, and Dom Jacques and Brother Antoine moved to one of the small barn windows to see rain beating against the road. Hail also bounced along the ground but quickly dissolved into the pools of water that had formed. They watched in silence. The yard had grown dark under the heavy cloud but flashed white for a second, and thunder shook the ground. The Abbot sighed.

"I'd best go and see about the hay," he said. "I hope that hail doesn't take the barley and wheat still standing in the field."

When the Abbot walked off, Antoine remained by the window to watch the water collect in splashing puddles. A fresh smell cleansed the barn. When the heavy rain eased into a light

shower, he noticed how grass had changed from dull khaki to
emerald green. As he watched, he imagined Brother Eli and Father Marie-Nizier at the Gates of Paradise. They argued about
which of them would enter first. Each knew that the other
would ruin his heaven, so Eli went after Marie-Nizier with a
cane, and Marie-Nizier taunted Eli about growing up in a shack.
They went back and forth at each other until heavenly clouds began to boil. Lightning flashed. God appeared, an old man with a
white beard. He raised his hands to cast them both into hell.

Antoine was jolted from this vision by a familiar sound. The
bell *Saint-Joseph* had tipped. A brilliant metal tone had already
disappeared leaving a sonorous hum in the farmyard air: five
pitches suspended together and disappearing in a murmur.

Shame struck at his heart. Antoine immediately left the barn.
A sweet drizzle beaded upon his face like sweat as he set off
through the mud toward the abbey. He wanted to make up for
having run away from Eli's deathbed. His shoes became heavy.
Marching along, he turned to see others following. These monks
moved solemnly as if already headed toward the graveyard. The
Abbot was among them. The bell *Saint-Joseph* tipped a second
time.

Under the tree-covered lane, Antoine glanced up to see the
vast wet canopy dripping down on him. His habit became moist.
For a brief moment, sunlight appeared, and the water on the
leaves became so bright he had to shield his eyes from the dia-
monds. The bell *Saint-Joseph* tipped a third time.

When he arrived at the west entrance, Antoine left his muddy
shoes outside the door and rushed up the stairs barefoot. The
thought of returning to Eli's bedside seemed somehow safe, now
that the old monk was dead. Antoine had been spared: no last
choking breath, no final flutter of the eyelids. He had no desire
to witness a man giving up his place in the world and his body
letting go of warmth and living tension. Although the thought

of seeing another corpse was unsettling, shame kept Antoine moving. He had run away. He had been a coward. The bell *Saint-Joseph* tipped a fourth time.

The familiar moldy smell met him even before he reached the infirmary. He turned a corner and walked toward Eli's room. Out in the hallway Father Jude was gesturing to Sauveur and Cyprien. Véran stood beside them. "I will wash body alone," Jude signed. "Go back to your work." The bell *Saint-Joseph* tipped a fifth time.

They turned to look at Antoine. With solemn faces they moved off down the hall. Jude, no doubt, would telephone the morgue. The others would return to their daily chores. Antoine was left alone outside the closed door of Eli's room.

The bell *Saint-Joseph* tipped again, but Antoine did not hear it, nor any of the subsequent tolls. He entered the room. There, at the bedside and holding the hand of the dead monk, stood Father Marie-Nizier. He mumbled.

"You old fart," he was saying. "You lame old fart."

By the time the Abbot reached the room with the others — all of them having scrupulously cleaned their shoes at the door — Father Jude had returned and was dressing the body. And beside him, holding towels with the timidity of a schoolboy, stood Antoine, assisting.

3

The Open Window

The wrought-iron gate that kept the public from the abbey yard looked less formidable inside than out. Except
for the seventy-six-year-old monk who tended it,
Brother Henri Artignan, the gate went largely unnoticed by the
monks, off as it was beyond the trees. The latch was operated
from the gatehouse porch. Henri had only to appear behind the
bug screen, push a button, and pull open the gate by a series of
levers. He did this rarely. The gate opened only for as long as it
took the milk truck to get through, then Henri left it to swing
back of its own accord and lock. Few besides the driver of the
Manitoba Milk Producers truck ever came inside that fence.

At the moment, Henri was in the scriptorium, well within the
enclosure of the abbey. Brother Antoine was there also, at his assigned desk. Windows had been left slightly ajar for an Indian-
summer breeze, but Father Jean-Marie, hunched and gnomelike,
came into the room and shut them. Aside from his quiet footsteps, not a sound could be heard. Franciscan and Dominican fri-
ars had their recreational periods every day, when rosy-faced
men sat around card tables telling jokes and laughing, but Cistercians were silent all the time. Aside from chanted psalms and the
monk reading during meals, an entire week might pass before

Antoine had the pleasure of hearing a spoken word, and then it was usually from the Abbot, during a formal chapter meeting, when conversation was forbidden; all were to listen quietly to the sermon.

With this near-perpetual silence, brother-monks seemed remote to Antoine at times, but cordial nods and frequent signs balanced the reserve with a feeling of goodwill. Quiet acted as a cushion and fostered tranquillity; Antoine was not oblivious to its riches.

As Jean-Marie went from window to window shutting out the September breeze, Antoine opened a note from Madame Seneschal; in it she wrote that she would be in Winnipeg the following Thursday, and would it be possible to visit? In the twenty months he had been with the Cistercians, Antoine had not seen his parents. Omer and Lucie lived only an hour away, but monks were rarely permitted family visits. "Really," she wrote, "it's about time I looked you over. I want to know if you're wasting away in that place." And if her simple request did not meet with the Abbot's approval, she said, she would run her car through the gate and confront the monks on her own terms.

Antoine got up from his desk and went straightaway to the Abbot's office. Rules were one thing, but he knew Dom Jacques Bouvray. Madame Seneschal would be granted permission to visit; he was almost certain of it. No, he was not worried about the Abbot. The person who concerned him was the gatekeeper.

Brother Henri was from the Beauce region of Québec. Of hardy stock, he was proud and stubborn. His people were potato farmers and they loved to talk. As gatekeeper he was allowed to speak with anyone and everyone, except the monks. People came to the gatehouse to buy honey or ask for prayers. Antoine saw none of them. But Henri spoke almost nonstop, from sunup to sundown, with a long line of visitors. This was his job.

Some came simply to speak with Henri. He had friends. All of them, as it happened, were women. He saved his talk for the opposite sex because he did not trust men and spoke to them as little as possible. But if a woman happened by — it mattered not who — Henri found a sudden gift for words. From woody bits of his own history he squeezed every ounce of juice. What was more, he shamelessly teased gossip out of them. He even lied at times. Antoine had heard him.

One day, while Antoine was painting the clapboard on the southeast side of the gatehouse, he heard Henri tell four Gray Nuns on the porch how he had electrocuted twelve horses.

"That was after I come here from Québec," he said in his clipped French. "Nineteen forty. The sky that day, it was black. I heard thunder. Me, I had twelve work horses harnessed in the field."

Although Antoine was out of sight, on a ladder near the eaves, he could imagine how Henri was using his hands as he spoke: fingers raised and spread wide for effect, then a hand shaking or sweeping before his face. Even using sign language with the monks, Henri was unusually expressive.

He told the Gray Nuns how he calmed the wet horses after the storm blew up, how he hurried them home through lightning and thunder, how a power line fell after a flash and a crack, sparks shooting from a dancing black wire, how that same snaking wire happened to touch a pool of water the horses were standing in, "and they all dropped dead," he shouted. "Electrocuted!"

"*Mon Dieu!*" the nuns cried.

"I could have been killed," Henri explained. "I could have been standing in the puddle myself." And, as he told the Gray Nuns, his superior wished he had been. "Oh, he was angry! He wanted to wring my neck!" Henri hushed his voice to dramatic effect. "You can imagine," he said. "Those horses, they were expensive. I killed them. Today it would be like if I smash tractors."

He was ordered to do ghastly penance. Every detail was delineated for the nuns and they were horrified.

When Antoine had finished with his painting under the eaves, he went to the Abbot to ask if Henri's story was true. Together they paged through the daybook of 1940. "August 6. Severe lightning and thunder," an entry read. "One work horse, Tchou Tchou, stunned by electric wire: addled but alive." This was the only entry they could find about work horses.

With his mother's letter in hand, Antoine knocked on the Abbot's door. He wondered how Henri would pull the wool over Madame Seneschal's eyes. She loved a good story, of course. As mayor of St. Jean-Baptiste, she considered it a duty to hear and pass on good gossip. She was a veteran listener. This was what worried Antoine. Henri recognized a good listener when he saw one. He would fill her with exaggerations and tall tales about abbey life that would take Antoine a lifetime to set straight again: overstatements about fasts and penances, imaginary humiliations and cult-like brainwashing. There was no telling what nonsense Henri might serve up.

The abbey has none of that, Antoine said to himself. *The place is quite boring. Wonderfully tranquil, really. But too boring for my mother. She'd be disappointed to know the truth.*

"Come in," the Abbot ordered.

Antoine entered the room and sat in a chair. Bright light from the window illuminated a pile of papers on the Abbot's desk. Dom Jacques was wearing a pair of reading glasses and pecking at a typewriter with two fingers. Antoine cleared his throat.

"*Benedicite,* Reverend Father."

"*Dominus,*" the Abbot said. "What can I do for you, Antoine?" He did not look up from the typewriter.

"Well, you see, my mother is coming to Winnipeg on Thursday, and I was just wondering if it would be all right if maybe she could stop in and visit with me. I mean, if it's not too much trouble. I haven't seen her in a long, long time, and I don't want to give my mother the impression that I'm living in a prison."

The tap of keys stopped for a moment and the Abbot shifted his attention to the desk, searching beneath the papers with a frown. "What is it?" he said. "Your mother? How is she?"

"My mother is fine, Reverend Father. I would like to know if she might stop in for a visit."

"A visit?" the Abbot asked, smiling at an unearthed paper and turning back toward the typewriter. "We haven't seen her in a while, have we?"

Antoine shifted in the chair. "I don't want to give her the impression that I'm behind bars," he said. "Father Yves-Marie told me that my parents could come and visit, now that I've been here for nearly two years, provided, of course, that you give permission."

The Abbot was not listening. He was looking out the window. "Brother," he said, "do you know anything about dogs?"

"Dogs?" Antoine asked.

"Yes. There are three large dogs sniffing the ground over there," he said, pointing. "You see them?"

Outside, three muscular German shepherds swept back and forth across the grass with their noses to the ground. They did not look friendly. They were agitated, as if they might pounce upon anything that stirred. Antoine was baffled as to why dogs should be inside the gate, on abbey property. The Abbot's face also showed confusion with eyebrows raised high on the ridge of his forehead.

From beyond the window, men in uniforms appeared, and it became apparent that the dogs were associated with these men. Words and short whistles made the animals freeze, then sent them searching. For what, Antoine could not imagine. When the dogs had passed out of sight, more uniformed men appeared. Most of them had guns.

"What is this invasion?" the Abbot asked, reaching for the telephone on his desk. He dialed and waited, the receiver to his ear. "*Benedicite,* Brother Henri," he said. "Why do I see dogs inside the gate? And who are these military men walking about?" He paused. "Is that so? Uh-huh. Uh-huh," he said. "The Royal Canadian Mounted Police. And the Winnipeg city police also." Not a hint of amusement registered in the Abbot's face, not even the familiar chiseled grin that he often wore. "And you have absolutely no idea why they are here? Yes, well, this is a surprise for us all. Thank you, Brother."

The Abbot hesitated before he put the receiver back on the hook; then he studied the police through the window again. "Brother Henri says they arrived in a convoy. He says he was trembling when they showed him their badges. No warrant is needed in Canada, of course, but Henri should have phoned me all the same. Instead, he simply opened the gate and let them in."

"Why are they here, Reverend Father?"

"I don't know," he said. "Henri didn't even think to ask."

Dom Jacques would have to make inquiries himself. He put on as pleasant an expression as he could manage and ushered Antoine out of the office. Then, having locked the door after himself, the Abbot walked down the hallway and disappeared. Only after Antoine was alone did he realize that the issue of his mother's visit was unresolved. He had no idea if permission had actually been granted.

Antoine next heard voices coming from the washroom. Such a thing was simply out of character. Why were people talking, and why in the washroom, of all places? To his surprise, he found twelve monks there, jostling for a place at the window. Something was happening outside. Antoine elbowed his way to see.

Because the abbey was built high on a bank of the LaSalle, the view from the washroom was a panorama of the river far below and the land beyond. Antoine could see the water, and the bushes and trees rolling up on the opposite bank. The air was still; saffron, scarlet, and orange leaves were motionless.

Directly in front of the window and slightly below it, a road curved around the abbey like an asphalt patio, just before the bank rolled out of view, down to the river. From their window the monks could see the policemen outside on the road, where they had formed a barricade with their vehicles. They were there for the same panoramic view of the woods on the opposite bank.

Antoine was scandalized. The washroom reverberated with monks' voices. He knew they had no permission to speak because he had just left the Abbot.

"Police brought those dogs into the dairy and they're disturbing the cows," someone said.

"And the chicken barn, too. The birds are hysterical. We won't have eggs for a week!"

"What do you think they're after?"

"Criminals."

"Criminals? Why here? Don't they have enough criminals in the city?"

"What else could it be? Look at them. Isn't it obvious with all those weapons that they're looking for criminals?"

Twenty-five policemen stood behind the barricade facing the river, and each of them had a gun. Old Father Claude Joly leaned out the window. He gained the attention of a young constable, who walked over to the monks.

"Pardon us, folks," the constable said in English. He was blond and fair-skinned. His high forehead and broad smile gave him an earnest, open look. "Bit of a problem, I'm afraid. A man robbed the co-op ten miles south of here and he's armed. We've formed a barricade for your own protection, you understand."

Father Claude stood straight and puffed out his chest officiously. The old priest wore bifocals and his head wobbled slightly as he opened his mouth to speak. "How much money did he make off with?" he asked.

"That I can't tell you, sir," the constable answered. He paused and then continued as if reading from a report. "Two suspects are involved. They stole a green Ford Fiesta and fled down County Road 330 for approximately ten miles while being pursued. Police managed to shoot out the left rear tire of the Fiesta and the vehicle rolled. At that time, the driver was pinned and was apprehended at 2:54 P.M. The other suspect fled on foot. He is armed and dangerous. The public is at risk."

Father Claude rubbed his chin with authority. "That suspect at large, is he in possession of the money?"

"I presume so, sir."

"Ah, yes," Claude said. "Well, how in hell are we to know how serious the crime is if we don't know how much money is involved? It could be twenty dollars. It could be twenty thousand dollars."

The constable blinked several times, then scratched his ear. Meanwhile, Antoine was scrutinizing the men positioned behind the barricade. They looked martial and intimidating. Although most of the window space was already taken up by Father Claude, Antoine managed to see how each policeman was shaved and scrubbed, stuffed into a uniform, face set rigidly and hair severely cropped.

"Will the fugitive go to prison if he's caught?" Claude asked. By now, he had his arm comfortably propped against the window frame.

"More than likely," the constable answered, glancing back at the river. He seemed anxious to wrap up the conversation. Claude, on the other hand, was just getting started.

"Say," he said, "have you heard the one about the monk and the convict?"

"No sir," the constable replied.

"Well, there's this monastery, you see, located right next to a prison. In fact, the monastery and the prison share the same stone wall. Monks and prisoners wave back and forth to one another. And this monk yells to a convict, 'How long you in for?'

"And the convict yells back, 'Twenty years. I stole money. I stole lots of it. Prisoners over here got respect for me because of my impressive sentence. How about you? How long you in for?'

"And the monk answers, 'For life.'

"Well now, that criminal's mouth falls open. He's impressed. And he's eager to know what the monk did to deserve a life sentence.

"'I took vows,' the monk says."

Claude began to laugh. "The monk said, 'I took vows.' Do you get it? Not bad, eh? The monk said he took vows and he's in for life."

The constable scratched his head while Claude kept laughing. Antoine bit his lip and looked at the other monks. They were not laughing either. Claude held his side and shook.

"What kind of vows did he take?" the constable asked.

Claude's face was flushed with mirth. He tried to steady his wobbling head and faced the constable directly. "I don't think you get it," he said, "about the vows."

"No," the constable said. "You're right. I'm sorry."

Antoine rolled his eyes and shook his head. He glanced down to the placid river. Brown water was visible, but from his position at the window he failed to make out the eddies, and could not, of course, hear the river's familiar gurgle in the reeds. The

LaSalle flowed smoothly in a deep, curving path, and Antoine often sat on a granite boulder near its edge. A scenic picture it made in the autumn, framed by the multicolored leaves of the woods. At that moment, however, instead of the tranquil water he wished to hear, he listened to Father Claude attempt to explain his joke.

"You see, monks are something like incarcerated criminals," Claude said. "That's the substance of the humor. Their lifestyles are the same. They both live behind walls. Both eat bad food. From what I know, prisoners do penance for their sins, same as monks. They work hard and follow strict rules. They wear uniforms and obey superiors. Monks do the same thing. We sleep in cells. We're allowed few visitors. Sounds like prison, doesn't it?"

Antoine rolled his eyes again, but the constable seemed fascinated. The comparison was interesting to him. Wide-eyed and mouth ajar, he gave his full attention to Claude.

"Well then, tell me," he said. "You people, can you come and go as you please, or are you forced to stay inside that fence?"

Claude rubbed his chin. "'Forced' might be too strong a word," he said, "but we aren't exactly free to come and go. Take me, for example. The last time I left this place was when I went to see a doctor in Winnipeg two years ago."

A monk behind Claude signed "poor father, sad father" by pinching the habit cloth at his breast, then pointing to imaginary tears running down his face. Antoine observed the amazed look of the constable and tried to guess the man's thoughts. Did he suppose that monks were shut away for the safety of the public?

"Do you have a television in there?" the constable asked.

"I'm seventy-three years old," Claude answered, buffing his glasses with a handkerchief, "and I've never seen a television set. I entered this community before they were invented. But the Abbot has a radio in his office, and he passes along any news he judges pertinent."

"Are you allowed to eat hot dogs?" the constable asked. And Claude had to admit that he was not. According to the constitutions of their religious order, he and the other monks were largely vegetarian.

"Oh yes, monastic life can be very difficult," Claude went on. "We rarely see our families. And I'm inside here with people I didn't necessarily choose to be with."

The other monks in the washroom had grown impatient. They grumbled and shook their heads. One of them nudged the old priest, but Claude seemed quite satisfied with the attention he had gained from the constable and continued.

"It's a martyrdom, really. A slow martyrdom. And in a sense, it's exactly like being incarcerated." He leaned out the window and put a hand near his mouth as a shield, but his words were perfectly audible to the monks behind him. "Some of these guys are not always friendly."

Laughter erupted from the monks. Even Antoine grinned. The constable seemed confused.

"Forgive my ignorance," he said. "I don't know anything about monks. If I may ask, why are you there in the first place? Are you being punished?"

Claude laughed. He began to tell his life's story, and he was thorough about it. As Antoine gazed out at the river, his mind wandered.

What, he thought, might a criminal look like? Antoine had nothing to go by except images from comic books and the films he had seen before coming to the abbey. Every criminal, he assumed, had a big neck, cauliflower ears, and a broken nose. A crewcut. Oh yes, and a tattoo on his upper arm. Such a man had to be big and swarthy.

His reverie was cut short by the laughter. Father Claude had made some sort of quip, and as the constable chortled, Claude said, "So you see, it was all a coincidence. I might as well say that because of my father's indigestion I became a monk." Antoine was very impatient with this. He wanted to see a criminal.

When the laughter stopped, Claude asked whether the police would shoot the burglar from their side of the river. The constable shook his head.

"Well, sir," he said, "we don't really shoot at people without provocation."

Antoine smiled. He was calmed by both the response and the tone of voice in which it was delivered. To him, the constable looked like a nice, generous person, someone who might be good at rescuing cats. Antoine could not say as much for the policemen behind the lineup of vehicles. With their hands ready on their weapons, they seemed poised to shoot.

"We won't shoot," the constable said, "unless the fugitive shoots at us."

None of this satisfied Claude. "Listen," he said, "you ought to wing him as he runs by. That's what I'd do. Because look at yourself. You're on the wrong side of the river. If you don't wing him, he'll get away through the woods to the highway, and you'll never see him again."

Once more the constable shook his head. "On the other side of the woods, Highway 75 is barricaded, just like this road is here," he said. "He'll eventually meet up with police no matter where he turns."

Father Claude kept talking. Antoine was astonished by how quickly the old priest had turned into a chatterbox, and how much he seemed to enjoy having an army of policemen on the property. Claude told the constable that he used plenty of guns in his day, back before sophisticated sights had been invented. Was there much kick in the high-powered rifles the policemen were holding?

The constable explained that the rifles had enough kick to "pardon me, sir, knock you on your ass."

"I doubt it. I doubt it," Claude said. "Give me one of them."

The constable grinned, but Antoine wondered if Claude really meant it as a joke. After witnessing this performance, Antoine believed him capable of any mischief.

Claude kept up a steady barrage of questions. What was the constable's name? Did he have a wife and children? Whereabouts had he grown up? What made him want to become a policeman? Was he Catholic? While the old priest grilled the policeman, boredom mounted in the washroom. One monk twiddled his thumbs. Another drummed the porcelain edge of a sink. The police had instructed them all to stay inside where they were unable to see the action, and they were restless. Several left to watch from the scriptorium windows a floor above, but high elm foliage made the river almost impossible to see from there.

The constable said his name was Jim Branaugh. He was Presbyterian and not yet married. He was twenty-four years old. Grew up in Miami, Manitoba, and knew he wanted to become a Mountie when he saw a constable on a horse in Ottawa.

"Ottawa? How old were you then?" Claude asked. "Twelve?"

"No, sir. I was nineteen."

Such news was heartening for Antoine. He was nineteen when he decided to enter religious life. And he had been influenced, too, by the sight of a monk in a habit.

Suddenly all heads turned in the direction of a muted sound down by the river. Antoine saw ducks fly from the reeds. He felt as if he were in a Hollywood movie, except that no director would intervene to cut the action.

The policemen remained where they were. Antoine thought their impassivity peculiar until he saw two of them he had not noticed before ushering a civilian up the riverbank toward the abbey. Guns were pointed at him. Briefly he tried lowering his hands from over his head, but one of the officers poked him in the ribs with a gun barrel. The man was burly. His hair was a mere shadow over his skull, and he wore wire-rimmed glasses. His big nose looked like a boxer's, battered and flat, and his expression was surly. This was almost exactly how Antoine imagined a fugitive to look, and he was pleased with himself. Evil always had a look to it, he thought.

When the suspect and the policemen drew closer, Father Claude craned his head out the window and adjusted his spectacles. His head wobbled. "Who's that?" he asked. "Wait a minute. Why, it's Brother Simon. It's our Brother Simon in work clothes! I'm afraid you have the wrong man."

When they drew still closer, Antoine saw that it was true: a disgruntled Brother Simon Montmayeur dressed in work overalls was being hustled onto the road.

"That one is ours!" Claude shouted, and Constable Branaugh rushed over to the advancing group, waving his arms. It was all a mistake, he explained, and the policemen lowered their weapons. Simon was escorted beyond the view at the window to the abbey door. Monks rushed from the washroom and down the hall to greet him. Coming toward them, Simon yanked his arms away from the police officers.

"Let go," he yelled. "*Décolle-toi!* This here is outrageous! A man can't even dig up the gladiola bulb without being molested by *police montée*."

"What happened?" Father Jude Sanders asked in English. "Tell us what happened."

"Me, I am minding my own business," Brother Simon explained, "digging up bulbs by the grotto. There am I, on my hands and knees with the trowel, when all at once I hear a voice, it is yell behind me in English, '*Drop the gun and raise slowly your hands.*' I turn, and there are they, the police. They have guns. They are aiming them at me! I scream. They yell, '*Shut up and drop you the gun.*' And then I tell them I have not a gun, I have the trowel, but they yell louder, *'Don't try nothing or we'll shoot.'* And what am I supposed to do? I drop the trowel and raise my hands like they tell to me. And then, what do they do? The crazy jokers. They frisk me! All up and down, and rough. And I'm getting mad. Then we are yelling at each other and they are not listening to me and they have the guns. They order me to walk slowly toward the building. They tell me to shut my mouth. Whose place is this, anyhow, I say? What's going on here?"

Simon was trembling. The stubby hair on his head was damp and sweat dripped from his forehead. Claude explained the situation in French.

"There's a criminal on the other side of the river," he said. "Police are everywhere. In their eagerness to catch this man, they must have mistaken you for him."

"Me?" Simon asked. "Do I look like a criminal?"

Father Jude took Simon's pulse. His heartbeat was rapid, and because Simon already had a history of high blood pressure, together they went off to the infirmary. In Simon's wake, tension hung in the air. The monks grumbled among themselves. Where had the Abbot gone? How long would they have to stay inside the building?

"This is what happens every day out in the world," one of them said. "I don't know how people stand it."

"Nothing but trouble," said another. "I have a headache already."

Antoine felt anxious and impatient. Even though he was afraid of what might happen once the fugitive arrived, he wanted something — anything — to happen so that the affair would be over and done with. Father Claude led the group back to the washroom. Antoine followed. From outside the window Constable Branaugh greeted them with a sheepish smile.

"Officers Jacobi and Daniels ask pardon," he said. "They will write an official apology once we have this business under control. You do understand, I hope, that we are only concerned for your protection."

The young man's face was a healthy pink, but his ears were as bright as boiled lobsters. Antoine felt sorry for him, for Branaugh had done nothing wrong.

Once more Father Claude dominated the window. He sucked air in through his nose and placed a hand on his hip as if he were chief of police. "You know what I think?" he said. "I think the fugitive got away. He has already slipped through your trap." Though his head was steadier than usual, his chin quivered. "You people may as well go home."

Constable Branaugh returned a weak smile, part camera-ready grin, part grimace. With a finger between his collar and neck, he eased himself into a more comfortable standing position. "We hate to impose like this," he said, "but our orders are to stay put. We have everything but a radio collar on that guy, and he's on his way up here, toward your property, sure as I'm standing in front of you."

Claude's head began to shake more vigorously, almost as though he were doing it on purpose. "I will remind you," he said, "that you're standing on private property." His chest rose with every word. "If anyone shoots, it should be me."

"I'm sorry, sir," Constable Branaugh responded, "but under the circumstances we have every right to be here, according to Canadian law. If you'd like, I could ask my sergeant to step over here. Would you like to speak with him?"

Antoine wanted to melt from the scene. He took a step back from the window, but his way was blocked by the monks behind him, and he found it impossible to ease out of sight. Everyone was silent. An unmistakable tension was building, and Antoine wished that the criminal would make an appearance before Claude did something stupid.

As it was, Claude simply stood there and stared at Branaugh

while Branaugh fidgeted with his collar, stealing glances at the river. A trickle of sweat emerged from the constable's hairline and in a slow, transparent glazing rolled down his cheek to his neck. Antoine was upset: once again the situation struck him as unfair. Constable Branaugh was not responsible for either the barricade or the police presence, yet Claude seemed to have focused his wrath upon him. Branaugh carried a gun at his hip, but he was not aiming it across the river like the others.

"Excuse me," Antoine found himself saying, "would you like some iced tea?"

Branaugh turned his head.

"Iced tea," Antoine repeated. "You look thirsty."

The constable opened his mouth, but no words came out. Antoine turned and glared at the monks behind him. In a moment, a path opened and he went to the kitchen for the tea. Soon, without discussion, a relay had been organized and cups were being handed out to Branaugh. He in turn took cold tea to every policeman along the road. Branaugh took his own cup last. By then, Father Claude had relinquished his position at the window and gone off sulking.

When Branaugh tasted his tea, he looked up. His glance caught Antoine's, and the constable smiled. A gush of pleasure went through the young monk and moved into his face so that he could not refrain from beaming ear to ear. To Antoine, the blue eyes of the constable were as vernal and full of life as any he had ever seen.

Meanwhile, the cups of tea backed up so that each monk had one. They stood drinking and chatting in a fashion that was rigorously forbidden by the customs of the house, but tension eased and faces were smiling. On the linoleum down the hall, a familiar tread was heard and soon Dom Jacques Bouvray approached them like an angry pontiff.

"What is happening here?" he asked. "Who gave you permission to speak? What on earth are you people doing near the window? These policemen have a serious job to do and the lot of you are clowning around in the washroom as though we had nothing to do all day but cavort in full view of these respectable public servants. The entire world will think that we are a bunch of buffoons! I've had my hands full since the policemen arrived and I don't need trouble from you."

The monks were not the least bit chastened by his scolding. Instead, they responded with a volley of questions. Had the fugitive been found? Were policemen still in the barns? Was the abbey surrounded? Would the Mounties question individual monks? How long before monks could return to their tasks in the garden and the farmyard? Would the abbey be in tomorrow's paper? Had the Abbot been interviewed for television?

Dom Jacques held up his hands until the room was silent. He explained that the policemen had found nothing in the barns, and aside from the contingent outside the window, they had gone farther southwest to a bridge on the river. The fugitive had nowhere to go. He was surrounded on the other side of the river, and the police were closing in on him.

As the Abbot spoke, Antoine glanced out the window and saw the frail figure of Father Claude, his head wobbling, standing in the middle of the road behind the police barricade shouting and shaking a finger at someone. Antoine presumed he was the commanding officer. Claude had worked himself into a frenzy and looked unsteady enough to topple over onto the pavement at any moment. Apparently no one had ever taken the barrel-chested sergeant to task, for Branaugh was clearly amazed. The other policemen gazed at Claude with their mouths agape.

Antoine intended to draw the Abbot's attention to the scene, but out of the corner of his eye he caught the enormous blue wings of a heron as it flew just above the water. Then he saw the fugitive.

On the opposite bank of the river, within the foliage of a yellow bush, the man's head appeared between branches almost like a big piece of fruit. Antoine squinted. His eyes, he thought, were fooling him. But then the bush moved. Leaves shook as if in a breeze, only there was no breeze, and the head did not disappear. Even from a distance, the man did not look like a criminal. His nose was small. His hair was strawberry blond. He had a light complexion that had turned red in the sun, and a large forehead, and he could not have been more than twenty years old. When he stepped out from the yellow leaves, Antoine saw that his clothes were muddy, but he looked as innocuous as a delivery boy except for the shotgun he carried in his left hand. Antoine's dilemma was clear. While the monks in the washroom listened to the Abbot, and policemen at the side of the road were distracted with Father Claude, was it right to allow the criminal to slip away? Or ought Antoine to shout and draw everyone's attention to him?

The fugitive seemed unaware of the police car palisade on the abbey side of the river. He put his hand to his forehead. Shielding his eyes from the rays of the sun, he looked harmless. Antoine could not bring himself to shout or point. To direct the policemen's attention upon the man seemed unfair: twenty-five guns would be leveled at him in an instant.

On the other hand, Antoine reminded himself, the criminal was in desperate straits. He had a gun himself. And if he should notice the inattentive Mounties, the man could easily fire, and perhaps kill one of them. From Antoine, all that was needed was a word of warning.

He was paralyzed; the moment seemed endless. How was

he to make a judgment? Criminals were supposed to look suspicious, weren't they? Evil had a face, didn't it? Just like in the movies.

The policemen around Father Claude began to laugh: the priest's scolding had apparently been sidetracked by his own joke, requiring posed hands under his chin and eyes crossed. The Mounties loved it. Everyone had forgotten about the river.

Inside the washroom the Abbot was still speaking to the monks. "The police have promised to get this business under control before nightfall," he said. "Now why don't we move out of here and leave them to their duties." He went out the door, and the others followed him. Antoine could not bring himself to leave the window. The criminal was still there, in full view, looking this way and that with a hand above his eyes, searching for clues that were directly in front of him.

Branaugh was the first to make a sign, and in a moment the policemen had scrambled into position, raising guns and taking aim. Before Father Claude knew what was happening, Branaugh shuffled him off to safety. Meanwhile, the barrel-chested sergeant whom Claude had been scolding raised a megaphone to his mouth. But before he uttered a word, the fugitive disappeared back into the bush. An elk might have vanished from hunters in the same way.

Antoine's jaw relaxed as he looked toward the yellow foliage where the fugitive had been. He was relieved. In his mind, the dilemma had come and gone before he was required to make an intelligent decision.

Only the bright twittering of birds was heard. The policemen remained still. Had the fugitive seen them? Would he show his face again?

The sergeant raised the megaphone and shouted, *"We've seen you."* His echo boomed back across the river like an alpine horn.

"Drop your gun and come out with your hands up. There's no escape. Patrol cars wait for you beyond the woods."

Birds stopped chirping and the countryside was quiet. Antoine leaned out the window into electric air. He caught his breath. Quickly he removed himself from the window, thinking that he might be a perfect target, cross-wired within the scope of the criminal's rifle. As he hugged the wall, he was momentarily distracted by a ping-ping sound above and to the left of his head. There, in the full light of the sun, a blowfly tapped angrily against the upper pane of the window.

Suddenly there was a sharp crack, like wood splitting, and Antoine expected the window to shatter. When it did not, he decided that it was not the criminal who fired but one of the policemen. He peeked out near the windowsill. The Mounties, at their positions behind vehicles, looked at one another in puzzlement. No smoke could be seen or smelled, but Antoine was certain that he had heard the sound of a gunshot. He withdrew.

A whole minute passed in heavy, second-by-second plodding, and although Antoine was anxious to ask the policemen what had happened, he was afraid to poke his head above the sill again. To him it seemed that the gunshot had come from far away, perhaps beyond the reach of gunfire from the abbey.

A sudden electric crackle made Antoine jump. Timidly he poked his head up over the sill. The crackle came from a police car radio. The sergeant with the megaphone leaped up to answer the call. Antoine could hear a squawking voice. The sergeant gave a signal and the policemen left their positions and surrounded him. Antoine could not hear what was said. After their huddle, they broke up and climbed into vehicles. Antoine leaned out the window. He waved at Branaugh, who was about to drive away.

"What happened?" he yelled. "Tell me what happened."

Branaugh stopped his patrol car near the washroom window and gripped the wheel as he spoke. "I don't think that fugitive saw us here on the road," he said. "Poor man. Apparently he heard the megaphone and started to run. The city police on Highway 75 heard a single shot and went into the woods to investigate. They found him dead. I would guess that he must have stumbled. He blew his own head off. Sorry to have bothered you folks with all this, but it's over." He waved, rolled up the window, and drove out, leaving a fine dust hanging in the air.

Antoine pulled his head back inside the washroom and stood for a while watching the fly bump against the window. He thought he should go tell the others what had just happened. Instead, he decided to stay in the washroom for a few days until he understood it.

If he had shouted as soon as he saw the criminal, would the man still be alive? Could Antoine have saved him, done something differently? With these thoughts, he was swept into sullenness. He fidgeted. *People are like bugs,* he said to himself. *They die.*

The angry blowfly pittered its way down the window. *Yes, people are like bugs. They bang repeatedly against invisible obstacles until they die.*

The fly pinged one more time against the wooden window frame and escaped into the mild autumn afternoon.

The following Thursday, Madame Seneschal waited inside the gatehouse. She was seated in the parlor with a copy of the *Winnipeg Free Press*. On her head she wore a purple hat with a feather in it, and Brother Henri was speaking a rapid French that sounded like German for its coarseness.

"Much more horrible than the paper," he was saying. "The police, they were all over the place. They turn everything upside out. Is a terrible mess they made."

Madame Seneschal shook her head and clicked her tongue. The feather moved languidly above her head. She tried to say something, but Henri cut her off.

"The newspaper," he said, "it's all wrong what they have in there. First, police come at the gate with big cars. I am standing there. I see with my own eyes. They get out with their big guns and their dogs. They tell me open up, they want to shoot somebody. I say, 'Who?' They say, 'None of your business. Open the gate.' I tell them I will phone the Abbot first. They tell me I will phone no one. They show me a paper. It's written in English. 'What?' I say. They ask me, 'Can't you read?' They say they will make me arrested if I don't open the gate. I open. They come in and turn everything upside out. A mess is everywhere: in the church, the sacristy, the dormitory, the barn. The Abbot, he blames me."

"*Étonnant!*" Madame Seneschal said, shaking her head. "I thought it was safe, here at the abbey. After all, it's so . . . quiet." She ran her finger along the windowsill, leaving a trail. "Peaceful enough for dust to settle, anyway."

Antoine stood unseen behind the door and peeked through the hinges while Henri told Antoine's mother how monks were threatened at gunpoint. Of course none of these details made it into the paper, he explained, because the police must own the paper.

"The people that write these words in the news, they should come ask me instead of ask all the time the police. I will tell them everything. How the dogs were here in the barn. Cows are still not giving milk."

Madame Seneschal shook her head again. Then Antoine stepped into the doorway and coughed.

"*Mon petit foin!*" she cried, and bounced up from her chair, grabbing him. "Oh, but you are nothing but skin and bones.

They are starving you here. My poor *petit foin,* you have no color in your cheeks!" She fussed over him, and pinched here and there. When finally she kissed him, Brother Henri frowned, got out of his chair, and left the room.

"Oh, that brother," Madame Seneschal said. "He is quite the *chouenneux,* eh? A storyteller. I can't believe it was like he says." She waved the *Winnipeg Free Press.* "Here, it reports nothing at all about the abbey. Only that a thief stumbled and shot himself by the LaSalle River. Is it true, what the brother says?"

Antoine hesitated to tell anything. He wanted his mother to believe that he was safe. Dom Jacques Bouvray, he thought, must have worked out a deal with the police to keep the abbey out of the paper, and consequently out of the public's attention. After all, the police had interfered enough. They probably agreed not to mention the abbey, in compensation for having disturbed the monks.

Antoine wanted to reassure his mother that monastic life was calm. "I guess I have to admit," he said to her, "that Brother Henri has a tendency to exaggerate somewhat."

"Ah, good," she said. "I knew it. He's a *bonhomme,* a joker. That brother was only entertaining me. Thank goodness. After all, am I expected to believe that there would be guns in *this* place? Or police dogs? Guns pointing at my son?" She laughed. "Around here there's no noise, even. A cricket couldn't sneeze without everybody knowing it. Anyway, I'm relieved that the Mounties got their man. And even more relieved that my little boy is safe."

An image of the fair-haired fugitive flashed through Antoine's head, a man much the same as Constable Branaugh. They could have been cousins. One could have been the other. The criminal's sunburned complexion, his youthful, innocuous appearance: what did it mean? Life seemed more complicated when appearances were not allies of truth and goodness.

"Momma, I'm safe," Antoine said. "And are you happy now, at my being here with the monks?"

"Happy?" she said. "Who said happy? You live inside a locked gate, for heaven's sake. Yes, it might be quiet here, but I haven't seen you in two years, and you look skinny as a bedpost." She crossed her arms and nodded her head. "Without women, you can expect such things. I'm surprised worse hasn't happened! With no women around, well of course you can expect turmoil, bad food, and dust."

4

The Baker Monk

B rother Antoine woke to sounds of groaning, then heard a name repeated over and over. The voice was soft and rich, and completely without the murkiness of dreaming. "Mary, Mary," it said. The voice came from behind a curtain, in the bed next to his.

The voice was recognizable. Antoine had heard Brother Martin Brown read aloud in choir: chapters of Scripture proclaimed in a resonant tenor, every *r* rolled in a manner peculiar to someone of Scottish origin. Martin had recently been assigned the bed next to his for reasons Antoine did not know, and the sound of his voice in the dormitory was unusual. Cistercian monks seldom spoke in their sleep; the abbey's rule of night silence seemed to have made its way even into their dreams.

Martin spoke softly again. "Mary, Mary," he whispered. A rustling of sheets accompanied the name. Antoine opened his eyes. *The monk is at prayer,* he thought. *He is whispering the holy name of the Mother of God.*

Their beds were in the middle of the dormitory, a vast room spread out on the abbey's third floor. Nearly forty monks — all but the Abbot and those in the infirmary — slept there under the mansard roof. On cold March nights the dormitory was drafty and difficult to heat. Curtains divided beds one from another. From every part of the room Brother Antoine heard a chorus of steady snoring: monks unaware of anything but the private and jumbled images of sleep. "Mary" was whispered again, and Martin's breathing became stronger, less measured. Antoine had never before heard such fervor in prayer. He tried to imagine Martin's face in ecstasy — eyes raised heavenward in detached bliss — but prayer had little to do with the expression he pictured on Martin's face.

Sheets rustled in a steady, rhythmic pattern. Something like a fever overtook Antoine. He imagined Martin whispering in his ear, the breathy warmth of it brushing his cheek. Perspiration broke out along his spine. His body seemed to act of its own accord, and Antoine pressed against the mattress in a rhythm that matched Martin's. Immense warmth and urgency came to him. Martin's breathing was rapid. Then he gasped and relinquished movement. Silence followed. Neither of them moved, though Antoine wanted to wake a priest and make his confession. Instead he waited, and after a moment the sound of Martin turning on his straw mattress made the event seem ordinary. Soon the monk was snoring.

Antoine rose quietly and wiped his thigh with a handkerchief. He removed his habit from a peg on the wall, dressed quickly and went down the stairs and outside. Snow lay on the ground. The air was chilled and fresh as mountain water, and he was completely awake. When his feet became too cold to stay out any longer, he spent the rest of the night in the scriptorium, walking back and forth along the rows of desks.

At three-thirty, under raw electric light, he saw Martin in choir with the others, alert and ready for the day. Some monks looked bloated and tired; from beneath the quilts of their half-open eyelids they followed chant texts. But Martin always stood with ramrod posture that made him appear tall among squat French-

Canadian monks. He had a Scotsman's square jaw with a shadow of black whiskers. His nose was straight and narrow. A thick, continuous brow ran above his eyes, and the hair on his head grew quickly after it was shaved. Antoine was especially aware of Martin's long lashes and his unusual purple-blue eyes.

After the office of Vigils, the cloister was still cold and the windows black. Antoine stood alone while the others walked to a breakfast of weak coffee and cold toast. He observed himself in the glass. A young prisoner of war looked back at him with a thin face, a shaved head like the other monks, and large, hungry eyes.

The following night Antoine heard nothing from Martin except soft, regular snores. For a long while he listened on the edge of sleep. But sleep did not come. He could not help but remain alert to Martin's every move. And in the nights following, Antoine listened vigilantly. He heard the monk slowly remove his habit, and soon after heard the crush of straw inside the mattress as Martin crawled into bed, the groan as he lay back upon the pillow, and the suck of air as he turned on his side. Antoine's nose was keen, too, for the faint, breadlike smell of Martin, for Martin was the baker monk. As breathing slowed and snores came from every corner of the dormitory, Antoine remained awake.

During the day his movements were slow, his feet heavy. Every task seemed arduous. Monks turned their heads, noticing how Antoine fell asleep as soon as he sat down in choir or in chapter. At meals, he seemed weary enough to drop off while chewing.

In the work line, when Antoine stood with the others waiting for daily orders from the Abbot, he was hardly able to stand. Father Yves-Marie's large eyes — swimming behind thick lenses — were upon him. Familiar with the young monk's even behavior throughout the novitiate, Yves-Marie quickly noticed the change.

"Sick?" he asked by placing his right elbow to his side, then dropping the forearm to the right.

Antoine signed back, "No worry. Just tired."

But when the Abbot came to him, after greeting each monk in the work line, he raised the question also. "You look tired," he said. "Antoine, are you getting enough sleep?"

"No," he replied. "But I'll be fine, Reverend Father. I have things on my mind, that's all."

The Abbot shook his head. "Lack of sleep is no good," he said. "Bring your problems to Father Yves-Marie or come to me. Don't bottle them up," and he continued down the line, greeting the new novice, Dominique Moulin, and a postulant, Charles Frémont.

Listless as Antoine was, unable to focus attention on anything for very long — except Brother Martin — shame kept him from admitting to superiors that he suffered from infatuation. Some nights he slept, but never for the seven full hours allotted the community. Weeks of insomnia upset his stomach. He ate less. His body began to feel like a rusted machine. Antoine had little energy for work. Nevertheless, at night, no matter how tired he was, his attention became riveted once again on Martin; Antoine imagined Martin asleep next to him, in the same bed, skin touching skin. And nothing Antoine did could drive these thoughts from his imagination. He tried lying on the cold linoleum floor. He tried sitting up in bed, propped against the wall. He stuffed his ears with cotton, and then with balls of soft wax from church candles. One of these balls lodged so deeply in his auditory canal that he had to go to the infirmary.

Father Jude, the tall freckled nurse, enjoyed a general permission to speak to anyone who came to him. "Why are you stuffing wax in here?" he asked as he dug into Antoine's ear with tweezers.

"Because I can't sleep for all the snoring," Antoine replied. "Give me some sleeping tablets."

"Pills are only a temporary solution," Father Jude explained. "Over time, more pills are needed, and a drug-induced slumber is never restful." He suggested long, brisk walks and a glass of warm milk before bed.

Walks, however, did not help. Neither did the milk. Antoine remained compulsively aware of Brother Martin, and sleeplessness caused his emotions to foment, enough so that Antoine developed a rash. Tears came easily. He could feel them welling. The washroom, or outdoors, became places of quick escape where he could be alone.

Brother Antoine's nose always seemed red. His face took on a puffiness that made Father Yves-Marie worry. More than once he was sent to bed in the middle of the day. But he did not sleep. When the community gathered in choir to sing the divine praises, Antoine was only vaguely aware of the liturgy. Monks turned to look at him, to see how distracted he had become, bowing at the wrong moments, staring off into space. Sometimes Antoine remained silent during hymns. When he felt their eyes upon him — their concern — he was unmoved, because for as many times as Antoine glanced up, Brother Martin's violet-blue eyes never met his. Martin was indifferent; his face was set in a stern expression that seemed to indicate an intense absorption in his own inner life. This coldness reminded Antoine of a statue he had seen in an art book: Moses holding the ten commandments.

Because he knew Martin's eyes never wandered, Antoine shamelessly observed him. Antoine's love was a constant scrutiny. Already familiar with the Scotsman's rigor, he came to admire the intensity with which Martin worked and prayed. But judging from the way Martin's jaw worked under the skin, monastic life seemed a strain. Other monks performed duties with detached ease, as if capable of nothing else, whereas Martin pushed himself through the day, slapping dough and banging bread pans. Other monks went from work to choir with vapid smiles on their faces. Apparently they needed the routine of the abbey as cows need a path from barn to pasture. But Martin walked the hall with authority, like a football coach or an executive. He moved with purpose. The hem of his robes hindered his stride somewhat, but he knew where he was going.

At breakfast one morning the toast ran out. Brother Roland went to Martin and signed for more, his forefingers and thumbs shaped into a triangle, followed by a sawing motion with the edge of his hand. Brother Martin ignored Roland's signs, because breakfast was to be taken in silence. That was the rule. As far as Martin was concerned, not even signs were allowed. Martin was scrupulous except, Antoine thought, for certain nocturnal indiscretions.

One day in the scriptorium Martin was reading at his assigned place when Antoine came upon him. With book in hand, Martin had drawn the chair back from the desk and hiked his habit up, exposing bare calves. Antoine stopped to observe. The muscles of Martin's leg tensed and relaxed, tensed and relaxed, as if he were ready to leap up even while reading. The shape of the leg became so absorbing that Antoine forgot what he had come to the scriptorium to find.

Wherever Martin happened to be, laxity in monastic observance was immediately checked. Once, Brother Roland and the new novice, Dominique, talked about Québec politics while shoveling snow near the pig barn. Antoine was working nearby. As he chipped ice from the concrete flooring at the doorway, the two yammered. They were breaking the rules, thinking they were out of earshot. But when Martin came out to help, Roland

and Dominique acted as though their tongues had been cut out. Inside the abbey Brother Camille was always whispering here and there, pestering others with his comments. But the mere sight of Martin made Camille's mouth snap shut. Martin did not notice this. His obduracy alone reminded others of the rule.

Antoine's obsession grew. During public prayer, at meals, and when the community worked in silence together, Antoine was aware of a single person only. Martin, for his part, took no notice of Antoine. That is, until they were assigned dishes together.

Father Louis Rondel complained of arthritis and asked to be relieved of dishwashing in the bakery. The Abbot asked Antoine to accept this duty. Every day, after taking loaves from the oven, Martin filled a sink with soapy water. Antoine came in, and the two worked in customary silence. Martin wore a white apron over his habit, the sleeves rolled up to the elbow, and Antoine noticed a profusion of black hair on Martin's forearms, wet, heavy, and glistening on his skin. Some days Antoine felt Martin's fingers touch his accidentally. They never looked at each other. When Martin pulled the drain, he often smiled toward the wall, displaying fine white teeth to no one, while Antoine hung towels to dry.

The bakery was a warm and cozy place, especially on crisp April mornings when the rest of the abbey felt like a walk-in refrigerator. Inside the bakery, fresh bread smelled sweet and pure, like the skin of an infant.

During the first week they were together, a wet china bowl slipped from Brother Antoine's hands and smashed on the floor. The shatter and spinning of chips made him tighten and he could not move. Martin got a broom and dustpan. He swept the pieces from the floor, then brushed Antoine's shoes with the broom while smiling at the floor. After the broom and dustpan were stowed in the closet, Martin brought his index and middle fingers to his forehead, then touched the tips of his little fingers together. "Abbot displeased," he was saying, but in fact no one would ever learn about the bowl.

Outside the bakery Martin remained distant and self-absorbed. When the community took their meals in the refectory, he never looked up. Chewing food, he held his knife and fork as if they were a hammer and pliers. Toast he tore into small pieces and popped into his mouth, back between the molars. He grasped the coffee cup by its rim, not the handle, then brought it to his mouth and sipped between index finger and thumb. When he swallowed, his Adam's apple vanished for a moment, then reappeared like a log rising to the surface of water.

During March and April, when not washing dishes in the bakery, Antoine was assigned to the cannery helping Brother Roland whitewash the walls. Roland covered twice the area that Antoine did, and Roland's clothes were far less splashed with lime. Antoine painted slowly and without concentration. Away from Martin, he was always tired. Not even the chalky-acid smell of whitewash roused him.

One day, when the tower bell announced the end of afternoon work, Antoine walked back to the abbey and entered the basement changing room. He rolled up his sleeves at a sink by the shower stalls and prepared to wash his face. Someone turned on the water in the shower behind him, and aluminum rings raced along the rail in a singing scuttle as plastic curtains were pulled shut. Seconds later Martin appeared, dripping and naked. He leaned over Antoine to grab a bar of soap from the sink, then disappeared back into the stall.

Antoine stood immobile at the sink. He felt cold air on his tongue. The image remained inside his head as clear as a photograph: skin wet as if oiled with balsam, an astonishing black mane funneled like an hourglass from the chest down the abdomen to where it bloomed again between the legs. Antoine shook his head, but the remarkable image remained. For a long while he felt Martin's warm breath on his neck, real as when the wet hand had reached for the soap.

The Scotsman's body was ordinary, really, with its pattern of hair and unexcused carnal weight and smell. But Antoine thought he was beautiful, so mesmerizing, so urgently attractive. That body could have been worshiped, as if it were the golden calf of the wayward Israelites.

In fitful sleep that night, Antoine dreamt he was snapping beans with the other monks in the cannery. Vegetables were piled in several green haystacks on a table. Walls were antiseptic white. Each monk worked with hood pulled up to hide his face. No one spoke. And while Antoine worked, he became aware of someone moving around the edge of the room. Wanting to lift his head, he could not. The figure moved closer. Steps were a barefoot pat-pat on the floor, and a buttery fragrance of baking bread filled the air. When the man stood directly in front of him, Antoine saw that it was Martin, naked except for a football jersey thrown over one shoulder. Sweat ran down Martin's chest to his groin, and he looked at Antoine with a lurid grin. His wet chest rose and fell, drawing in air with a slight rhythmic whistle, as if asthmatic. He seemed ready to laugh. Although Antoine tried to speak, his mouth refused to open. He woke with a start and saw nothing but blackness, Martin's snores coming from the bed next to his, a rhythmic whistle. Antoine threw back his sheets, put on his habit, and went to choir.

The church that night was dark and cavernous. Only one tiny flame danced in a glass lamp by the tabernacle. Wind beyond the windows caused the building to creak, as if the very bricks made fitful noises in their sleep. Antoine knelt. Alone in the church, he tried to pray, but only a single word came to his mind. "Lust," he said aloud. "I desire. I want so badly it is making me sick." The tiny vigil light kept dancing. No angry words came back at him from the shadows. Antoine was relieved. The building continued to creak as it had before he arrived and no anger came from heaven. Neither did any answers.

The next morning Antoine trembled as he took dishes from a silent Brother Martin. Throat dry, underarms soaking wet, Antoine clutched slippery plates with both hands in an effort not to drop them. At last Martin pulled the plug on the drain and wiped his hands. As he headed out of the bakery, he punched Antoine playfully in the arm and smiled at the wall.

After Martin had gone, Antoine felt so lightheaded he could not walk. He grabbed the edge of the sink and stood still for several seconds, reviewing in his mind Martin's punch again and again, wondering exactly what it meant. Did Martin have any interest in him? Was Martin perhaps attracted to him? Such a possibility spelled danger indeed, for what then would keep them apart? What would prevent Antoine from tumbling headlong into sin, if it was true that Martin wanted him? Antoine shook himself out of his terrifying reverie and went outside.

The sun was bright. Buds on trees looked ready to burst while snow melted slowly into the ground. The air was cool and damp. Antoine walked unsteadily on a gravel path until he happened to see the Abbot in his black skullcap standing near the river. Antoine approached and touched the tip of his right forefinger to his mouth, requesting permission to speak.

"*Benedicite, mon père abbé.*"

"*Dominus,*" the Abbot answered. His cheeks were pink from the early spring temperature. They walked together. "What's on your mind?"

"Pardon me, but I would like to move to a new bed in the dormitory."

"What's wrong with the bed you have now?" the Abbot asked. They had reached the bee yard. Sunlight filtered through the bare branches of the trees to highlight a single hive, the only one warmed and active with humming insects.

Antoine paused for a moment. "Well," he said, "my mattress is very uncomfortable. Whoever had it before me wore it down in all the wrong places, you see, and I can't get to sleep." Amazed by his rationalization, he elaborated on how the bed had been shaped to someone else's body, a shape that had nothing in common with his own. He and the Abbot turned away from the bee yard and walked back toward the abbey. The Abbot had his arms folded in front of him all the while.

"Don't expect comfort in the monastic life," he said. "Besides, I don't see what I can do for you. No mattress in the dormitory is shaped to your body. We have no new mattresses, to my knowledge." They stopped walking. "How long have you been using that bed?"

"Two and a half years."

The Abbot scratched his nose. "And you just now thought to mention it?" He looked Antoine in the eye. "Soon you will petition the monastic chapter for first vows. You ought to behave yourself. Now is no time to single yourself out with special needs." He pulled a rosary from his pocket. "Besides," he added, "I only just moved Brother Martin to a new bed four weeks ago. He complained about a draft where he was before. If I move you, it might seem as though Martin is the culprit."

The Abbot waited for Antoine to say more, but the young monk remained silent. How could Antoine explain his obsession, especially in light of the impending petition? Antoine would indeed be asking to take vows for three years. After living in the cloister as a novice, it was the custom for a young monk to petition for a trial period of vows, and it never occurred to Antoine to do anything else. The Abbot spoke again.

"On second thought," he said, "lately, you don't seem to be

getting enough sleep. And if a mattress is to blame, such a thing shouldn't be allowed to ruin your life."

Antoine hung his head in silence. The Abbot resumed walking and Antoine followed.

"Reconsider your situation for a day or two," the Abbot said, "and come back to me if you still want to move." Antoine bowed and plodded off toward the barns.

He knew there was more at stake than a mattress, or even a change of place in the dormitory. Antoine was not altogether convinced that he wanted to move away from Martin. And suddenly he was not convinced that he should pronounce vows, either. Monastic life seemed to lack a certain middle road. Monks rarely spoke to one another, never touched, and seldom even looked at one another. In monastic life, radical separation by silence had an odd partnership with extreme physical proximity. Antoine had been largely unaware of this polarity until he found himself sleeping next to Martin, and now there seemed nothing between the two poles to assuage a need for emotional warmth: no recreation, no comradeship.

But who was he to judge the ancient tradition of the Cistercian Order? Such extremes must somehow ensure progress on a spiritual path that, for hundreds of years, had brought many others to sanctity.

Now at the chicken barn, he leaned against it. Antoine wanted to blame monastic prudery for his infatuation. But was monastic custom really the cause? He wondered if silence did not sharpen his desire for intimacy. But if he *could* speak freely to Martin, would his feelings fall into place, or might they actually escalate? As it was, Antoine thirsted for the forbidden, the dark and mysterious pleasure of sin.

He pushed open the creaky door of the chicken barn. The interior smelled of hay and sun-bleached cotton. Six hundred newly hatched chicks had arrived, and the gnomelike Father

Jean-Marie Orève hunched over a feed bag in the corner, digging into it with a wooden scoop. A series of heat lamps had been arranged two feet above the floor and the tiny puffball chicks ran underneath, lively and curious, pecking at everything. They were shielded from drafts by a wide cardboard skirt that also acted as a fence, keeping the birds on sawdust litter. Jean-Marie lifted his head out of the feed bag. He scowled at Antoine until the young monk closed the door behind him.

Contented cheeps — a bright baby noise — filled the room. Antoine forgot about polarities and became absorbed in the birds. Contentment overwhelmed him; his chest expanded. Drawing close to the yellow chicks, he took in their fresh, eggy scent and picked one up. The chick felt no heavier than a leaf. It observed Antoine first with one eye and then the other, and turned its attention to his palm, where it began to peck. Father Jean-Marie hurried over. By scratching under his right ear, he gave the sign for a reprimand. Antoine set the chick down and left the barn.

Cool air bathed his face again; the day smelled as if it had been scrubbed. Without the chicks, thoughts of polarity returned, and Antoine became aware of another pair of contraries that was woven into the fabric of his monastic life: celibate monks earned their living on the fecundity of animals. Chickens laid eggs daily until their feathers fell out and they were sold to the Campbell Soup Company. Sixty dairy cows spent their lives either pregnant or lactating. Each cow gave birth every year, so frequently that she might drop a calf during a mere pause in chewing. Two Holstein bulls spent their lives servicing the cows; more than once Antoine had stared wide-eyed at them while they went at their business. Even bees participated in this ironic marriage of celibate and sexual. Fertilized queens laid thousands of eggs in brood comb. Their offspring emerged from hives as honeybees gathering nectar from fields for the hives, but their honey was harvested by the monks and sold for income. The interplay between abstinent monks and their sexual animals was a paradox that fascinated Antoine.

Near a decaying snowbank, big as an overturned rowboat, a wild crocus lifted its pink bloom an inch above the mud. Rather than pluck it, Antoine gathered small stones and propped up the flower. He was thus occupied when someone behind him laughed. Antoine lifted his head. He turned but saw no one. Leaving the crocus, he searched for the person who had observed his foolish stone collecting. Once more he heard the laugh, this time down by the river.

Antoine ran there, bent to look through budding branches near the bank, and saw a tall, fat figure by the water. It was Father Alcide. White fuzz covered his scalp. His forehead sloped into a long, narrow nose between small black eyes. He looked like a polar bear standing on its hind legs. A burlap bag was in his hands and he jostled it, then tied a rope around the opening. Lifting the bag, he spun it around his head, and let go. The burlap alighted in the middle of the river with hardly a splash.

As it drifted in slow circles downstream the bag seemed to float just above the surface of the water. Inside, something began to move. With each twitch, the burlap lost some of its raft tension, absorbing water. Alcide laughed. His bearlike belly shook as he looked out over the river, the bag slowly disappearing below the surface, even as it jerked.

"What do you think you're doing?" Antoine yelled.

Father Alcide spun around, surprised. He held a finger to his lips.

"I don't care if it's forbidden to talk," Antoine shouted at him. "I want to know why you laugh when you drown kittens."

With a frown the fat monk gazed at Antoine. The bag had vanished, and he pulled on a length of rope until it reappeared on the riverbank. He refused to speak. Instead, he made a series of gestures — some of them newly invented — to explain the situation in crude terms. "Barn cats fuck. Make kittens." He laughed out loud and his belly shook again. "Many kittens. Must kill," he signed.

Antoine's face flushed and tears began rolling down his cheeks. "My God! You keep the bag? For when you need it again?" he said.

"Shhhh," Alcide hissed, with a finger to his lips. He signed again. "Fuck is bad. Fuck is bad."

Antoine backed away. His hand was at his stomach. For a moment he thought he might have to sit in the dirt, but he turned and ran.

Hours later, after the sun had set, he entered the confessional box in the rear of the church.

"Bless me, Father. I saw Father Alcide drowning kittens today and I nearly became sick."

"That's not a sin."

Kneeling in darkness, Antoine could see a grid pattern of Father Yves-Marie through wooden laths. Yves-Marie turned to look at the screen, and a naked bulb above him reflected in his spectacles. Magnified eyes came into view, huge watery olives. Then, once more, all that could be seen was his profile. Antoine cleared his throat.

"Yes, but you see, Father Alcide was laughing when he watched the kittens drown. How could he be so cruel? Did a life of celibacy make him that way?"

"Of course not. Father Alcide has personal problems, and celibate or not he'd laugh at the kittens. Now, what do you wish to confess, Brother?"

"I don't think I have a vocation to be a monk anymore." Antoine went on to explain that he was not worthy to remain in the abbey because of temptations against purity.

"Temptations?" Father Yves-Marie said. "Give me a penny for

every temptation *I've* had, and I could pave a copper road from here to China."

"But Father, I can't take vows. Whenever I sit down to write my petition, all I can think of is sex."

"Young men are tempted against purity," Yves-Marie said. "It's a fact of life."

Antoine ran a thumbnail along the frame of the confessional screen. "You know, Father, I don't understand why that has to be," he said. "Why can't I put sex out of my mind? Why can't I get rid of it? It's nothing but misery, and if there's any way I could escape it, I would. But I can't escape it. Does God really want me to be a monk, then? Am I worthy?"

"None of us is worthy," Yves-Marie said. "God has called us, and we have no choice but to respond."

Antoine remained silent. He could see Yves-Marie scratching his forehead under the harsh light. His thick glasses hung on the end of his nose.

"Bear in mind, Brother," he said, "no human longing can be filled by the things of this world. Human beings are thirsty for all kinds of pleasure, but God alone can slake that kind of deep human thirst. To think otherwise is to make an idol out of what we see, and that's foolishness. The earth is transitory. But look on the bright side. Thirst means you're alive. It's good to be thirsty. It should turn your attention to God. And if you have a vocation, nothing will give you peace but to be here. So, be thirsty for God. And be patient with yourself, Brother. Remember that temptation, in and of itself, is no sin. Pray to God to fill you, and you will find peace."

But Antoine wanted relief, not peace. How could prayers possibly slake a thirst like his? Monastic life was meant for angels and he was just a man, filled with earthly desire. Surely the priest was wrong. Antoine could never be a monk unless he was able, somehow, to leave sex behind, to crush it, or deliver himself of it. And how was such a thing possible?

"How can I know God's purpose?" he asked. "How can I be sure I have a vocation?"

"You came here of your own free will, didn't you?" Yves-Marie said. "And the Abbot hasn't sent you away. If the community votes in favor of keeping you, then you must assume it's God's will." The priest raised his hand to give Antoine absolution. "You have begun God's work," he said. "God rewards those who are faithful."

The next morning, having listened all night to Martin's snores, Brother Antoine sat down to write a petition for vows. He took up his pen with trepidation, but in the process of putting words together, remembered calm days filled with ordinary tasks. The last two and a half years had been free of worldly cares, dressed simply in an unpretentious rhythm. That life he had grown to love. If Antoine had done little to distinguish himself, neither had he caused the monks any trouble. He bottled beets and scrubbed floors, dusted choir stalls and cleaned toilets: one day had been like the next. But he knew that a balanced life created balance within. Regularity suited him. And if he was thirsty for touching, emotional satisfaction, and sex, the haunting plainsong of the choir nourished something deeper: it nourished his soul. He loved the way the monks sang the psalms. Perhaps if he sang with more passion, more sincerity, all troubles would melt away and God *would* give him peace, just as Father Yves-Marie had said. Antoine wrote in the petition that he never felt alone. "Maybe I'm always in someone's way, but it's a comfort, having people around." He had the example of forty men engaged in the same honest, simple, peaceful way of life, and hoped that his brother monks would accept him for vows. He wanted to live their life of obedience, stability, and monastic conversion.

When the petition was finished, Antoine was ebullient and re-lieved. He gave himself no further opportunity to hesitate. He rushed off to the Abbot's office, slipped the paper under the door, and went to morning dishes.

Brother Martin had already filled the sink with soapy water; his sleeves were rolled up, exposing his hairy forearms, and all Antoine's ebullience seeped away like air squeaking out of a bal-loon. He was left with confusion. As Martin passed dishes to be dried, Antoine asked himself over and over again: Why do men become monks? No simple answer occurred to him. Instead, memories of childhood flooded his head. He thought of sweet occasions as a boy, walking alone on sunny afternoons, enjoying the pleasure of his own company without a single anxious care. That same innocence and sun-drenched peace he had felt at mo-ments in the cloister, and he saw innocence in the eyes of old monks who had spent their lives in prayer. Faith had transformed them. He wanted to be transformed, too.

At the same time, Antoine — feeling warmth from Martin's arm only inches from his own — had thoughts not so innocent or pure. Celibacy seemed unnatural whenever he was close to the Scotsman, and he was hungry for physical relief. The fact that Martin was celibate occurred to him, of course, but Antoine remembered those sensual groans in the night, and the man did not seem so holy, so untouchable.

After the dishes had been dried and put away, Antoine spoke. "Do you ever think about sex?" he asked.

Brother Martin turned to look at him and lifted a finger to his lips. "Shhhhhhh."

"No one is around," Antoine said, "and the bakery door is closed."

Martin made a series of signs. "I am no priest. Go see a priest." But Antoine shook his head.

"What can a priest tell me about sex? Besides, I'm asking *you*.

How is it possible, to lead this life of complete abstinence? Is it even normal? I mean, didn't God create sex? Weren't men created with sexual hunger on purpose? Isn't that to be respected?"

Martin moved backward toward the door, but Antoine blocked the way. Surprised by his own boldness, Antoine said, "Don't you wish someone would touch you once in a while? I Iold you, maybe? Rub your back after a hard day? Aren't you hungry for that?"

Martin's neck flushed and he could no longer look at Antoine. He put his hands over his face in a sign that meant "shame."

"I don't think sex is shameful," Antoine said. "God invented it. It must be holy. But that's not my question. I want to know how I can be celibate when sex is always on my mind. Do you have that problem?"

The Scotsman grew impatient. He lifted a fist as if ready to punch Antoine in the stomach.

"Let me by," he said loudly. "I know nothing. If you want help, go to a psychiatrist."

"I'm asking a simple question."

"Well, don't ask me," Martin said.

Antoine would not move. "Do you care for me at all?" he asked. "Am I appealing?"

Martin looked startled. "I'm no homosexual," he said.

Antoine sucked air through his nose. A current of nervous energy passed through him and he had to steady himself against the door frame. "Homosexual?" he whispered.

"Get out of my way," Martin yelled. "I want nothing to do with your problems." He tried to push through to the hallway, but Antoine would not let him by.

"Who's Mary?" Antoine asked.

Martin jerked back, and Antoine, not knowing what to say, wiped his nose on his sleeve. For a moment, Martin moved his mouth, hesitating, but then shoved Antoine aside and hurried away. When he was gone, Antoine felt remorse. The last thing he had wanted to do was hurt with words. He left the bakery and spent the remaining hours of the work period in the cannery, scrubbing the cement floor.

Antoine allowed his mind to replay every detail of the exchange in the bakery. Over and over again he heard Martin's voice say "homosexual." More than once, he found himself motionless, not scrubbing at all, overcome by wave upon wave of alternating feelings: shame and love. He wanted to hide himself. He wanted to run away. He wanted to leave a note on his bed that said, "Thank you. I've had two and a half interesting years here in the abbey, but I can't go through with it. I can't take vows that confuse me." Where would he go, Antoine wondered. What would he do? Where was life easy for a homosexual?

He decided to visit the Abbot and take back the petition for simple vows. This time, he would not lie about an old mattress. Neither would he lie about his infatuation. Rehearsing words in his mind, he wanted to tell the Abbot about his confusion and ask whether or not anyone was morally capable of taking vows when strong sexual desire did not ebb. If the abbey rejected Antoine for his honesty, he felt ready to give up and cast himself into the dark world, and suffer whatever fate awaited him.

He knocked on the Abbot's door. There was no answer. Antoine knocked again and placed his ear to the wood. Shouts and angry words came from within, and he thought he heard Martin's voice. Antoine backed away from the door, then turned and walked down the hall. Suspicion took hold of him. Martin had gone to the Abbot first and was explaining what happened in the bakery. And having heard Martin's side of the story, the Abbot would have no sympathy for Antoine. He would never believe anything about Mary or suspicious movements in the night. "You're dreaming," he would say. "You're in love with Martin and you imagine things."

Antoine weaved down the hall. The end was near, he was sure
of it. Why bother to retrieve his petition for vows when the Abbot was ready to throw him out anyway? He sat in a heap, in the
middle of the hallway, dabbing his nose with a handkerchief.
Nothing mattered anymore.

The Abbot's door opened. Martin walked out without noticing the slumped figure on the floor. He slammed the door and
stomped down the hall, away from Antoine. For a whole minute,
the tick of a clock could be heard from somewhere within the
building, and only because Antoine knew he could not remain
on the floor all day, he got up. What puzzled him was the anger.
If Martin had just complained to the Abbot about the discussion
in the bakery, why did he storm out of the room? More likely
he'd have been relieved, consoled and confident, because someone else was at fault. What happened? What had they discussed?
Antoine was more confused than ever.

That night, nothing was heard in the bed next to his. No
snore or faint rustle of sheets came from behind the curtain,
and Antoine lay awake for hours, alert for the slightest move.
Through an open dormer window he could hear two cats hissing
and screaming. He finally threw off his bedcovers. After putting
on his habit, he touched the curtains of Martin's cubicle; he hesitated, then slowly drew the fabric aside, only an inch. The bed
was empty. Martin was gone.

Cats continued to hiss and whine outside the windows in the
bushes three stories below the dormitory, and Antoine crept
about, overwhelmed by curiosity. He wondered if Martin had
left the abbey, if the monk had given up in anger and walked out
without telling anyone. He wondered again about the words exchanged between the Abbot and Martin and how much of it concerned himself.

After stepping quietly along the cubicles of sleeping monks,
Antoine reached the end of the dormitory and pushed his head

out a window into cool air. He half expected to see Martin on the sidewalk below, hurrying away in trousers, wearing a big hat and carrying a suitcase. But the moon was only a sliver, and the yard was dark and mysterious. He hung out of the window in a sullen mood. The cats had gone away. Because the season was too early for insects, silence prevailed.

Antoine had decided to go back to bed when he heard a faint voice. At first he thought it came from somewhere near, out on the mansard roof, but after pulling his head inside, he knew it came from among the straw-filled beds in the dormitory. The voice was unmistakable.

"Mary, Mary," it said.

Antoine could hardly breathe. Soundlessly he crept along the row of curtains until he discovered exactly where Martin was, in a corner, far from where he had been before. After a minute the name was whispered again. Martin's breathing became heavy. He moved on the mattress. The whispered name took on a slight edge and then the voice became a dangerous murmur, enough to wake the others. Antoine began to perspire, and his own body absorbed an agony of longing. He opened his habit and touched himself. Caressing his skin, he imagined Martin touching Mary. Without any difficulty, Antoine gave himself up to fantasy and intense pleasure.

He was very near losing control when he heard Martin's breath stop short, followed by a moan that seemed like the last bit of machine-pressed air, the release and ease of it falling away to silence. Antoine's eyes were wide and he dared not make a sound. Quickly he stepped out of the dormitory and ran down three flights of stairs to a small water closet in the basement.

For a long while he sat on the closed lid of the toilet, trembling. Tears ran over his chin and down his neck. Antoine was exhausted. Though he did not want an erection, he still had one, and waited for it to subside so that he could go back to bed. Saint

Benedict, he remembered, threw himself into the nettles of a rose bush as a cure for lust. Saint Francis had done the same. Saint Paul described a "thorn" in his flesh sent by God to keep him humble. Had they been homosexuals, too? Antoine wondered.

For nearly an hour he sat alone, but his bloated penis would not relax. He became frantic. Though he refused to touch himself now, weeks of emotional torture had worn down his will. The more he tried to push thoughts of sex out of his head, the larger they became, and the more he tried to ignore what was between his legs, the more he felt like one gigantic penis.

All of it seemed a cruel joke: God giving him sexual desire that was never to be acted upon, his efforts to resist depriving him of sleep. Night after night of torture. He had no energy left. These temptations, and his inability to cope with them, pointed to the lack of a vocation to monastic life. But what would his leaving accomplish? The Church condemned homosexuality. He had to be a monk, whether he lived in a monastery or not!

The stubble on his head had become damp. Sweat ran down his face along with tears. Antoine was not impulsive. Never in his life had he been given to extremes, but this time he saw only one solution to his problem. Yes, only one solution. He stood. With sudden boozy assurance unlike anything he had ever experienced, he knew what had to be done. He left the toilet with dizzy fervor to collect razor blades from the commissary. When he returned, he locked the water closet, stripped, and took up a razor.

If he cut quickly, he thought, there would be no pain. His breath became rapid and shallow. He felt cold. When he grabbed his scrotum and held the blade to skin, his body responded with excitement. His penis grew even larger at the cold touch of the blade, as though his body did not know what was in his mind. Body and soul seemed completely separate. He closed his eyes.

As he cut, the pain was sharp and alarming. Immediately he felt a warm flow down the side of his leg. He opened his eyes and saw blood running in a wide rivulet, though the razor had only nicked the scrotum. When the blood reached the floor, it made a slow thick line to the drain. For a whole minute Antoine watched the blade without moving. He realized that if he continued to cut he would bleed to death.

This was insane. He had wandered to the edge. He knew it was mad. God's will could not possibly involve castration. Calmly he placed the razor on the sink. He took wads of toilet paper and stuffed them between his legs. As they turned scarlet, he threw them into the toilet and took more. The blood slowed but never seemed to stop. Antoine remained naked for a long while, flushing red tissue down the toilet.

After what seemed like an entire day, he heard the bell for rising. Stuffing fresh tissue on the wound, he made sure there was no sign of blood in the water closet and left the basement.

Two days later, he was still daubing iodine on his scrotum. But he took comfort in the relatively small red line, two centimeters long, near the pubic hair. Had he lost his head, cut a few centimeters more, an ambulance would have been necessary. And how would he have explained such a thing to the monks? To his parents?

Martin no longer slept beside Antoine. The absence relieved much of the trouble. At night, Antoine fell asleep without distraction and dreamt about things other than Martin.

Dishes in the bakery continued as a tight-lipped affair. Just as before, Martin never looked at Antoine, but his occasional smiles were now replaced with a wordless antagonism. Outside the bakery Martin avoided him. Antoine felt despised, and knew Martin's patterns well enough to stay clear of him when they were not at community prayer or meals.

But full nights of rest restored Antoine's alacrity. Sleep deprivation had contributed greatly to his emotional imbalance, and once he began to recover, a measure of peace returned. He let the rhythm of monastic life maintain him with its balance of work, prayer, reading, and quiet. He tried to forget the frantic episode with the razor.

Calm took away his frazzled look. Monks no longer turned their heads to observe him. In June, the Abbot took Antoine away from dishes in the bakery and assigned him to the dairy. Brother Gennade had sprained his arm there and needed help milking cows. Together they carried smells of manure into the church and whiffs of incense into the barn.

The fecundity of the livestock continued to amaze Antoine. More than once, he assisted Gennade with a distressed heifer, reaching inside her to run a rope around the unborn calf's hoof so as to secure it to pulling chains. With the calf safely out, the cow always forgot her discomfort and began immediately to sniff and lick the small creature.

Brother Martin was not forgotten. Often, Antoine looked at him in choir — a sullen face, the violet-blue eyes angry, the mouth rarely opened to sing anymore — and questions arose as to the responsibility of his own actions. Should he have said anything at all about sex to Martin?

At last, the day of voting came. On an evening in mid-June, the Abbot entered the chapter room with his monks while Antoine was left to stand alone in the church. Behind closed doors, the formal petition for vows was read. Monks were then to discuss Antoine's character and weigh the matter. Each monk was to vote according to his conscience, whether to accept Antoine or to send him packing.

It was a long wait in the church. At first he heard nothing. The chapter room door remained closed. He did not expect to hear anything, and thought the discussion would be straightforward, the vote taken quickly. Antoine fidgeted. Thirty minutes later he was still alone in the church. Then forty. The hands on his wrist-watch read fifty-five minutes after the hour.

Antoine heard the sound of a heated discussion. Two people. Yelling. Antoine hung his head. As the shouting continued, he felt tears collect on his eyelashes. He wiped his nose.

Alone in the church with muted voices of anger coming from behind the chapter room door, Antoine nearly fainted but knew he had to act like a man. He must show no emotion when told to leave. He must pack his bags and go without a word. Yes, he would miss the monks. He had come to rely on the collective discipline of their life and their silent companionship.

The shouting became louder; it seemed incongruous in a cloistered atmosphere, the sifted quiet of the church. Antoine's shoulders slumped. He felt heat rise out of his chest to his face. The yelling went back and forth between two voices, climbing in tempo and pitch, growing and growing. Then, suddenly, it broke off. There was silence. Antoine waited, his hands up around his throat. Finally the door opened.

Martin strode out of the chapter room and slammed the door, muttering as he walked into choir. They looked at each other. Violet-blue eyes had turned black. Martin ignored Antoine as he walked past, taking a stall several feet away. Moments later, the chapter door opened again and the Abbot entered the church. The other monks followed. Each appeared shaken but took his place in choir to sing the office of Compline. When they began, the steady rhythm of their chant slowly cleansed the air of tension until an equilibrium was again established. For Antoine's part, he could not keep his mind on the psalms. Mouthing the words, he wondered what had been discussed in the chapter room. How had Martin affected the vote?

Compline ended with the plaintive antiphon *O dulcis virgo Maria*. The monks sang from memory. An elegant musical line rose and fell in immaculate unison. Antoine turned toward Martin to see if the words had any unusual effect upon him — the hymn to Mary in Latin — but the monk stood in choir like a statue, his arms crossed and his mouth shut.

Feeling a heavy pulse in his neck, Antoine turned back to his choir book and continued to wonder about the vote. When the singing had ended, the monks left the church in single file. Dom Jacques Bouvray sprinkled each of them in turn with holy water, and they walked down a dark corridor to the stairwell. Antoine followed. But before reaching the stairs, he felt a tug at his sleeve. It was the Abbot. Dom Jacques beckoned Antoine to follow, and they walked to his office.

"*Benedicite*, Brother," he said once they were inside the room. He closed the door.

"*Dominus.*"

"This is the Grand Silence. Forgive me," Dom Jacques whispered as he sat down at his desk, "but I wanted you to know that the lengthy chapter had nothing to do with you. We took the vote before any shouting began. In five minutes, that was all over. We've accepted you. Congratulations." He pointed to a chair, and Antoine, shaking in the knees, went to sit. Relief washed over him so suddenly that he nearly missed the chair and fell on the floor.

"You should know," the Abbot continued, "that Brother Martin and I have been at odds." His expression was sober. "An argument broke out between us over the possibility of his transfer to another abbey. I was thrown off balance, I'm afraid. Not prepared for an outburst in chapter, I lost my temper." The Abbot folded his hands. "And as it stands, I think Martin is resolved to leave religious life altogether."

Antoine's mouth dropped. Though tension had melted when he learned of his acceptance, this was now checked in thinking that he might have had something to do with Martin's leaving.

"Reverend Father," he said, "there's something you should

know." He blinked several times. Straightening his back, he stumbled on, hardly knowing what to say. "When I asked to be moved in the dormitory because of my mattress, I told you a lie. My request had nothing to do with a mattress. Truth is, I am strongly attracted to Brother Martin."

"The mattress?" Dom Jacques asked.

"Yes. I told you that my mattress was shaped for someone else and kept me from sleeping. But you see, it was really Martin who kept me awake."

"Martin?"

Antoine closed his eyes for a moment and tried to rephrase his tumble of words. "Yes. Please understand, I'm . . . I think I'm attracted to Martin. What I mean is . . . I think I'm a homosexual."

The Abbot waited for more, but Antoine had nothing more to say. A moment went by and the Abbot looked at his watch.

"Yes," he said. "Each of us has his burden to bear. Listen, Brother, it's getting late. You'd best get to bed."

Antoine stood and walked to the door on unsteady legs. He hesitated, thinking the Abbot had not heard correctly. Perhaps he should repeat the confession. The Abbot spoke again.

"Antoine," he said. "Pray for Brother Martin. Pray for God's blessing upon him. You of all people might be in the best position to do that."

"Yes, Reverend Father." Antoine stood at the door for a moment, then left the office and made his way to bed. There it was, simple and straightforward: a request for prayers. Nothing more. His heart pounded as if it had slipped into a higher gear. He felt winded. Even *if* the Abbot had completely misunderstood his confession, the deed was done. He had claimed something sexual about himself, and what was more, had announced it aloud. There was no going back. He did not want to go back. A new sense of identity had begun to bloom, and he felt he knew himself far better than before. The confession left him stronger. Still,

II

Antoine's thoughts were tempered by the realization that Martin would disappear from his life.

Two days later, Brother Antoine spotted Martin coming from the attic with a suitcase. Antoine hurried to the Abbot's office.

"May I speak to him? Please, Reverend Father? When will I ever see him again?"

Dom Jacques closed his eyes and nodded.

Antoine hurried away, looking about the building until he found Martin in the wardrobe packing the suitcase with trousers and shirts. After an awkward exchange of words, the two agreed to walk outside, along the river.

Sunshine warmed new grass the color of limes, and birds carried twigs to fresh nests. Martin seemed interested in none of this.

"Will you still take your vows, then?" he asked.

Antoine rubbed his hands together. "Yes. I think so."

"And your questions? About sex? Have they been answered?"

This time Antoine felt embarrassed, and a rash of color spread across his forehead and cheeks. Words escaped him. Martin seemed more at ease than he had for weeks and rescued them both from vexing silence.

"Big step," he said. "When I took solemn profession five years ago, I felt a wonderful relief. I thought my life was squared away. Everything was settled. My troubles were over. Now, look at me."

"Did I have anything to do with your decision to leave?"

"No, of course not."

"You can always come back," Antoine said. "Who knows? You might change your mind. The community would take you back."

"No," Martin replied. "I've had enough. I want to go."

They listened to cows lowing in a far-off pasture. Antoine wanted to know about Mary but feared that any such question might spoil the moment. "Celibacy is making you leave, then?" He fumbled with his hands and put them in his pockets. Martin looked down at the grass.

"No," he said. "Listen, you must have heard me in the dormitory. I'm no angel." He spoke carefully. "But celibacy is not why I'm leaving. In fact, celibacy is one of the reasons I came here. I know what's good for me." Martin paused. "I'm leaving because I don't get along with Dom Jacques. He and I do not see eye to eye. For years I've been perfectly candid with him about the abbey's business affairs and it's got me nowhere. He's afraid of my ideas. Look at me: I have a degree in management and what does he make me do? Bake bread. That's it. For eight years, I've been baking bread. He won't let me near the bursar's office, and I'm tired of fighting. When a monk fails to get along with his abbot, life becomes impossible. I hope you have better luck than I did."

Antoine studied the Scotsman's profile as they walked along the road.

"Don't worry about me," Martin said. "I'll be fine."

A fragrance of wild plum blossoms carried on the wind. They reached the apiary and saw how sunlight had flooded the place. The spring air was alive with a feathery buzzing as the two men paused under the arms of a spreading elm tree. Antoine heard the far-off chuck of a tractor. He wanted to remember every detail, standing next to Martin.

"Who is Mary?" he asked.

Martin shook his head. "Does it matter? A woman is a woman, and Mary is a hell of a lot easier to say than Alexandra, Elizabeth, or Magdalena."

"I don't believe you," Antoine protested. "You whispered the name with such passion."

"Did I?"

"Oh yes! You had me all steamed up."

Martin barked a laugh. "All right," he said, "I do remember

Mary. She was well worth remembering, but nobody I'd introduce to my mother. And she was only one of many. All that I got tired of. I couldn't control myself out in the world, you see, and I wanted an escape. Back in the world, I probably won't keep my virtue long. Not that I have much virtue to keep.

"But it's more than escape I was looking for. I found something here. Believe me, there's a good measure of peace to being a monk. I sensed peace when I first visited this place many years ago. So I stepped out of my past life, all that constant looking at and sizing up, all that appraisal. It's hunting, and it happens all day long, every day. I left it behind. Because it's like a drug, you know. There's never enough of it. No, I came here because I wanted some peace. And I've had peace on that score. It's the obedience that I can't take. The Abbot won't let me be my own man."

The wind shifted and the tractor became a faint hum to be confused with the bees. Antoine looked at Martin's shoulder and felt an urge to put his hand there, to comfort him. He held his hand up for a moment, then ran it along the rough bark of the tree. "Tell me," he said. "Do you think I should take vows if I have sexual temptations?"

"Who doesn't?" Martin said. "Chastity is like poverty and obedience. Monks simply embrace as vows what every man has to accept whether he wants to or not. In the world, there's no such thing as having too much money, for instance, and a monk knows that. He embraces a life of communal ownership so that greed won't destroy him. In the world, even a married man has to be chaste, and he has to abstain once in a while. A wife is ill, or pregnant. But hell, I know I could never be faithful to one woman. A monk, he not only accepts the chastity, he *embraces* it. And in embracing it, in a paradoxical way, I was at peace."

"And obedience?"

Martin was silent. Bees flew by with a light business of their own, but he did not seem to notice. "I guess everybody's got to obey," he finally said. "Obey a father. A boss. A wife. Or even the laws of the land." He shook his head. "But I can't obey *this* boss anymore. I've had it. I'm leaving."

The sound of the tractor stopped. They stood together for a moment. Then Martin stepped backward. "I wish you luck," he said, raising a hand. Antoine embraced him.

Martin Brown walked away along the path, moving with ease and authority like a man of business. Brother Antoine stood anchored to the soil near the apiary.

5

Cello

In chapter, Dom Jacques Bouvray informed the assembled community that they would soon receive four Buddhist monks as visitors. Brother Antoine sat near the door. Thirty-six of his brothers shared benches along the walls of the room while the Abbot spoke from a raised throne at the end, under a crucifix.

"As you know," Dom Jacques said in French, "Benedictine and Cistercian monks have been given a Vatican mandate to establish dialogue with monks of other religions. This is why we have invited the Buddhists. I am certain that if we are open-minded and hospitable, this exchange will be a singular learning experience for us."

Old Fathers Cyprien, Marie-Nizier, and Ignace were asleep, their heads shamelessly bowed to their chests. Other monks stared at the Abbot with open mouths and raised eyebrows. Antoine wondered if Buddhist monks fell asleep while their abbot addressed them, too.

"We need a volunteer," the Abbot said, "to look after details of the visit," and he peered out over his reading glasses. Antoine saw no hands. After an awkward moment, the Abbot spoke again.

"We need someone friendly and open-minded, someone interested in world religions."

Still no hands. Antoine nervously scratched at a spot on his scalp, behind the left ear.

"Thank you, Brother Antoine," the Abbot said. "You're just the person for the job. I appoint you our official East-West Dialogue Contact Person."

Antoine was caught by surprise, but in the days following his job grew on him. At first it sounded ridiculous. How many Buddhist monks lived in Manitoba anyway? Whom would he contact? In what language would he dialogue, he a monk who used more sign language than speech? What was East? What was West? He had no idea where these monks would come from. A Buddhist monastery in Asia?

Antoine read the stack of material given him by Dom Jacques and discovered that Dharmsala, India, was exactly where the visitors were coming from, about as far east as he could imagine. Several Roman Catholic monasteries had combined efforts and shared expenses to bring them to North America.

Six places were on their itinerary. Brother Antoine's Cistercian abbey was fourth on the list; the Buddhists would arrive from Québec, and travel on, after Winnipeg, to visit an abbey in Saskatchewan and another in British Columbia. Many details of the tour had not yet been arranged, however, and Antoine wrote and received several letters. He even spoke on the telephone when necessary. At first he was shy, but quickly became more forward, even officious, receiving calls from Québec and India with the full approval of the Abbot. Often he had to leave work in the dairy barn to handle this or that pressing detail.

Antoine soon found himself studying with enthusiasm. Because he knew next to nothing about Buddhism, the Abbot allowed him to read any Buddhist-related book he could get his hands on. He ordered exotic tomes through interlibrary loan, and Brother François picked these up whenever he went to Winnipeg for supplies. He read about Zen monks in Japan who spent whole days sitting in a lotus position like the Buddha, impervious to disturbances; such self-mastery seemed worthy of monks. Why were his own brothers not able to do likewise? They did not sit still for a moment, fussing and passing gas in choir during the most sacred moments of the liturgy.

Antoine learned of Tibetan Buddhist monks exiled to India. He read of monks who ate nothing for weeks at a time. This seemed inhuman. But surely the intense discipline they practiced led to high levels of spiritual enlightenment. Otherwise, why would they bother? Cistercian monks, by contrast, grumbled if they were made to give up desserts for Lent. The more educated Antoine became about Buddhists, the less edified he was by his own brothers.

It began to dawn upon him that perhaps somewhere there was a better, more fervent monastery in which to live. He imagined rows of motionless figures seated upon the floor, solid and stonelike, their lips moving in a salubrious whisper. These were spiritual masters. He wanted to be with *real* monks who ate tiny portions of boiled rice and pickled vegetables, who slept on the floor, who remained motionless for hours at a time in stationary meditation, unperturbed by one another and, in a state of nirvana, detached from the world.

As Contact Person, he was told that the visiting Buddhists were Tibetans living in India, and that one of them could speak both French and English. This was exciting news, and Antoine prepared himself to discuss topics of a religious nature by reading the Tibetan *Book of the Dead,* none of which he understood. He repeatedly attempted to gain some insight, some small handle on the subject of Buddhism, by an ambient washing of words as he read books aloud in the pig barn. Several times he tried to sit in the lotus position, but after his legs had been forced into a knitted arrangement in front of him, his feet went to sleep and he found it difficult to walk when he stood up. Still, Antoine eagerly kept up preparations for the Tibetans, even though Contact Persons were advised to "be themselves" and present the Buddhist monks with "living Western monastic traditions."

What living Western monastic traditions? After reading about the great feats of Buddhist monks, he felt embarrassed by Western monasticism. Seeing nothing extraordinary about his own abbey, he was ashamed. Antoine became anxious to lift, by his own efforts, this low assessment. He corseted himself with Buddhist meditation practices described in books by Western writers. He painted himself with a hodgepodge of Eastern attitudes he had lifted from footnotes.

"Dear Brother," Dom Jacques said to him one day after seeing Antoine build a Tibetan prayer wheel, "the Buddhists are coming here to see Western monks. Take pride in yourself and in your own monastic heritage. Why be embarrassed by your abbey's peculiarities? We will receive the Tibetans into our home under our terms."

"But *mon père abbé*," Antoine answered, "I don't want the Buddhists to think we are ignorant of their ways."

Secretly, Antoine cut back on food. He hoped to become accustomed to less so that if the Tibetans should, by chance, notice him in the refectory, they would be impressed with his nibbling on a piece of dry toast while his brothers shoveled oatmeal into their mouths. All Buddhists ate rice, he assumed. So he heaped his bowl with the slimy rice that was occasionally served at the abbey, and passed on the cheese that everyone else loved. If no rice was served, he ate gruel, usually with only one slice of bread. After a few weeks of this imagined Buddhist diet, Antoine became anemic. He fainted one day in choir, and when he opened his eyes, Dom Jacques was slapping him on the cheek.

"Brother Antoine," he said, "why aren't you eating properly?"

He told the Abbot he had a delicate stomach. Dom Jacques ordered the kitchen to serve Antoine whole milk at every meal, and from his place at table the Abbot watched the young monk until he swallowed it down.

Anemia was not what bothered Antoine. He was hardly aware of symptoms, except for vague aches and pains when working among the dairy cows in the barn. He was preoccupied with a more acute psychological discomfort. The more he studied Buddhist monasticism, the more he felt deceived. After all, he had been with the Cistercians for four years, and to what effect? He was no spiritual master. All the while he had believed that these austere-looking monks, shaved and scrubbed as they were, would draw him up a ladder of monastic discipline that led to perfection. Antoine wanted to be flawless. He wanted to be a saint: as clean as a piece of carved ivory, as pure-smelling as beeswax. And why had it not happened? Why was he still so unaccomplished in the spiritual life, bored with the everyday sameness of it all? Why had he made so little progress in four years?

Because he did not live with real monks. Real monks do not scratch in odd places when they assemble to hear their abbot speak. Real monks do not belch in choir. Real monks do not shovel food into their mouths in the refectory. Real monks have manners.

One evening during supper, Brother Antoine was called to the telephone to speak to a Cistercian monk from Québec, Father Léon Gaide-Chevronnay, who reported that the Tibetans would be coming early, and he would be coming with them to insure that they made all the proper connections.

"The tour schedule has been moved up," he said in French. "Two abbeys of nuns have withdrawn from the itinerary. We'll be arriving five days earlier."

Antoine gasped. He felt unprepared. "Why did they back out?" he asked.

"Papal enclosure," the priest explained. "We all have enclosure, of course. Men are strictly forbidden to enter the cloister of nuns, just as women can't enter cloistered areas in our abbeys. That makes this tour easy for us. The Tibetans can stay anywhere inside our abbeys. But the nuns had to find sleeping quarters for the monks outside their enclosure and the arrangements fell through."

"That means my abbey is now second on the list."

"Yes. But don't worry. I'm in complete charge of their tour in Canada," he said. "I've been to Japan, you see, and I'm quite familiar with Buddhism. You need not concern yourself about anything, Brother, except for transportation to and from the airport and, of course, our lodgings."

The hair on Antoine's neck bristled. "I am the official East-West Dialogue Contact Person for our abbey," he said. "I will not relinquish my responsibility for their visit. And I know a good deal about Buddhism myself, thank you."

Father Léon apologized. He only wanted to be helpful, he explained, and thought that his being with the Tibetans would relieve others of a burden. Antoine detected trouble, however, and did not look forward to fighting with Léon over these monks.

Further complications arose. Brother Norbert Gignoux, who was assigned to work in the forge but in fact could never be found there, took Antoine by the sleeve one day and hauled him into the scriptorium.

"Brother Antoine, I've a question for you," he said. His white bushy eyebrows twitched. Antoine was already late for the afternoon milking.

"We're not allowed to speak in here," he reminded Norbert.

"When you get to be seventy-four," Norbert answered, "you can do exactly as you like. Now Brother, I want to know if these monks who are coming, are they Catholic?"

"As in Roman Catholic?"

"Yes," he said. "I want to know if these Buddhist people are Catholic."

Antoine had to close his eyes for a moment. "No," he said. "They're Buddhists, Norbert. There is no such thing as a Tibetan Buddhist Roman Catholic monk."

Norbert's eyebrows kept twitching and he snorted. "Well," he said, "we ought to pray for their salvation. Perhaps we could baptize them while they're here."

This was exactly the type of nonsense Antoine feared. He had no doubt that the Tibetans were monks of spiritual depth, far beyond anything Brother Norbert could imagine. Antoine did not want someone of Norbert's ilk offering bidding prayers for the Christian conversion of the Buddhist visitors in their very presence. He asked the Abbot to silence Norbert, to prevent him offering public prayers, but the Abbot refused.

"Norbert means well," he said. "The Tibetans will understand."

They arrived on a weekend. The air was cool, but ice had not yet formed on puddles along the road. Leaves had turned into cascading colors of lemon, orange, and raspberry, and a vague smell of apples hung in the air. Brother François and Brother Antoine met them at the airport. Among the first of the passengers to disembark was Father Léon. He wore civilian clothes in public, just as François and Antoine did. Moments later, three Tibetan monks appeared, all clothed in robes the color of oxblood. The first was Geshe Chouzin Gyaltsen, professor of dialectics. He was supported by two younger monks. Léon explained that Geshe Chouzin was not feeling well, having caught a severe cold in Montréal. He was supported on his left by the eighteen-year-old Venerable Sering Dechen, the geshe's English and French interpreter. On his right was the Venerable Tenzin Wangchuck, who also spoke some English. He was fifteen but looked more like twelve. Father Léon presented everyone and asked the Canadians to return the goodwill gestures of the Tibetans: they folded their hands and bowed. The Tibetans then put white scarves over their hosts' necks as a sign of best wishes. An awkward moment of silence followed, and just when Antoine was about to ask where the fourth monk was, a small, shriveled peanut of a person appeared with the last of the passengers from the airplane. He wore the same oxblood robes and smiled broadly without benefit of a full set of teeth. This was the Venerable Ngawang Damchoe.

All the Tibetans' heads were shaved. Sering and Tenzin both possessed smooth, walnut-colored scalps. Their luminous eyes made them seem happy even when they were not smiling. The geshe had several weeks' worth of stubble on his overly large head. He looked sick and puffy in the face. Patches of yellow skin framed his eyes. On the tiny, shriveled one — the old monk who got off the plane last — a lack of hair revealed a bumpy, gourd-like skull, discolored in places as if he had slept in the dirt. He smiled incessantly.

Because of the sickly geshe, they returned to the abbey straightaway. Father Léon proved to be pushy and difficult about all the arrangements, just as Antoine had expected. He demanded changes of schedule and accommodation, along with certain dietary adjustments.

"No meat," Léon said. "And, of course, they want no milk."

The Tibetans were given rooms inside the cloister grounds, in what was called the old seminary house, a big white clapboard building sheltered by trees near the river. The geshe went to bed at once, while the old peanut Ngawang, who never left off smiling, put a pillow on the floor in the hallway and sat on it to say his beads.

"Mantras," Sering explained. "We're obliged to recite one

thousand mantras a day, but Cello says ten thousand or more. The beads help keep track of the number."

"Cello?"

"Yes," Sering answered. "It's a nickname. You may use it if you like."

Because Antoine found the name Ngawang unpronounceable, Cello was a good alternative, and the little man did seem a brown, worn-out old instrument.

Dom Jacques Bouvray came to speak with Father Léon, and while their guide was thus occupied, the young monks asked Antoine to give them a tour. He took them to the wine cellar, where old Father Cyprien made wine from Australian raisins; to the bakery, where Brother Jules made heavy whole wheat and honey loaves each day; and to the scullery, where Father Casimir sliced cheese and laid out portions for the nightly collation. He also took them to the bee yard, where Father Anselme examined hives without needing the protection of a veil; to the forge, where Brother Emery repaired brake shoes and tractor gears; and to the barn, where Brother Gennade milked sixty Holstein cows by machine. When the Tibetans saw the cows, they began to speak rapidly to each other in their own tongue; the flow and contour of it sounded like a gentle agitation of smooth stones in a brook. Tenzin became very shy and covered his face. Sering spoke to Brother Antoine in English, asking if they might have a drink of fresh, unpasteurized milk. Antoine hesitated for a moment, remembering Father Léon's orders, but then went to fetch cups.

"We like," Tenzin said after he drank the foamy liquid. "We very much miss yak milk."

"Yes, yak milk," Sering said, looking at Antoine with large, shiny eyes. "It tastes very much like yak milk."

Tenzin held a hand in front of his mouth to hide the mustache that had formed there. "Hot yak milk with tea and butter and salt. This is our very best favorite drink."

The information surprised Brother Antoine, and it made him question the books he had read. It also caused him to wonder how precise was Father Léon's knowledge of Tibetan monasticism. Perhaps Buddhist dietary laws in Japan differed from those in India.

Meanwhile, Father Léon Gaide-Chevronnay had finished talking with the Abbot and had come in search of the young monks. He went through the abbey, and when he could not find them there, looked around on the farm. He found Sering and Tenzin in a chicken coop with Antoine.

A bantam rooster had been holding the attention of the Tibetans. They were amused with his crowing and how he strutted before hens twice his size. When a hen fell down on her breast before the little cock, he proved too small to climb on her back. Sering and Tenzin whooped and laughed.

With a sharp cough, Father Léon cleared his throat. "The Tibetans have their own schedule for meditation," he said. "We mustn't be keeping them."

Antoine glared at the priest. He was about to voice a complaint, about how some people can ruin a good deal of fun, but Sering and Tenzin had already dropped their interest in the rooster and waved good-bye to Antoine with polite smiles. They walked away with Father Léon.

Chickens had never been so interesting, Antoine thought, delighted with these new young friends and amazed by how lively monks could be. He enjoyed them even more than he had anticipated, but was also confused. They seemed such ordinary people. Antoine had to remember that they were really only teenagers. What if, for instance, Brother Norbert Gignoux had laughed at the rooster? Would Antoine have found that so delightful? No, he had to admit. Brother Norbert annoyed him, no matter what he did.

★ ★ ★

The next day in the chapter room, the Tibetans had their first formal encounter with the entire Cistercian community. The Abbot asked Father Léon to introduce the guests. Antoine closed his eyes and frowned: he considered Léon's words unctuous and his tone condescending. Besides, Antoine should have been the one to introduce the Tibetans.

The geshe was asked to speak first. Because of his learning, he held seniority among the group: geshe meant "doctor" in their language. Although his face was sallow, he stood for the entire address. He did not flag at all. Speaking in a monotone that sounded almost like chant, he went on and on, sentence by sentence, for an hour and twenty minutes. Sering translated with confidence, as though he knew the geshe's words by heart. It was all about bad thoughts. When someone raised a hand, it was ignored. Later, Antoine learned from Tenzin that Buddhists consider it bad manners to question a geshe before he is finished speaking.

Fathers Cyprien, Marie-Nizier, and Ignace were the first to drop off during the homily on bad thoughts. Nizier snored loudly, but this did not seem to affect the geshe's concentration in the least. Others began to drop their heads and breathe heavily. The geshe continued in his trancelike tone, moving his mouth in a steady, monosyllabic pace, without any hint of excitement in his eyes. All the while, Antoine kept his eye on Cello, who paid no attention to the geshe's address. He smiled broadly while reciting mantras on the rosary. His murmuring lips produced the sound of a baby chick calling in distress.

"Bad thoughts lead to bad actions," the geshe explained. Bad actions create more bad thoughts. A vicious cycle results, and produces unhappiness. "There is much unrest in the world," Sering translated. "People are not happy because of their bad thoughts. And they take their bad karma with them into the next life. Over and over there is a struggle with bad thoughts and bad actions, while souls are reincarnated into worms or angry, howling ghosts. We must put away bad thoughts and keep our minds at peace." This was the essence of the geshe's vast speech.

When at last he bowed, all rose from their benches and left the chapter room for common prayer. Lunch followed in the refectory. Boiled potatoes and green beans were served, along with a noodle soup and thick slices of buttered bread. To Antoine's dismay, the geshe ate as heartily as anyone, shoveling potatoes into his mouth with evident relish. No one seemed to notice that Antoine nursed only a small cup of broth. The Abbot pulled him aside after the meal.

"The Tibetans look uncomfortable to me," he said. "I think they're cold. Perhaps you could find some coats and shoes." Robes and woven sandals were the extent of their dress, Antoine had noticed, and he was perturbed that Father Léon had not thought of their comfort in Québec. He went to fetch coats and sweaters, thick socks, and shoes from the wardrobe in the attic and brought them over to the old seminary house in a wheelbarrow. When Sering and Tenzin saw the pile, they poked through it, examining each article, pulling at it and trying it on while laughing at each other. Tenzin went inside with a thick coat and threw it over Cello. Sering selected a coat, sweater, woolen socks, and shoes for the geshe. Then each of the teenagers chose something colorful for himself, articles that seemed to blend well with their oxblood robes and saffron undergarments.

The next day the Cistercians were given the opportunity to question the geshe. He sat alone under the crucifix, on the Abbot's throne, while Sering translated questions. Someone asked how old he was. Another asked at what age he had become a monk. A third asked if Buddhists believed in a heaven, and Brother Norbert wanted to know if Cello was saying the same rosary as Catholics said. To all these questions the geshe re-

sponded with the same answer: bad thoughts must be banished
from the mind.

While this was going on, Antoine nervously pulled at his ear.
He began to realize that for as long as the geshe was present, the
other Buddhist monks would remain silent, except for the necessary translation and Cello's incessant whispers. He made plans to
get rid of the geshe.

That evening, he tapped lightly on Father Léon's door. A moment passed and he heard footsteps.

"Yes?" the priest asked. Only one eye and a nose were visible
through a crack in the doorway.

"Excuse me, Father, but I noticed today at the conference that
the geshe is not looking well. In fact, I see that his color has become worse since he arrived."

"Really?" Léon said, opening the door wider. "I thought he
was perking up." He held a book in his hand, a thumb stuck between the pages. He wore odd half-moon spectacles. Antoine
continued in an evenly paced whisper, the most authoritative
voice he could muster.

"Did you have a doctor look at him in Québec?"

"Why, no," Léon said, rubbing the book against his nose. "We
didn't have time, what with our schedules. Besides, it's just a case
of the grippe, don't you suppose? I feel rather bad about hauling
him all over the country this way, but we do have a schedule to
keep."

Antoine lifted a hand to his mouth and paused for what he
hoped would seem a grave moment of consideration.

"Well now, Father," he said, "imagine the consequences if the
geshe were to have serious complications. How would anyone
know until it was too late? What if he has walking pneumonia,
for instance? Or it could very well be a rare bacterial infection of
the lung. Who are we to say? The geshe could become danger-

ously weakened. And what would happen then? Your tour might be held up. You'd have to explain to everyone how seeing a doctor had never occurred to you. And if the geshe should die . . . well, Father, you must understand how I want to save you embarrassment."

By four o'clock the next afternoon Father Léon and Geshe Chouzin were at Winnipeg's Victoria Hospital. While they were away, Antoine went to the Abbot and told him that the remaining Tibetans wanted to speak to the community. Then he told the Tibetans that the community wanted to ask them questions. By this subterfuge a conference was quickly arranged.

They gathered in the chapter room. This time, Cello was given the Abbot's throne. He crawled up into it and sat on a cushion with his feet dangling over the side. Thus seated, he smiled and muttered his prayers. Sering and Tenzin sat on either side of him. Cello took questions, answering them without hesitation. Sering translated.

"How many vows do you take?" someone asked.

"Tibetan monks take a vow to abandon each of the two hundred fifty-three downfalls," Cello said. "Nuns vow to avoid only the eighteen root downfalls."

"Why do women take less?"

Cello rubbed his nose. "Because vows must be received by the novice from a living monk or nun, and the tantric tradition died out among Tibetan nuns."

"When did you enter the monastery?"

Cello laughed. "I was given to the monastery as a child," he said. "Most monks and nuns begin their monastic lives this way. In fact, the best monks and nuns are those who spend their early years memorizing all the necessary Scriptures and living monastic life while they are most impressionable. Adults may enter the monastery, of course, but they never make very good monks or nuns because they haven't memorized the necessary Scriptures."

"How old are you?"

Cello had no idea. No record existed. He explained that he had been given to a monastery in Tibet, and when the Chinese occupied the country, his monastery was destroyed with all its records. The Chinese put an end to religious freedom and Cello fled to India with thirty companions. Only three of them survived the trip through the mountains.

Brother Norbert raised his hand. Antoine felt blood rush to his head. He thought Norbert would ask if Cello believed in the Virgin Mary, if the Tibetans would consider giving up the error of their ways and being baptized as Roman Catholics. Antoine feared that Norbert would offer a prayer, on the spot, for the conversion of the heathen and the liberation of the world from the dark fog of Buddhism. Antoine imagined Norbert informing Cello how stupid it is to believe in reincarnation, to believe in howling ghosts or prayer wheels. But Norbert did none of these things.

"What does the name Cello mean?" he asked.

Sering translated the question. Cello raised his eyebrows, then spoke briefly in the bubbling language they used. The whole room waited for a translation, but Sering hesitated. Cello waved a hand to encourage him.

"Cheh'leh," he said, "is the word for nun . . . You see, Cello is a woman. She is the abbess of the Geden Choling Nunnery in India."

Mouths dropped open and Antoine heard gasps. No one said a word. It took some time for the Cistercians to absorb the fact that the short, wrinkled Cello sitting under the crucifix was not a monk. The cloister had been invaded. A woman had taken the Abbot's throne.

Everyone turned to the Abbot. He sat on a bench with the others, portly and overheated. At first Antoine thought Dom Jacques's face was red with anger, but then he noticed how the

Abbot's shoulders rose and fell. For a moment Antoine heard only the thick sound of his own pulse in his ears while wondering whether the Abbot was laughing or weeping. Then he saw the Abbot's eyes: how they sparkled. Dom Jacques Bouvray's mouth fell open, and he let out a short hoot that began the rumble of his laugh. This set off a chain reaction throughout the room.

Cello smiled broadly, showing her four little teeth. Even with laughter coming from all around her, she took up beads and continued her mantras.

The laughter died down, but no one knew what to do next. Tenzin covered his mouth. Sering's cheeks were rosy with embarrassment, and he cleared his throat.

"We didn't want to tell you," he said, "because it seemed to us a discourtesy. We had no idea, in India, that you wanted only monks. We didn't know how very important it is for you to exclude women from your monasteries. After we brought Cello all this way across the ocean for our tour of North America, we thought it ungrateful for us to disappoint you, so we said nothing. After all, what were we to do with Cello? Besides, who would know that she is a woman? Our heads are shaved. We wear the same clothing. She might as well be a monk. In our world, because we remain celibate, we are equal. We are more alike than different. And even without such considerations, it is all relative. Each of us has been a man or a woman in a past life, and each of us will be a man or a woman again, unless we are reborn as higher spirits. So you see, it makes no difference."

The Abbot rose and adjourned the meeting. He immediately summoned Brother Antoine to his office. Antoine worried. As official East-West Dialogue Contact Person, he might be blamed for this debacle. He slumped in a chair facing the Abbot's wide oak desk and stared at the floor.

"Brother Antoine, I thought it best to inform you about things as they are," Dom Jacques said. Antoine's palms began to sweat. "You know," the Abbot continued, "that Father Léon insisted upon taking Geshe Chouzin Gyaltsen to the hospital. It was a very wise decision. The geshe has a bad cold, of course, but the doctors have discovered an aortic insufficiency near the lower left chamber of his heart. This condition may be life-threatening, and he has been persuaded to give up his tour. Father Léon will accompany him to a Tibetan monastery in Colorado where he will be looked after by American doctors. Meanwhile, Sering, Tenzin, and Cello will continue on to Saskatchewan."

Antoine looked up. The Abbot sat comfortably at his oak desk, and his folded hands were mirrored in the glassy finish of the desktop. Antoine wanted to tell the truth: that *he* had insisted the geshe see a doctor. *He* deserved to be the hero of the hour, not that bloated, egotistical Father Léon. The Abbot continued.

"I will notify other abbeys that Cello is a nun," he said. "She will be respected as an abbess, of course, but the cloister must be observed. I was startled and amused by this revelation, but I must uphold the rules about cloister."

Antoine nodded and smiled. He kept silent but still fumed about Father Léon.

"A magnificent human being," the Abbot said, "this woman who has suffered grave injustice, in the mountains watched her companions die, been in exile all these years, yet she is so cheerful. So humble."

Antoine nodded. But in his head he said to himself, *She has four teeth. How can anyone be magnificent who has only four teeth?* "She's not what I expected," he said to the Abbot. "I mean, even beyond the surprise, her being a woman, she's too odd to be an abbess. I had hoped for someone more dignified."

The Abbot opened his mouth to say something, but tapped his fingers lightly against his lips instead.

"Brother Antoine," he said after a moment of silence, "I want to thank you for your assistance as Contact Person. The Tibetans are scheduled to continue their tour tomorrow. It's been a rare opportunity, this exchange of cultures. Perhaps you've some private questions for Cello? I give you my permission to speak with her."

Antoine rubbed his chin. "Oh, I don't know," he said. "I don't think I need to talk to her. I want someone more interested in meditation. She just says those mantras over and over."

The Abbot leaned back in his chair. "You're missing a golden opportunity."

The only opportunity Antoine wanted was to take rightful credit for having saved the life of Geshe Chouzin Gyaltsen. An idea flashed into his head. He could explain to Cello, Sering, and Tenzin that it was *he*, Antoine, who had saved the geshe. If he could tell them how it happened, how he had gone to Léon and begged the priest to take the geshe to the doctor, they would realize Antoine's virtue.

"Yes!" Antoine said to the Abbot. "On second thought, there might be something I could discuss with Cello."

He went off to the old seminary house. Sering and Tenzin were outside pushing the wheelbarrow. Cello was seated in it like a small Oriental dignitary. All her earthly belongings, Sering told him, were in the little felt bag she carried. In a soft and bubbling tone, she spoke to her carriers without the usual rosary in hand. Antoine made them stop.

"What are you doing?" he asked. "Where are you taking her?"

Cello stopped speaking. Sering smiled and said that they had been told to move the abbess out of the cloistered grounds to the gatehouse, where Brother Henri would give her a small room.

"Oh yes," Antoine said. "Such a bother." He stood in the path of the wheelbarrow. All three Tibetans smiled at him, but he did not move.

"I've come to set something straight," Antoine continued. "The geshe's being in the hospital, that was *my* idea. I'm the one who told Father Léon to take him there."

Sering looked at Tenzin and they spoke briefly in their native tongue. Sering looked back to Antoine.

"This hospital is not a good idea?" he asked. "The geshe is in a bad place?"

"No," Antoine said. "You misunderstand. *I* am the one who saved Geshe Chouzin Gyaltsen's life. That was not Father Léon's idea."

"That is fine," Sering said. "We are not upset."

Before Antoine could further explain, the wheelbarrow was taken up, and he had to move out of the way. Cello continued speaking in a thin but expressive tone, much like a grandmother telling a bedtime story. Antoine followed alongside. The little procession moved down the road and past an orchard where red nutlike crab apples hung profusely in the trees.

"What is she saying?" Antoine asked.

"She is giving us a teaching," Sering explained. "Her subject is Gelugpa, or the Yellow Hats, one of the principal sects of Tibetan Buddhism, to which His Holiness the Dalai Lama belongs."

Her cheerful, rocking words seemed somehow connected to the movement of the wheelbarrow, and Antoine found it hard to believe that she was talking about anything serious.

"Can you tell me exactly what she is saying?" he asked.

"It's very complicated," Sering answered. "In general, she explains that the real ground of Gelugpa is knowledge of suffering. Only when a person is fully convinced of the immensity of suffering can there be enlightenment."

"Oh," Antoine said.

"This suffering," Sering continued, "must be recognized as a universal condition, and the monk or nun must want deliverance for *all* beings from this suffering. Only then can enlightenment, or *sunyata*, be understood."

"Really," Antoine said.

They had reached a picket fence and Antoine opened the gate for the wheelbarrow. After they passed through, he turned back to check the latch, just above a yellow sign that read MONASTIC ENCLOSURE in black letters. Cello had finished speaking, and she pulled from her felt bag the old discolored rosary. The road ran ahead of them into cool shadows of elm and ash trees, and just beyond that was the gatehouse. When they arrived there, Brother Henri was waiting for them on the screened porch. Rubbing his purple-veined nose, he offered no words, not even to the abbess, who seemed not to have changed, a man even yet, the same person as when she first arrived, bald and stooped with years. Henri came down the steps to collect her little bag, and the two of them disappeared into the gatehouse.

"Is she upset?" Antoine asked.

"Upset?"

"At being moved," Antoine said. "Is Cello upset inside?"

"Oh no," Sering answered. "She is perfectly healthy."

"I mean, is she angry, about being put out?"

Sering laughed and said something in Tibetan to Tenzin. The blush on Sering's face was of unmistakable innocence. "Cello would sleep on the sidewalk without hesitation," he said.

Presently, Brother Henri appeared on the porch with a rubber ball. "Eh?" he said to the Tibetans, and before an answer came back he threw it out at Tenzin. The boy was delighted, and the ball was soon going back and forth in a wide arc from Sering to Tenzin and back. The teenagers whooped and laughed, and Henri, without so much as a grin, turned and re-entered the gatehouse. *Just as I expected,* he seemed to be thinking. *Boys are the same everywhere.*

Antoine took the ball once but then waved himself out of the game. The Tibetans ran down the road from which they had come, looking spry in the late afternoon light. Antoine followed them as far as the crab apple orchard. He felt sad that they would leave soon. He wished that he were taking Father Léon's place with them, but had to admit that he knew next to nothing about airports, probably less than the Tibetans, and besides, Brother Gennade depended upon his help in the barn.

With the Tibetans gone, Antoine would no longer be official East-West Dialogue Contact Person. Life would sink to the ordinary again.

He opened the picket fence and went into the orchard. Sitting beneath an apple tree, he asked himself what he had learned from contact with Buddhists. The first thing that came into his head was how little he had learned from books. "People are far more complicated than books!" he said aloud.

The short, twisted trees in the orchard offered their tiny crab apples. The fruit, though abundant, was a dull red and therefore inconspicuous even as the branches were losing leaves. From where he sat he could see the white seminary house flanked by several yellow elms. The air was cool and ripe with the smell of pumpkins that grew just over a hedge and down by the river.

Antoine felt on the cusp of grasping something important about monasticism, some common thread between East and West that he could identify and present to the Abbot, who would be suitably impressed with his insight. And then perhaps Antoine would discuss it with the Tibetans before they left in the morning. Yes, but he could not quite name it, the lofty idea he was after, and he decided that what he needed was a bit of meditation to shake the thought loose.

Though he sat for some time under the tree, no profound thoughts came to him. The sun was not visible behind the abbey to the west, but the evening sky was bathed with its scarlet influence. Birds sang across the fields up and down the river, all of it creating a sweet air.

Antoine pulled out his rosary and made the sign of the cross. He said his prayers with a little whisper. Wrapping his feet beneath him, he attempted to be very solemn. He wanted to banish all bad thoughts and put his mind perfectly at peace.

His prayer went well. He imagined looking like the Buddha himself, under a flowering lotus tree, serene in meditation. He imagined being Saint Benedict or Saint Bernard, caught up in sweet and undisturbed prayer.

On a nearby tree, a flock of cedar waxwings pecked at crab apples. They exhibited identical rose plumage with tiny crests of feathers. Suddenly they all flew up at the same instant.

A gentle breeze played at Antoine's ears. He closed his eyes to the birds. His mind was nearly empty of distractions when he heard something peculiar: a dull repeated noise. It would not go away. Antoine whispered his rosary louder, but the noise continued. It sounded like heavy apples falling on the ground, one by one, in a methodical pattern. He struggled to put the noise out of his mind but could not, and the more he tried, the more exasperated he became.

The rhythmic thuds persisted. Antoine ground his teeth. Sweat rolled down his forehead. He simply had to know the cause of the noise.

He opened his eyes. Slowly he came to his feet and, hunched and stalking, began to walk toward the sound. Over the short grass, a few trees away, he saw the small, bent figure of Cello in her oxblood robes. With her bare feet she was stomping on fallen crab apples, one after another, breaking them open, beating them with her heel into a pulp. This done, she bent low and picked at them, putting bits of apple paste into her mouth.

From a distance she looked like a hungry abandoned child.

Antoine was transfixed. He had never seen anything so peculiar: there she was, the Venerable Cello, abbess of Geden Choling Nunnery, foundress — he would later learn — of five other nunneries like it and spiritual mother to six thousand nuns, eating crab apples from the grass.

As sunlight drew away from the orchard, it came to him, the thread that bound their lives together. Cello *was* abandoned by society. She was marginal. The abbess was as defenseless and as irrelevant to the world as an orphan. And as a monk, so was he.

The experience of many days clicked into a clear order in his head. Antoine saw before him a Cello who had survived immense suffering in the Himalayas to offer a living witness to anyone interested: nothing less than the reversal of world order. As weak as she was — as weak as all humans are — Cello was fully awake. The wisdom of peace was hers, an old woman grounded in "suchness," her smile shining through all things and meeting no opposition.

He saw that his own behavior was to blame for his sour discontent. His growth as a monk had been checked by his own longing for a better place to live, better people to live with. Even after reading about Buddhism, he had failed to understand that nirvana meant the extinction of dissatisfaction and petty longing. Full awakening called for humility in emptiness.

Cello seemed unaware of Antoine's flabbergasted stare. She straightened her rounded back. Then, brushing her knotted fingers back and forth over the trunk, she appeared to thank a perfect living thing for its fruit. And when the wind died and the birds stopped singing, Cello walked back toward the gatehouse, making her way to bed.

6

Fires

Long before he set fires, seventy-six-year-old Father Ignace Lacan was told to keep the abbey roads clear of weeds. Dandelions, creeping jenny, and wild chamomile grew everywhere in the gravel. Cost ruled out asphalt, and because Ignace had nothing to do, the Abbot told him to work at his own pace, two or three hours a day. "Fresh air and sunlight will do you good," the Abbot yelled. Ignace claimed to be deaf.

Brother Antoine overheard. He looked to the west from the abbey church and saw the old monk with the Abbot on the elm-covered road. A large potato field spread out to their left and a cornfield to the right. The dairy was a fourth of a mile farther on.

Antoine surmised that fresh air was the Abbot's last hope of clearing the old monk's head and keeping him out of mischief. Ignace was a handful. Yes, weeds grew on the roads. And it was true that Ignace did nothing. But Antoine had learned, in the five years he had been in the abbey, that any truth about a monk was complicated.

Dom Jacques Bouvray found it difficult to assign Father Ignace responsibilities because no one wanted to work with him. Ignace proved incompetent at everything. For a brief period he had been the cook. The entire community complained because at nearly every meal the soup was sour. Nevertheless, the Abbot kept him on. Finally, when Ignace made everyone sick on frozen and reheated leeks, Dom Jacques relented. Ignace was dismissed. But before he left the kitchen, he managed to kill all the laying hens in the barn by feeding them a gallon of boiled oatmeal into which he had accidentally dumped a large quantity of salt.

Antoine did his best to suspend judgment on all this, but it seemed that everyone knew and accepted Ignace's incompetence. He was a troublemaker. Cows were upset whenever he visited the barn. Tools were bent and machinery ground down in the forge. Brother Edouard kept the carpentry shop locked after witnessing the horrifying way in which Ignace used a table saw.

With persistent calamities, the old monk managed to worm his way out of any gainful employment. He was a man of leisure by design. And although his mischief was well known, few caught him in the act. His wooden expression never gave him away.

The old monk was thin. Skinny ankles jutted out of enormous black shoes that must have been too large for his feet. Wispy hair grew like cobwebs from his scalp; how Ignace escaped the razor Antoine did not know, since everyone was required to wear the same short stubble. Big ears sagged on his head, nearly touching the back of his jaw. And his nose was so large and fleshy, it seemed to belong on some other face. If his expression ever betrayed a hint of attitude, it was that of determination. Ignace always appeared to have somewhere to go and something to do, which was rarely the case. He did nothing but smoke. Each morning his infirmary room was so filled with fumes that it rolled out into the hallway and others complained. Fresh air never reached him. That was one reason why the Abbot assigned Ignace the task of killing weeds.

Antoine worked in the dairy barn. Late mornings, after

Ignace's new assignment, Antoine often saw the old monk pausing from his work of vegetal removal, his hands gripping the small of his back. Bending with a trowel from the waist all day, clearing an area no bigger than a porch stoop, Ignace got fed up and threw the trowel away. Instead, he began using a mixture of Clorox bleach and water that he sprayed from a plastic pump bottle. The weeds died, but only after persistent applications, while the hem of his black scapular absorbed droplets of Clorox and turned a violet and purple splash. And when Ignace spilled the bleach mixture on the new carpet in the gatehouse, Dom Jacques ordered him not to use it anymore. Ignace obeyed, but found bottles of Roundup in the garden shed that killed weeds so effectively he expanded his attacks beyond the gravel road. Roundup killed dandelions on the lawn in the abbey yard. Unfortunately, large patches of grass also died, in a pattern that resembled ringworm. The Abbot hid all the Roundup, but this only led Ignace to hunt for a cheaper and more readily available poison. He soon noticed the diesel tank in the middle of the farmyard.

The tank stood by itself in the weeds like a giant pig carcass suspended from a wooden frame: a bloated, salmon-colored metal container with rust stains running in bloody patches over its belly. Between it and the abbey church was the flat, ten-acre field of potatoes and the elm-lined road. Twenty yards behind the tank loomed the granary and the big horse barn where Jean-Marie kept chickens. The massive dairy was to the right of the horse barn; behind it, and out of view, was a pasture that bordered the long road to Winnipeg. In the diesel tank Ignace recognized a virtually unlimited supply of weed killer that would prove effective in extinguishing green things everywhere.

The first time he drew fuel, his plastic bottle dissolved, but he found a tin sprayer in the garden shed, and he was back at the tank. With a thin coating of rainbow-colored gas on them, weeds relaxed their rigid stems, slumped over, and turned brown. Pigweed, burdock, thistle, lamb's quarters, kochia weed, crabgrass: nothing survived Ignace's sprayer.

Success did not satisfy, however, and he was driven to experiment. Ignace was one to press the boundaries. On a rough patch of thistle he sprayed a thin line, set a match to the fuel, and watched the lapping blue and yellow flames melt the weeds.

Brother Antoine happened to witness one or two such productions. Although the old monk's expression was remote, Antoine noticed that Ignace held his breath just before setting a match to the diesel trail, as a baker might pause before cutting into a cake.

Weeks went by, and Antoine began noticing evidence of little fires where there had been no weeds: charred paths in the gravel, sooty shadows of flames that had danced there, perilously close to dry grass. Antoine also noticed that Ignace's stiff seventy-six-year-old pace seemed to pick up every time he went back for more gas. Whenever Antoine peered out of a dairy barn window, it seemed as though Ignace was after more fuel. Fire was his only pleasure.

Working in the barn had become Antoine's pleasure. He cared for cows with names like Claudine, Daphné, Françoise, Irène, Josephine, and Nadine. They were milked at four in the morning and four in the afternoon every day of the year, and his work followed him everywhere, even into the church, where he could not pray because his mind wandered. When he heard the gospel words about seed in good soil, he thought of oats and the number of bales a given field might produce in the fall. When the monks sang of a land filled with milk and honey, he thought of Pauline and the mastitis in her left rear teat. When he heard Scripture about God's dreadful judgment upon the disobedient, he thought of Irène, how she had jumped the fence for alfalfa and then needed treatment for bloat. Antoine had become a dairyman. The farm and its many concerns absorbed his attention. But he felt guilty. Prayer did not concern barnyards. The Bible was not about dairy cows and mastitis and silage. The Bible, he thought, was about holy things. Details of ordinary life had to be left where they belonged — outside the church door — if he was to hear and understand the mysterious secrets of Scripture.

Antoine began to find the frequent bell for prayer rather irksome. Barn duties had to be left behind as he rushed off to the church. It did not occur to him to think of work itself as a prayer, the care of animals as a vehicle to holiness. Mucking out stalls, he whistled "Yesterday" by the Beatles. Sometimes he wailed with pleasure under the roar of the manure conveyer. Rinsing the milker, he remembered his first day in the dairy. Back then, he did not know how to milk a cow. Brother Gennade slapped the rear end of a big Holstein named Emma and made a monastic sign, two fists banging together: "Get to work." And Antoine took to milking almost instinctively. He liked cows, and they sensed this. Antoine came to recognize each animal by her spots. He touched the cows with fascination, and spoke to them. Even Irène — temperamental and unruly, pushing her way to feed and jumping fences for green grass — never seemed out of sorts around Antoine.

By and large, his cows were uncomplicated. They readily took to a schedule, and each occupied the same stall, day after day, with stolid contentment. To them, the beaten path was sweet.

To Antoine, however, the path between barn and church was not an easy one. After five years of the same prayer schedule — repeated day in and day out like a broken record — it had inevitably become dull. Antoine wanted to be a good monk but was not one to quickly drop work for prayer. He enjoyed the barn: a new calf was frequently being born, or a cow was stealing oats from her neighbor. In the church, he struggled to sing psalms sweetly, but the ritual did not always move him. Psalms were a penance: they were always the same. And however earnestly he sang with the other monks, his mind wandered. If this was a contest between work and prayer, work was winning out.

Bells and communal prayer were part of monastic life. Antoine knew this. He also knew the difficulties involved in any communal effort. While an outsider might think that monks slip into church now and then for a refreshing pause from labor, Antoine experienced prayer *as* labor. Monks were taught to sing the psalms as the *opus Dei*, the work of God, and if that chant was beautiful, it was in direct proportion to the careful preparation that went into singing in unison. This was difficult. Idiosyncrasies had to be left aside. The voices needed to blend, with enough attention and energy for proper pitch and tempo. To be sung well, the chant required as much work as went into a fine drill team or a good string quartet. Every time Antoine walked into the church he was there to perform this sacred duty, and it was *work*. He knelt on the tile floor until the superior gave a rap on the oak platform. He and his brother monks came to their feet and sang. The entire psalter was sung within the course of a week, with many hymns besides. Vigils began at three-thirty in the morning, and roughly every two and a half hours throughout the rest of the day the monks assembled for common prayer: seven offices each day, besides the Mass.

Physically, he was present for communal prayer; he rarely missed an office. But mentally he was nearly always absent. At Vigils, for instance, his mind was soaked in dreams: automobiles, scenes from movies he had once seen, songs from albums he had owned, the faces of friends and the ruckus of the life he had left, all this stitched together on the flank of a cow, with the hard pulling of teats in a bleary-eyed quilt of memories. All the while, he mouthed words of the psalms, and bowed, knelt, sat, rose, and moved in procession with the choir.

To begin the milking at four, Antoine was permitted to leave

Vigils early, but not one sacred image from the Bible followed him to the barn. And throughout the day, at Lauds, Terce, Sext, None, Vespers, and Compline, he returned to the church with waking concerns, mostly of cows and grain.

Still, every now and again, he woke at prayer to the beauty of men's voices singing in unison. Every now and again, the fog of routine dissipated and the music of plainsong dovetailed with his mood and swept him into an age-old current.

Antoine likened monks to oarsmen on a ship, lifting a sheet to catch a sacred wind, the breath of something holy. Because plainsong moved in free rhythm, the notes rose and fell until a secret breeze caught the phrase and filled it out, let go, then caught it again and made it strain against simple understanding, pulling the choir along with the force of an unseen power: monks taken away. The movement of voices was then imbued with a higher significance. All things were possible during the work of God. Occasionally, Antoine recognized these subtleties.

The choir was of no interest to Father Ignace. His knees bothered him, he said. He also claimed to be too deaf to follow music. When the Abbot demanded he attend the office, Ignace pointedly demonstrated an inability to sing, and was thereafter allowed to stay in his infirmary room to recite the breviary alone.

In the infirmary, located on the second floor of the east wing, near the scriptorium, all sorts of strange behavior was overlooked. Old monks occupied private rooms there and did as they pleased. The corridor smelled like rancid butter. Father Joseph washed underwear in his sink and hung it out to dry on the fire escape. Father Marie-Nizier attended the holy Mass from the infirmary balcony overlooking the altar and snored through the orations. Both of them smoked. Ignace had started the practice. For years he bummed cigarettes from the milk-truck driver and transient guests until the Abbot agreed to give him three packs a week, provided there was no smoking in church. After that, Joseph and Marie-Nizier wanted them, too. The Abbot reasoned that once a monk reached a certain age he was entitled to endanger his health.

Father Joseph smoked in the belief that cigarettes helped him cope with the pain of crippling arthritis. Besides, he had been a cigar-smoking parish priest before he entered the abbey. Father Marie-Nizier smoked as a consolation in his old age: he was ninety-three. But Ignace was only seventy-six, and smoked — it seemed to Brother Antoine — simply to enjoy the bright red glow of the burning punk while it ate at the tobacco. While smoking, he drew hard on the filter and his eyes crossed as they followed the progress of the smoldering tip. No one made a connection, at the time, between Ignace's smoking and pyromania; that realization occurred later. Although Antoine never saw Ignace smoke at the diesel tank, he did see him with a cigarette while spraying fuel over weeds. Ignace pumped his tin can with both hands while holding a live cigarette in his lips. Ashes fell. How he avoided burning himself was a mystery. But Ignace had the makeup of a stupid and reckless hero. In another context, he might have been decorated for foolishness. But the abbey afforded no bombs to detonate, no foxholes to explore, no enemy to distract, and Ignace had to make do with a little diesel fuel and a cigarette.

Brother Antoine was curious to know whether the wooden face Ignace wore showed indifference or courage. Mishaps seemed to follow him everywhere. Once, in the pantry, Antoine found him pinned by his sleeve to the wooden countertop with a cleaver. The old priest explained that he had used the cleaver to open a five-gallon plastic pail of all-purpose joint compound for Sheetrock. He had positioned the sharp edge of the cleaver against the plastic lid and hit the flat edge with a hammer. Antoine pointed to the joint compound.

"Why this?" he signed.

Ignace answered in a loud voice; often he did not bother with signs. "It was the only thing I could find," he said. "I needed it because I punched a hole in the kitchen wall." And in the kitchen, there it was: a ragged three-inch puncture with a bread hook hanging from it. "I couldn't get the damn hook on the mixer, so I threw it over my shoulder," he explained.

Once, shortly after Ignace had been dismissed from the kitchen, he was asked to wash kitchen pans. The detergent was weak, he decided, and he dumped a gallon of lime solvent into the water with some bleach. Then Ignace went off in search of lye powder. Monks soon noticed a smell like solder smoke and traced it to fumes rising from the sink. The aluminum pots had turned black and the stainless steel washbasin was permanently damaged.

Such things were but a prelude. Fire now occupied most of Ignace's attention, and he became more and more brazen. Antoine watched him spray patterns in the gravel with fuel and light them for the sheer spectacle of it. He staged miniature burning landscapes with tin cans, rocks, and twigs. Ignace was no longer interested in weeds. He discovered that when motor oil and diesel fuel were mixed, flames lasted longer. After heaping piles of sticks and dry kindling, he set a match to twisting fire paths that ran under his feet, licking the hem of his habit and causing the wool to smolder before he put it out. Antoine observed all this from a barn window.

Ignace scratched phosphorous to grit and a delicate flame appeared for a moment. The fires he created lasted briefly. He might have benefited from the calming effects of a log fire, his feet up, smoking a pipe, but the abbey had no fireplace, and even logs burn to ash in an evening.

★   ★   ★

It was always dark when Antoine began early morning milking. Brother Gennade arrived first to set up the equipment and feed mash to the cows while Antoine went from stall to stall with the milker. In the quiet of the morning he stripped the cows by hand. After taking off the machine, he propped a three-legged stool next to Pauline or Daphné and rested his forehead upon her soft flank. Rhythmically, he worked warm teats. The cow's udder was like a pillow, and her teats heavy-gloved fingers filled with rich liquid that foamed in the pail. He loved the zing zing music of milking, and the cows seemed to enjoy his hands. Pauline and Daphné, especially, preferred Antoine's hands to the milker. Their hind legs did not move. Their tails switched to the rhythm. Antoine found hand-milking a pleasure, especially on cold mornings when a cow's body warmed even the soul and made him grateful for health. He would get to wondering how long the cow might live, how long he himself might be around to enjoy early mornings. He was twenty-four years old that summer when Ignace was playing with diesel fuel.

Once, on an easy Friday afternoon while Brother Antoine was walking through the pasture, he caught a whiff of something dead. Magpies flew nearby; he saw the flash of their black and white plumage in a grove of trees at the property line. These birds were like vultures: he knew they gather for a corpse. Antoine went to the grove and found a cow that had been missing: number thirty-two. It was Irène. She was bloated to great size, with legs stretched out to the sky, and her mouth was open wide. Entrails had begun a slow push out of her back end. Death was a stinking business. Flies covered her like a moving blanket. Nevertheless, Antoine could not bring himself to turn away from the sight. He was fascinated. In her long life Irène had produced enough milk to swim in, and many calves besides. Now, there she was, a pathetic pile of rotting flesh.

He went to the barn and told Brother Gennade about the dead cow. Two fingers were held like horns to his temples, then he pressed a thumb against the bottom of his chin. "Cow dead." Gennade held his right hand up to his cheek like a telephone, and Brother Antoine went to ring up the Hide & Fur. A man answered with a thin voice and promised to come haul the carcass away. He spoke in English.

"You're the Trappist place, right? The farm just south of St. Norbert?"

"Yes," Antoine answered, feeling uncomfortable about the businesslike disposal of Irène. "Stop by the dairy and ask for directions," he said. "The cow is far enough away from the barn, but if she's left for very long, the flies will become a big problem."

"Okay. Monday or Tuesday, eh? If I'm down that way. We'll get her eventually."

After the man hung up, Antoine listened to the dial tone for a whole minute: an odd buzzing connection to the world.

Irène's empty stall was reserved for a heifer named Bernadette, almost old enough to be bred. She recognized Antoine because he had fed her as a calf. A slight thing, she had been born in the pasture during the summer. The entire herd of lactating cows gathered around, each of them licking the calf and offering an udder. They seemed delighted. And when Antoine hoisted little Bernadette onto his shoulders and took her off to the calf barn, every cow but one followed him; the real mother stood several yards away, chewing the afterbirth.

Antoine loved animals because they spoke to him. Calves bawled for their bottles and cows lowed at milking time. Even the two bulls, Julius and Caesar, bellowed for attention; each of them wanted to be scratched behind the ears.

In the barn, Antoine felt a sense of equilibrium. While the atmosphere in the church was abstract, the barn housed a tangible drama every day. The earthiness of feeding and milking and mucking stanchions was robust and full of sense. In the barn he had a place. But under the high vaulted ceiling of the church he was bored. Prayer seemed empty but for words: the same formulas endlessly repeated. He enjoyed sacred music, but his mind wandered from Scripture because of the endless monotony of it.

"It happens to everyone," Father Yves-Marie said. "Monastic life becomes dull with routine. Every monk becomes weary after a while. It's a phase. And meanwhile it ought to remind you that a real monk is not necessarily someone who obeys, much less someone who is merely celibate. The real monk is someone who freely turns to prayer, and prefers it to other things."

"Then why," Antoine asked, "is prayer in the abbey compulsory? Why is it built into the schedule like a never-ending drill? Why not let real monks freely turn to prayer?"

Yves-Marie let out a long sigh. "Because," he said, "if a bell didn't ring, you probably wouldn't go to prayer. And if you didn't go to prayer, you probably wouldn't learn the habit of prayer. It's the *bell* that drills prayer into us until it's second nature. The bell is your friend, despite the annoyance."

Frequently, on the way to church, Antoine walked through the infirmary and glimpsed Ignace through the open door of his bedroom. Cigarette smoke was nearly always billowing out into the hallway. Ignace had a habit of reading the breviary in a rocking chair by the window. Although Antoine had his own difficulties with the psalms, he thought Ignace's attitude toward the work of God a little too casual. Was Yves-Marie right? What would become of monastic life if each monk were to say the breviary in a corner, smoking a cigarette or eating a sandwich? Was this what Antoine wanted? Would this be the result of an unscheduled day? Did he really want to be delivered from communal obligations to prayer? Would he really perform the work of God alone in the barn, at his convenience, never entering the church to pray with the others? Yes, Yves-Marie was right. Given Antoine's own will, he probably would not think of saying the breviary at all. And he tried to imagine life without prayer: the vaults of the church silent of ethereal music, plainsong no longer floating up like incense into the air. Without prayer, monks would no longer be monks — this much he knew — and the church might as well be nailed shut, turned into a giant storage crib for corn. Without prayer, Antoine told himself, the monks could just as well leave, each of them, and find something better to do.

And what would that something-better-to-do be, exactly? Selling automobiles? Counting money at a bank? Running machines in a factory? Watching television?

But Antoine *did* have prayer to go to because the bell never ceased ringing, no matter what his mood. Yet again, he walked into church and took his place in choir, straining to make something meaningful of the monastic liturgy, trying to hear as fresh the worn-out psalms within the never-ending tedium, the dreary sameness of it all. In his mind, the most profoundly sacred had become mechanical. And despite his efforts, even while mouthing the words of sacred Scripture, he thought about dirty teat sockets on a milker. While singing hymns at the holy Mass he thought about how cow shit is green and runny when the animals are first put to spring pasture. His feet moved in single-file formation with the others as they walked to and from holy communion, but he realized only after he swallowed the host that his mind had been wandering yet again. What had he missed? What sacred opportunities had passed him by? Had there been a divine whisper in the church? Had a heavenly sigh been heard amid the human voices raised in lilting music, floating softly as feathers in a breeze?

"I'm still not attentive in prayer," Antoine told his confessor, Yves-Marie. "My attention is always on my work."

"Never mind," the priest answered. "It's all of a piece. The chores, the prayer, the silence. Each flows into the next, and one without the other would be incomplete. Trust it. Monastic life transforms you as you live it."

Antoine had been in the monastery a short time compared with others. Brother Gennade had been a monk for twenty-five years, Joseph for forty, Henri for sixty years, and Marie-Nizier for nearly seventy. At times Antoine thought that perhaps he was not mature enough in monastic life to pray well, and believed that good things come to fruition slowly. A monastic life of penance — early rising, field work, plain but sufficient food, cloistered detachment and prayer — had a cumulative effect. That is, on all but the crazy Ignace, and that polar bear Alcide who had made a hobby of drowning kittens. How they escaped transformation Antoine did not know. Probably because they were psychotic. But he did not want to be judgmental. After all, the community accepted them and protected them, conceding only that they were a bit odd.

The majority of monks set a good example, which meant that they had become invisible for their quiet fidelity to the life. Yes, Brother Henri loved to gossip in the gatehouse, but he was faithful to prayer and to his duties. And Father Yves-Marie peered out at the world from behind his thick glasses with a trace of condescension now and then, but he was forever ready to help. Brother Bernard was almost completely invisible. An old, crippled monk with a preternaturally wide smile and no hair — not even eyebrows — he sat in the church whenever possible, for hours on end, quiet as a whisper.

Father Ignace was anything but invisible. He grew bored with cigarettes and demanded cigars. The Abbot refused. Ignace became indignant and compared himself to a martyr, but the Abbot still refused. Trying another tack, Ignace said he was willing to compromise with a pipe.

"You ought to be an example to the young ones," Antoine heard the Abbot say. "And besides, you should be preparing yourself for heaven. Do you think the souls of the just smoke cigars?"

Ignace began dropping cigarette butts in the hallways, and he regularly beat a tin cup against water pipes that led to the Abbot's room. When cigars still failed to appear, he pissed on the Abbot's geraniums near the cemetery. On a sunny day in July, Antoine was on his way to the afternoon milking and saw Ignace through the trees, hoisting his habit over the flowers. But the flowers only grew bigger. Ignace finally killed the geraniums outright with diesel fuel. The Abbot said nothing. Unable to provoke, Ignace poured gasoline into an empty soup can and sprayed an oil path away from it, then lit this elaborate firecracker in the cemetery. The Abbot came running.

"Stop squirting fuel all over the place!" he yelled. "I have had enough of this idiocy, you *cabochon!* When will you act your age? You might have killed yourself." He grabbed Ignace's spray can out of his hands and ordered the old monk to stay in his room. The Abbot also confiscated Ignace's cigarettes because it had become common knowledge that he smoked in bed. But Ignace simply wrote a sad letter to his niece in Duvernau, Québec, and she sent Cuban cigars. These were delivered in plain parcels and placed unopened in Ignace's room.

After weeks of smoking the finest tobacco, he grew bored again and roamed the hallways. He had learned to enjoy the outdoors. And without distractions, life was too tedious. For long moments he stopped and stared at the novice, Brother Charles Frémont, making him nervous sweeping floors. The novice asked, "What am I doing wrong?" by shrugging his shoulders and pinching his nose.

"Matches," Ignace signed back, passing the tip of a forefinger across his wrist, then blowing out an imaginary flame at his fingernail. "Get me more matches."

The novice rushed off and returned with a big box of farmer's matches. Ignace lit these one by one and tossed them out the window of his room.

Once a day Ignace knocked on the heavy oak door that led to the Abbot's office and went in to beg Dom Jacques Bouvray for cigarettes. The Abbot waved a blessing instead. Ignace soon turned his attention to the bursar. He went to sit in Father Pierre Ollier's office for an hour, not saying a word, until Father Pierre lost his patience; he shooed Ignace out and locked the door. Pierre did not enjoy being stared at by an expressionless old man.

Then Ignace came back to church. For lack of anything better to do, he sat in the balcony while the community chanted psalms. But Antoine could see that Ignace was bored. The old man buried his head in his hands, and after a week of prayer asked to see a doctor.

He was taken into Winnipeg in the abbey's green 1973 Chevrolet, and the doctor told him to quit smoking. He also told Ignace to eat better food and get some exercise. Although the symptoms were vague — something to do with stomach cramps and rectal pain — when Ignace returned home he was regularly given old plucked hens from the poultry house boiled with vegetables and served with cream. The Abbot assigned him light yard work pushing an old compactor with a rusted handle, tamping already well-worn gravel roads. Ignace performed this useless task every day. He wore his wool habit. Over his head and neck he draped a large red handkerchief as protection against the sun and held it in place with a baseball cap. He looked like Lawrence of Arabia. His expression was ever the same: disengaged eyes and a mouth that seemed not to close anymore because of a bent hinge. After a few hours of pushing the compactor, he always left it in the ditch by the cornfield and went off to smoke with Father Joseph.

Exactly when he started lighting fires again Antoine was not certain, but three nanny goats that lived in an old toolshed showed signs of distress. Their keeper, Father Denys, could not understand why they had become so skittish until he let them out into the harvested cabbage field and called Antoine from the dairy to witness what he had found: traces of fire behind the shed.

"Shall we tell the Abbot?" Antoine whispered.

"Surely he already knows," Father Denys responded, poking at scorched vegetation. It looked as though the old monk was back to killing weeds, and they assumed his spray can had been returned to him. What business was it of theirs to question the Abbot?

Yet when Antoine saw Ignace with his spray can again, he noticed that the priest was enjoying himself a little too much to have been given permission for what he was doing. Ignace did not smile, but his weed-burning was more elaborate. As an artist sizes up a canvas with crayon lines, Ignace drew patterns around weeds with a stick before actually spraying fuel, and when these little masterpieces were lit, they proved to be quite inventive: a flaming face with weeds for hair, or a circle of flame around a burning mayonnaise jar. Fuel-soaked string hanging upon tall thistle made it blaze like a small Christmas tree. On occasion, Antoine could not resist standing over Ignace to see these patterns of fire, and the old monk was so absorbed it was hard to say if he knew someone was watching.

What was it about fire that fascinated him? Antoine wondered. Ignace found matches so amusing he let them burn almost to his fingertips. Who was Antoine to judge? He himself could never pass up a big fire, the spectacle of a wooden building buckling and folding in on itself as it glowed hot with color, gnawed and eaten in a violent outpouring of energy that bellowed and dissipated into a cloud of smoke.

Fire, Antoine knew, ate everything but rock. Fire could solve a problem of his; the Hide & Fur had never come, and when the wind blew from the southwest, a faint odor of rot floated in the air. He considered asking Ignace to burn Irène, who had ripened beyond usefulness even to a glue factory, but thought better of it. Ignace could easily burn off the entire pasture.

Leaves of summer dried into paper colors. Every day Ignace placed a red handkerchief under his cap and pushed the compactor in front of the Abbot's window and down the farm road to the end of the potato field. There he collected his spray can from a hiding place in the granary and prepared little fires. From the hayloft of the dairy barn, Antoine saw him throw a match onto a trail of oil that circled a garbage can with an inch of gasoline inside it. That particular explosion went unheard in the Abbot's office because Father Philippe Fluet had three grain augers going at the elevator, churning out a noise worse than grinding gravel with a rotary tiller. Ignace stood motionless, as if all his energy had been consumed in some secret voluptuous frolic. Perhaps he was stunned with the realization of his own destructive power.

Wind blew leaves from the trees. The dry autumn turned chilly. One day, before the afternoon milking, Brother Gennade sent Antoine from the barn to look for a cow that had not returned to her stanchion. He set out across the pasture north of the barn. A brisk October air washed over his nostrils like clean water. He expected to see the cow along the fence line nearby, waiting to be fetched; she had a big, uncomfortable bag, and nothing would have kept her from milking except a lush stand of grass. But the pastures were brown by then; cows had begun to eat hay.

To the north, a grove of trees marked the property line and beyond it a gravel road wended its way to St. Norbert. To the northeast, the abbey gate was visible with its white gatehouse. Directly to the east was the cornfield and beyond it the abbey yard and the church. Bordering the cornfield to the southeast was the elm-lined road to the farm. And to the south, all Antoine could see was the dairy barn. The farmyard beyond the barn was not visible.

He moved quickly. The idea that the cow might have a broken leg or bloat had occurred to him, and Antoine felt anxious. As he walked through the short, dry grass, he pictured the empty stall in the barn, clean and ready, and then his own choir stall in church. His place might as well have been empty because he could not remember which monk had been reading the lessons the whole week. Seven times a day for several days he had been in choir but now failed to recall even the most basic elements of the weekly prayers because his mind had wandered so persistently.

As he neared the grove of trees at the property line he saw no living cow. Instead, the carcass of Irène came into view. She was half gone; her skeleton seemed to have slipped out of her. What was left of the body looked like a pile of wind-damaged rugs behind the white bones. The exposed ribs protected a mound of dry grass, the remnant of what she had eaten. The guts had vanished. Irène's tag — she was number thirty-two — lay in the sun-bleached grass near her skull. Antoine remembered how fond she was of being scratched on her right flank before milking. She always backed out of her stall until she felt his hand.

As he studied the carcass, he felt the urgency of life, how brief it is and how it should be used well. At the same time, and with sudden clarity, he understood that none of his efforts had been in vain. His project in this world was neither the abstraction of a holy life nor the rootedness of mucking out animal stalls, but both of these. The project was to discover his weight as a human being. And as he stood there, Antoine thought that the purpose of monastic life, riddled as it was by human weakness, was sealed in a kind of obedience to a very high order; that peace would come to him no matter what, even after many head-on encounters with his own faults, and those of others. He had only to heave a sigh and accept all that life had to offer in its very plainness.

A sudden buzzing made him lift his head and look for a bee. The sound grew to a mechanical whine, and it occurred to him that something like a police car was headed toward the abbey.

He looked at the road. There, in the ditch outside the fence, was the living cow he had been searching for. She held her head down and raked back and forth through a stand of meadow plants, the last green taste of summer. Beyond her was a fast-moving firetruck. Pulsating lights, red steel, and chrome left a long trail of dust in the air over the road. As the truck sped by, the cow never even lifted her head.

Brother Henri came running from the abbey to open the iron gate for the truck. Monks had already appeared in the yard, but from his spot in the field, Antoine could see no smoke from the abbey. The truck slowed and cautiously moved through the gate just as Father Philippe arrived to point the way. It moved on through the yard, in front of the abbey church, then turned down the elm-lined road toward the farm. Soon it disappeared behind the dairy barn.

From where Antoine stood, nothing but clear blue sky framed the farm. But the forge and pig barn, as well as the old horse barn and the grain elevator, were obstructed by the large dairy barn that was planted solidly between him and the firetruck. He left the grazing cow and ran across the pasture toward the elm-lined road.

"*Non! Non!*" Father Philippe yelled to him from across the cornfield. "*C'est très dangereux!*" Antoine stopped. Only then did he notice that the monks had remained at the head of the road near the abbey church. No one was going near the farm.

Antoine pulled away from the dairy barn and crawled over the pasture fence. He ran through the cornfield in less than a minute and reached the monks. Philippe and the Abbot were among them. Everyone gazed toward the farm with a look of horror.

Ignace stood within a ribbon of flame surrounding the diesel tank. Even while he stooped to spray more fuel with his little can, dry weeds ignited and disappeared. He seemed unaware of the dilemma. Ten feet from him the tank was suspended from the ground with its diesel hose lying in the grass like a giant wick.

Father Philippe had seen Ignace from the grain elevator and called the fire department. Then, rushing out into the yard, he had yelled to Ignace, but the old monk only waved and continued pumping his sprayer.

The firetruck came to a stop near the dairy barn and men jumped to the ground, where they stood motionless, calculating. Apparently they decided to abandon the tank and save Ignace. Three of them rushed through the burning weeds and snatched the old monk from behind. Together they raised him high above their heads and scuttled, single file, back toward the truck. His sprayer dropped from Ignace's hands, and a few moments later it exploded in the burning weeds.

Meanwhile, the firetruck backed away from the tank. Someone released the dairy cattle from the barn, and the monks watched them move off into the north pasture, away from danger. They smelled smoke and broke into a trot, swaying together as herd beasts, their udders bouncing back and forth in rhythm. The last cow in the line glanced back with her ears raised.

An electric pop came from the firetruck, and one of the men shouted into a loudspeaker. "Get away from the diesel tank!" his voice boomed. *"S'en aller de réservoir d'essence.* If you hear me, get out of the farmyard and move away from the diesel tank, anyone in the barns, as quickly as possible."

Ignace was still riding above the heads of the firemen, a distance from the perimeter of flames. They moved less quickly and with more care toward the firetruck. The old monk did not stir. He looked like a scarecrow being moved to another field.

Grass ignited around the tank's wooden frame only inches from the diesel hose. Several monks standing near Antoine turned away and covered their ears.

The explosion was louder than anything he had ever heard. The ground shook, and a wave of heat swept out and across the yard to where the monks stood. It lifted their habits and stripped leaves from the trees.

What happened in an instant Antoine saw in slow motion. Flames crossed the ground like liquid wind. The firemen fell over in domino fashion while Ignace rolled above them in the air. Dry grass ignited everywhere. Ignace's wool habit collected flames as he moved downward. He landed in a tall patch of weeds that ignited as soon as it received him. After this, black smoke obscured Antoine's view just as the firemen came to their feet, looking about in confusion.

"*Mon Dieu,*" Antoine whispered. Then, standing on the balls of his feet, he shouted, "Save him! Save him!"

Ignace reappeared of his own accord. Standing up, he seemed not to notice that flames were eating his clothes. He moved hardly a muscle. Instead, he looked down at his feet as if he had mislaid something.

The next moment the firemen were upon him. They rolled Ignace vigorously on the ground as if they were dealing with a boy instead of a seventy-six-year-old man. They could not save him. By the time he reached a hospital, Ignace was dead.

In the following days, Antoine went from the barn to the church and back to the barn, tending his duties in a stupor. Strangely unaccustomed to his body, he seemed almost to have lost a limb in the explosion. His heart pounded. Cows picked up on his nervousness and fussed with the milker, kicking and switching their tails.

When Antoine was in choir with the monks, he felt a jolt every time the word "fire" was mentioned. "Can a man take fire into his bosom?" He raised his head. "Fire will test the quality of each." Antoine's eyes widened to see Brother Théodore or perhaps Father Philippe at the podium. "He will baptize you in fire and the Holy Spirit." Now, Antoine's complete attention was on the reading. Words were charged.

The funeral was a calm affair. No one blamed Ignace for foolishness. No one blamed him for the iron shrapnel all over the yard, or for the forty-six shattered barn windows, or the grass that burned all the way to the foundation of the dairy before it was put out. The farmyard looked as though it had been bombed from the air. And as a final tribute to the old monk, a shallow crater remained barren of weeds for years in the spot where the fuel tank had been.

Ignace was alive in Brother Antoine's dreams for a long while. He appeared in a manner akin to the bush that spoke to Moses: engulfed in flames, yet never consumed. An image of him with arms outstretched seemed to burn away Antoine's mundane memories of the dead priest. Ignace became a mythic figure, remembered in one flaming image, in a purer state than he possessed while walking in the yard with a tin can full of fuel and a lit cigarette.

The Ignace in Antoine's head was always on fire, hands lifted to the sky with extended fingers like so many lit candles. Antoine had no desire to remember the corpse as it lay upon the catafalque: head and neck bound in cloth so that embalming fluid might not leak from the burns and stain the habit; the mouth, nose, and eyes set in a mannequin's wooden expression; the raw hands hidden from view. Antoine avoided the priest's grave. Instead, he went often to view the bones of Irène, an ever less gamy picture of death. By then, her skeleton was picked clean and cornflowers grew between her ribs. The eye sockets of her white skull stared up at the sky and her lower jaw remained open at a slant, as if she might sing.

Antoine did not stay in the dairy. The young Brother Dominique was assigned there, and Antoine was told to help Father Casimir in the cheese house. He missed his cows. Although he visited from time to time, care of the animals had to be left to Gennade and Dominique.

In his new duties he had much to learn: the exact temperature for heating milk, the amount of rennet to add to hot vats, the proper feel and heft of curd, the correct mold for aging. Father Casimir was painfully specific about the washing and handling of the cream-colored wheels of cheese. Only a perfect product was sold, and the soft brie, with a delicate hazelnut flavor, was called Port du Salut.

In the months following the burial, Antoine prayed in the church with his brothers and his mind still wandered. Any mention of fire, however, and his attention was brought back to plainsong and its delicate suspension of ancient phrases. Then he'd notice the stained-glass colors washing the floor, and the incense that filled the air with a heady clove scent. Crossing himself, he bowed, knelt, and received the bread along with the rich wine of communion. A disciple does not look for compensation. The road is the promise, even if not easy. To walk in faith is enough.

7

Heaven Abroad

Three monks died in October: Father Ignace Lacan, Brother Gabriel Eremasi, and Father Louis Rondel. In the graveyard beneath the windows of the abbey, three fresh mounds appeared in a row. Each man had died in a different way. Their absences were keenly felt in a community of only thirty-five, and the funerals, coming so soon one after another, left the monks in a somber mood.

Brother Antoine had attended five funerals in five years. In that same length of time, no new monks had made solemn profession of vows. Empty places in choir remained empty. And judging from old faces in the community, he knew he had not seen an end of death and burial.

Some younger monks were present in choir, too, of course. Three were in their forties, three in their thirties. And Brothers Dominique Moulin and Charles Frémont were juniors in their twenties who, after Antoine, would join the ranks of the solemnly professed. Overall, however, the balance tipped toward the elderly. Nine were retired. Six of these were in the infirmary. And because several years had gone by without a single inquiry or young person coming in, the community itself seemed to be dying.

The first to pass away after Ignace was Brother Gabriel Ere-masi. Even beyond the walls of the abbey he was known for his holiness. People from Winnipeg came to sit in the back of the church just to catch a glimpse of him walking into choir. He had an aura: at times he seemed to glow, and not especially when praying but perhaps while digging through pockets for a hand-kerchief or attempting to untangle a black rosary. Gabriel had no idea he was being observed. He was nearly blind and deaf, and completely unassuming. Looking different from the other monks, he was one of the last of the laybrothers to keep a beard, and the long, snow-white whiskers set him apart in choir and made his face seemed scrubbed and pink. He loved flowers, birds, trees, butterflies, and especially his pigs. Every day he walked the path to the barn with a bottle of green tea tucked un-der one arm and a plastic bucket of kitchen scraps in the other. If the animals escaped into the garden, he called them back with a gentle *"Chouchou! Chouchou!"* They ran to him like fat puppies. He sat on a stump and fed them while drinking tea and reciting the rosary. But in September a stroke sent him to bed in the infirmary. The pigs were sold. People expected Gabriel to die peacefully, but instead he suffered a horrible agony that went on for three days.

At night his shouts were heard in the dormitory, where they kept Antoine awake. Brother Gabriel was terrified, it seemed, of an imaginary demon, and Antoine wondered why Father Jude did not sedate him to ease the passing. Jude explained that be-cause of a deep reverence for death, monks preferred not to in-terfere. Cries were heard throughout the abbey. Whenever An-toine saw Father Jude in the hallway, the priest signed, "Poor pig brother. Sad." When the cries stopped, Jude made that sign, too, by pressing a thumb up under his chin to close the mouth: "Dead." Gabriel was buried on the tenth of October next to Fa-ther Ignace.

Though Antoine missed the pig brother, almost the whole of his attention was absorbed with work in the cheese house. Father Casimir, who looked like a thin, bald woman, kept him busy. Nearly every day, heavy oak weights, or followers, were placed upon curd in chisset molds, to press the whey out of it. Both the chissets and the weights were one hundred years old, made by monks from wood harvested on the property. Antoine handled them with care. When the unripened cheese was tapped out of the chissets, each wheel had to be rubbed with salt. He wore thick gloves to scour this gritty seasoning into the cream-colored curd.

Cheese was left in the salting room for twenty-four hours so that the salt could migrate into it. The next day Father Casimir poured boiling water over each wheel, to harden its surface protein, the first stage in forming a nice buttery rind. Then the cheese was returned to the chissets for two hours to cool and firm up.

Antoine tapped the heavy cheese wheels out of their molds and stored them in the loft and cellar for both drying out and ripening. He checked each wheel every day for visible defects; any mottling, dirt, splitting, or discoloration and they would be discarded. Most of the wheels were good, however, and were left on shelves with older cheeses; their heft was familiar to him, and Antoine had learned to appreciate the look of a good six-pound wheel. In the loft and cellar, unripened cheese caught a powdery blue bacteria from the older cheeses, and in two months it matured to a good *fromage* with a white creamy inside and a firm crust. Healthy wheels had a slight spring when pressed with the fingers, and the delicate aroma of the loft reminded Antoine of hazelnuts and ripe apples.

The abbey's cheese recipe dated from 1865, the formula of a French Cistercian house. Monks considered whole, unpasteurized cow's milk essential to a good aging process and flavor. Father Casimir was proud of his natural cheese. He adamantly refused to process or film-wrap the product for cold storage, like modern-day cheeses. It was sold only in wheels. That way, the business was deliberately kept small: a cottage industry for the monks. Cheese was made from start to finish in a modest-sized clapboard house, heated in winter by its own coal furnace and conditioned in summer by water pipes that ran from the basement to the roof, cooling the slates during hot weather.

Antoine would have been content with his work, were it not for his headaches. After being taken from the dairy and sent to the cheese house with Father Casimir, he began to suffer from an ache near his eyes. At first he thought he needed glasses. Inspecting mold in a poorly lit cellar, he squinted at wheels of cheese and experienced a dull, tedious pain that made his eyes throb. Eventually, simple eye discomfort became migraines. By the middle of any given day the pain was intense, burning having spread backward under his scalp and ears. And thereafter his attention was divided between duties and his throbbing head. The heat from the aching, he imagined, could melt sugar, turning a saucepan of it, if placed on his scalp, brown and bubbly. And the pain was inexplicable: he knew no real cause or connection.

Although Antoine was inclined to blame conditions in the cheese house — poor lighting, cheese mold, or the salt — he kept silent. The way he looked at it, someone had to help Father Casimir. And the Abbot had far too much on his mind to shift a half-dozen monks into new assignments so that Antoine might follow a hunch. Of all the monks, only the infirmarian knew about his headaches.

Tall, freckled Father Jude dispensed aspirin and various herbal teas. But nothing relieved Antoine's pain, not even a relic of Sainte Thérèse de Lisieux, a fragment of her holy habit that Jude touched to Antoine's forehead.

"Your headaches have to be psychosomatic," Jude said. "You didn't have them in the barn."

"That's true," Antoine answered, with his hands over his eyes. "But it could be anything. Maybe I'm allergic to cheese mold. Should I see a doctor?"

"It certainly wouldn't hurt. I'll ask for the Abbot's permission."

Antoine shook his head. "Oh no, please. Never mind. I can brave it out for a while longer. It's embarrassing, really."

"Does the Abbot know about your headaches?" Jude asked.

"No. But let me explain it to him myself. I'll ask for permission to see a doctor."

A week went by. Antoine said nothing to Dom Jacques. Wanting to avoid fuss over his health, he had a reputation to worry about. On October 20, the monks were scheduled to vote on whether or not to accept Antoine for solemn profession of vows. Upon profession, he would become a lifelong member of the abbey community. He wanted no impediments to stand in the way of a favorable vote, especially not that of poor health. Antoine did not want to be seen as a liability. Besides, he had a hunch that after the vote he'd be headache-free. At least, this was what he hoped.

In any event, an appointment with a doctor was something Antoine did not look forward to. He was afraid of a diagnosis. Mold was the least of his worries. When pain hit, the intensity frightened him. Cancer came to mind. He imagined a slow and painful death until he pushed those thoughts aside, preferring to believe that the headaches were connected to anxiety and would disappear after the vote.

On October 18, another funeral was held; Father Louis had died. Compared with Brother Gabriel's death, Louis's was less of a mystery. He had lived in the infirmary for years and never came to choir. Subject to tantrums, he was avoided by other monks. Once, he threw a tin cup from a window that hit Father Anselme squarely in the jaw. *"Chéti!"* — good-for-nothing — he yelled down to the sidewalk. The Abbot went up to Louis's room to reprimand him, but Louis refused to open the door. From inside he said that he ought not be disturbed, he was saying his rosary.

Louis hated people, or so it seemed. He hissed at Father Denys St.-Pieters, though they were both from Belgium, because Denys spoke Flemish while Louis spoke only French. Louis also hated Father Jude Sanders because Jude was "English," although in reality Jude had been born and raised in Orangeville, Ontario. Louis perceived all English speakers as interlopers into his French-Canadian abbey. He even shouted at Antoine whenever he saw him, *"Des Anglais! Des Anglais!"* simply because Antoine spoke English to Jude. When Antoine tried to explain that he himself was French Canadian, Louis put his hands over his ears. *"C'est en masse,"* he said. *"That's enough!"*

When Louis came to die, he begged for painkillers. The Abbot had too much heart to refuse, and a doctor came out with a morphine drip. This was not enough. A bolus was administered, but it was still not enough. Louis wanted alcohol. The Abbot agreed, and Jude gave him tumblers of cheap brandy. This had a calming effect, but toward the end Louis sobbed. All of life had conspired against him, he said. And then he quit breathing. His eyes turned toward the ceiling like a pair of glass marbles. His grave was next to Gabriel's.

At times Antoine wished for a morphine drip himself. No clear pattern existed for his headaches. Each morning he felt comfortable folding out cardboard boxes for cheese. He also spent time salting and turning wheels. The peaceful atmosphere changed as soon as fussy Father Casimir entered the cheese house. The man henpecked. Even his sign language grated on Antoine's nerves. Nothing was right: either far too many or not enough boxes had been folded out, the floor should have been swept properly, the stove temperature was set too high, a stainless steel kettle was not scrupulously clean. "Cold," Casimir signed, blowing on the back of his hand and then pointing at the open window. "You waste heat." And the headaches began.

Some days, however, and for reasons unknown, Antoine felt fine. Casimir's nagging did not bother him. Sunshine seemed wonderfully new and fresh. Birds sang the opening measures of a cosmic symphony. He wanted to dance through his chores and found it difficult to keep silent. Happy people are not silent. Sometimes he finished in the cheese house early and took the bicycle — the one Father Denys used to collect the mail — and rode to the dairy to visit the cows. Josephine, Nadine, Daphné, Françoise, and Pauline licked his palm, each in turn. Others had forgotten him; it had been so long since he had worked there.

But the headaches always returned. Three consecutive days never passed without pain. He wondered whether he was manic-depressive, if he had a chemical imbalance of some sort. Anything was better than cancer. But suffering was suffering, nonetheless, and it occurred to him that all human beings start dying long before the grave: slowly, daily.

Setting water to boil for Casimir's rind-rinsing, Antoine often experienced a vast deflation of energy, as if the headache were burning away all his body's fuel. But he forced himself to continue his work. Only when Casimir's hands were occupied was there a measure of peace.

Sometimes Antoine's pain became so severe he found it impossible to see clearly, and then he left the cheese house to sit outside in the cold for a few moments. Most mornings, Father Alcide, the fat polar bear, was nearby shoveling snow. On a tree trunk, the black outline of a crucifix nailed there made him remember that Jesus had suffered. Nails held his body to the cross. Antoine knew that headaches were nothing compared to such torture. Nevertheless, he longed to exchange psychosomatic pain for physical wounds that doctors could see and treat.

Not even his confessor, Father Yves-Marie, knew about the headaches. Antoine found no moral reason to lay such trouble out, and so refused to mention them in the confessional. Furthermore, it seemed like so much whining over conditions, something he had gotten away from since his novitiate. Yves-Marie had little patience for hypochondria or anything that seemed remotely like it.

Soon after Louis's burial, Dom Jacques Bouvray called Antoine to his office, wanting to schedule a date for the vow ceremony.

Antoine was surprised. "The community hasn't even voted yet," he said. "What if they should decide not to keep me?"

"Nonsense," the Abbot answered, sitting back in the chair behind his desk. "You've been here for nearly six years. The vote is a formality, really, because we know you by now. In all my years, I've never experienced someone being voted out before solemn profession. I think you'd have left by now if you didn't have a vocation." Dom Jacques had not changed over the years, except perhaps for more gray hair near his temples.

"Dominique and Charles?" Antoine asked.

"Oh yes. They'll be petitioning for vows. Dominique next year, Charles the year after. We're blessed. But meanwhile, pray for novices." The Abbot flipped through a calendar. "I'm afraid I'll be away the last two weeks of November for canonical visitation of nuns in Québec. December?"

Antoine tried to imagine a vow ceremony during the octave of Christmas, perhaps on the feast of Saint Stephen or of the Holy Innocents, but an idea suddenly popped into his head. "On my mother's birthday," he said. "Why not on her birthday?"

"And when's that?"

"The fourth of November. Is that too soon, Reverend Father?

She'd be pleased that I remembered. You might know that she still isn't entirely won over to my being here. Having the ceremony on her birthday might soften her."

"Well, there you have it, then," Dom Jacques answered. "The fourth of November. I'll write that on my calendar. I expect everything will go well."

Yes, Antoine thought, *if I don't have a headache. What if I should get one of those horrible migraines just as the ceremony begins? I won't be able to function. I won't be able to smile or look comfortable. My mother and father will think I'm being forced to take vows. My family will see that this life pains me.*

Dom Jacques looked up from the calendar at Antoine. "Anything else?" he asked. "Anything on your mind? You look worried. The vote should go well, I assure you, if that's what you're concerned about."

For a moment Antoine considered telling his superior about the headaches. He was tempted to relieve his anxiety about brain cancer, to obtain permission for an appointment with a specialist. The whole matter might be dealt with. And even if the headaches were revealed as psychosomatic, a possible cause might be explored: perhaps it was anxiety over working conditions, or worry about the future. Perhaps his headaches were not psychosomatic at all but the result of an allergy to cheese mold. And then the Abbot might arrange for him to take a new job, or to go back to the barn.

Antoine rubbed his nose. "My aunts and uncles," he said. "May I invite them to the ceremony? Cousins, too?"

"Yes, yes, of course," the Abbot replied with a smile. "Solemn profession ought to be a public ceremony. Ask whomever you like. But we'll need some idea of the number, for the reception."

Nodding, Antoine closed his mouth. Five years of sign language left him mute. He did not quite know how to wrap words around the complicated matter so as to express his anxieties with

the sort of care and discretion they needed. Without lucid clari-
fication, the disclosure of headaches might be taken as a sort of
whimpering complaint. Antoine wanted the Abbot to know that
the pain had no connection with unhappiness or lack of motiva-
tion. *The headaches will disappear,* he thought. *It's nothing to be
troubled about. As soon as I mention them, they'll go away and then I'll
feel like a child.* He bowed and left the Abbot's office.

That evening, he wrote to his mother and father asking them
to invite what relatives they wished to the profession ceremony.
The letter seemed awkward somehow, and he thought to keep it
back until after the chapter vote, when arrangements could be
made with certainty. But because the Abbot had instructed him
to do so, the letter was sealed and placed in the mailbox outside
the bursar's office.

On the day of the vote, he suffered another headache. He felt ill
already in the morning and had to pull himself through the day's
work in the cheese house. By evening he was nauseated.

"No need to be nervous," Father Yves-Marie signed in the hallway, displaying clenched teeth because there was no sign for
"nervous." In answer Antoine offered a weak smile, but as the
monks entered the chapter room to vote, he escaped to the cool
air outside.

The sky was grim and muddy, like dark felt. Flakes of snow
shimmered in a cascade before the yard light. He realized how
senseless it was to have a headache just when the Abbot and
community expected a smile, announcing the news of his acceptance. But pain controlled him. Although joy was in his heart,
smiling produced a driving ache behind his temples so that his
mouth stopped rising upward and reassumed a flat position.

He had heard pious sermons encouraging acceptance of suffering. Trials were sent to teach a lesson, sent as a vehicle to earn
merit for heaven. For his part, Antoine thought that suffering

ought, at least, to open his heart to sympathy. Knowing what it is to suffer, he could commiserate with others. He winced. Such notions were good for later. Pain-free, he might have some energy for virtue. As much as Antoine wanted to think that headaches had some value, under the circumstances the idea only annoyed him. He wanted to be rid of the throbbing pain. Like a wounded animal, he was ready to bite anyone who came near.

The chapter vote was affirmative. Only the next day did Antoine discover the results because he had gone to bed before the Abbot could find him.

"Are you feeling well?" Dom Jacques asked.

"I'm much better today," Antoine said. "I was upset by all the excitement. Really, I'm just fine today."

But by noon the headache was back, and this time Antoine was especially alarmed; he could not see to distinguish mold on the wheels of cheese. When he attempted to read simple instructions posted by Father Casimir on the bulletin board, they blurred, became clear, and blurred again. Bulbs and lamps were a torture. Bright lights waved on the periphery of his vision.

Anxiety sent him looking for Father Jude Sanders. He had reached his limit: no longer would he keep the headaches a secret from anyone. He would tell Jude to inform the Abbot so that they could take him to the hospital. The only solution, he thought, was to find out exactly what was wrong.

Antoine walked slowly toward the abbey. Footprints he left in the snow looked like those of a drunken man. He carefully climbed the doorsteps and went through the west entrance, but before he got anywhere near the infirmary, pain drove him to a bench in the hallway. There he remained with his hands over his eyes, unable to move.

All of his attention was absorbed in pain. For a long while he remained undisturbed. But at the top of the hour, a hall clock chimed three metallic pings, and his head felt each ping like a brass hammer against his skull.

Someone shuffled toward him. It was a slow, methodical movement. Antoine looked up and Brother Bernard Touzin was standing near. The old monk was smiling; he could see at least that. The top of Bernard's bald head had a shine. On his face there was no trace of hair: no shadow of a beard and no eyebrows. Antoine's vision blurred, then sharpened again, but he was already familiar with Bernard's bright little eyes. They were set within wrinkled flesh, and big rubbery lips spread across the face like the mouth of a horse. His teeth came from Toronto.

Bernard's hand opened before Antoine's nose, and a Tylenol nestled there like a chickadee's egg. Antoine took it. Then the old monk offered a warm glass of water carried all the way from the washroom. A trail of splashes indicated the path. Antoine drank the pill down while Bernard's smile spread to a ridiculous width. He looked like a bald Martha Raye. Because of this, Antoine choked on the water and coughed, but could not laugh because the stabbing pain at the base of his skull locked his head in place and left him without air. Brother Bernard took the glass and shuffled off in his arthritic way.

Antoine never suffered another headache.

There is an innocence about miracles. Almost always, they are small, private goings-on, easily overlooked. Jesus cured a woman in the crowd. Who knew but she? And his miracles were so often ambiguous. A wedding at Cana: the assembly was obviously unaware how the wine kept coming; it just did. Miracles can as easily be credited to a natural cause as to a divine one, as if out of consideration for delicate human sensibilities one is given a choice, whether or not to believe. Was it the Tylenol that cured Antoine's illness? Or did Bernard, through divine grace, restore some invisible balance in his brain?

In the days following, Antoine had unbounded energy. He salted cheese in half the time, and Casimir seemed astonished. But after scrutinizing the work carefully, the older monk found no grounds for complaint, and soon a pattern developed: by three in the afternoon, the cheese house was closed for the day so that Antoine could go to the barn and visit cows.

Secretly he credited Bernard with the cure. How else could sudden health be explained? He felt marvelous. More than once, Father Jude, the tall, freckled infirmarian, asked with gestures about the headaches, gripping his temples and rocking the upper half of his body back and forth. Antoine simply laughed. Or, after a shrug of the shoulders, he patted his head to say that everything was fine.

The same could not be said for Brother Bernard. The old man suffered a great deal from rheumatoid arthritis. In choir, he sat on the edge of his stall in an attempt to find a comfortable position for aching bones. Stooped, with a crooked spine, he did chores. Some of his vertebrae had fused into an inflexible mass of bone. His knees were swollen with inflamed fibrous tissue. Fingers were bent every which way. Nevertheless, Bernard performed his duties with calm regularity. No one especially noticed him. He drew no attention to himself. The sound of his voice was rarely heard; when it was, it was unforgettable because of its high, unnaturally pitched timbre, like the voice of a child.

Four days after the headaches vanished, Antoine received a letter from Madame Seneschal. She enclosed a newspaper clipping about herself as mayor of St. Jean-Baptiste and a photo of her shaking the lieutenant governor's hand.

> My little chipmunk:
> I thought you already took vows. Three years ago we came to watch you do something. I thought it was vows.

You threw your life away by promising never to have my grandchildren, and now you have to do it all over again? Why? Didn't the first ones take? If that's the case, think twice. Jeanne-Marie Loubier is still not married. You remember her? She is a sweet girl, and her father lives right here in St. Jean-Baptiste.

I spoke to your grandmother. She is proud of you. She wonders why none of her boys became a priest. But then with plenty of grandchildren she doesn't see things the way I do. She says she will come to your profession and has already invited the relatives. Your father and I will bring her.

Behave yourself in that place and brush your teeth.

Much love & kisses,

Momma

Antoine looked up from this letter with a smile. He noticed six of his confreres standing in the corridor near an oak statue of the Virgin and Infant. The monks were engaged in silent discussion with their hands, using animated signs and exaggerated facial expressions. The wooden statue itself seemed to preside over the conversation, the Infant looking out from its mother's arms with a raised hand, participating. *I'm one of them,* Antoine thought. *I'm really one of them.*

Before October ended, Brother Bernard died. His death was easy compared with the hard life he had led. Long ago, as a young monk during the Great Depression, he was sent to the LaSalle River to remove a stump. The river was, in fact, gone. It remained dry from 1932 until 1936. Bernard asked the superior if he might use the tractor for the removal, and with permission he chained the tree stump to the tractor frame and drove up the riverbank incline. Wheels spun. The tractor reared up, and the big machine rolled over him. When the monks found Bernard, they decided against the hospital because he seemed so close to death. But for days he drifted in and out of consciousness in the infirmary. He woke, recognized faces, and smiled. In the end, he lived, but his body mended poorly and for the rest of his life he remained stooped as though carrying an invisible burden on his back. He was also destroyed as a man — or so Brother Antoine believed — which might have explained his high, flute-like voice and lack of facial hair. As age set in, Bernard acquired acute rheumatism from poorly set bones, but he never complained. Instead, he sought comfort in prayer. He often sat in church on the edge of his choir stall, rocking back and forth like an old granny.

Bernard had seemed in relatively good health that summer because the heat suited him. But autumn temperatures were cold. Snow came early. The ground froze. He took ill with the flu in the last six days of October and stayed close to bed. Early one morning, Antoine noticed him wandering the hallway, listless and without his usual smile.

"Where's the infirmary?" he asked, looking about with tired eyes.

Although it was still the Grand Silence, when even signs were forbidden, Antoine spoke to him. "Are you all right, Brother?"

The old monk nodded. But he looked ready to drop. Antoine led him to a bench inside the chapter room, then ran off in search of Father Jude. Moments later, the two of them returned to find Bernard lying on the floor. Father Jude immediately took a pulse. While Bernard's frail wrist was held high above his head, he opened his mouth and sighed. That was his last breath. No moans. No clutching. No tears. The flu had weakened his heart, and in a moment he was gone.

Antoine remembered the words of a psalm used every Saturday at morning prayer: *A short span you have made my days, O God, and my life is as naught before you. Only a breath is any human exis-*

tence. You dissolve like a cobweb all that is dear to him. The psalm
was a bald lament, with no excuses or apologies.

The Bible offered innumerable images and symbols to Antoine.
He noticed some of these only after reading a passage many
times. These images were an invitation, he decided, a tool for de-
ciphering latent meanings within the whole mystery of living.
Rich mental pictures from the Book of Psalms, for instance,
made visible again the life from which those poems had come
into being — poems full of emotion — and he could then apply
the ancient prayer to his own life. While he read, the lesson
seemed always to be that appearances are but a clue to God's
work: inscrutable, too vast to comprehend.

The Bible was slowly becoming part of his blood. Verses of
the psalms he knew by heart, and he recited them in the cheese
house. Business was steady.

Antoine was returning from work when Bernard's body arrived from the funeral home. The corpse was delivered without
a coffin. This was the Cistercian custom. The funeral home had a
standing order to embalm the abbey dead as the law required
and do nothing more, adding no extra costs, particularly not for
makeup. The Abbot stood by the hearse and waved Antoine
over. He wanted help.

"I can't find anyone else," Dom Jacques said. "We need to
carry the body into the church."

The corpse was surprisingly heavy. After they had eased the
catafalque into the vestibule, Dom Jacques thanked the undertaker, speaking to him in French. "He looks very dead. In fact, he
looks a little too dead, don't you think?"

The undertaker put on his glasses and leaned forward to ex-
amine the body much as an expert would scrutinize a piece of
art.

"But it's what you wanted," he replied. "I'm not supposed to mess with the faces. Of course, if you're displeased, I could fix it for a small fee."

"How much?" the Abbot asked.

"Normally a hundred, but for you, I'll do it for fifty."

"Fifty?" The Abbot lifted a hand to his forehead and tipped slightly. "Just for the mouth?"

"Oh, for the mouth? Well now, let's see. Twenty-five."

"Mon Dieu!"

The Abbot showed the undertaker to the door. Antoine leaned close to the corpse. Bernard did indeed look dead. His face bore an expression of grief, as if he had just learned of the punishment of purgatory.

"Brother, you grip one edge," the Abbot said. Antoine turned to him, puzzled.

"The mouth," the Abbot said. "Grip the mouth. We can't let the monks see this."

Together they stretched. But rubbery and difficult to shape, the lips assumed their original position no matter how far they were pulled. Still, the Abbot and Antoine kept trying; after much tugging, the mouth eventually took on something of a smile.

They stood back to appraise their handiwork. Antoine felt as though he had committed sacrilege. The corpse no longer bore the grimace of purgatory, but neither did Bernard appear to be hearing the music of angels. His expression showed exactly what had happened: someone had fooled with his mouth. The Abbot was satisfied, though, and together he and Antoine moved the body into the church.

Bernard's burial was stark. In Manitoba, the Cistercian custom of placing the body in the ground without a coffin was legal as long as the grave was dug to six feet and the body embalmed. Although Antoine had witnessed several monastic burials before,

Bernard's was unique. For one thing, his grave was not dug next to Father Louis's, in the order of death; it was dug between a large elm and a lilac bush, next to an iron fence, in another part of the graveyard entirely.

The gravedigger, Brother Roland Roy, had already dug three holes that October. In the manner of a stout Russian peasant, he chipped the frozen clay with a pickax. Roland was strong: he could carry two hundred pounds of dry cement on one shoulder. But he was exhausted with grave digging, and as a concession, the Abbot told him to choose an easy spot. Roland found a dry place near the elm tree where the dirt was frozen only an inch or two. Below that was dry, sandy ground that moved easily with a shovel. The Abbot released Antoine from his duties in the cheese house to help. The two were given permission to speak.

"Oh, brother," Antoine said as he picked at the ground. "So this is what it's like digging graves in winter. I'm exhausted."

Roland spoke in halting English because Antoine could not understand his Acadian dialect. "Here, is no bad," he said. "Over there," and he pointed to Gabriel and Louis's graves, "is like to break up a sidewalk. In, down under, maybe two feet, come better. But you rest and mud maybe, how you say, it freeze. Very bad. Is very different here."

They dug all morning. The finished grave seemed a beautiful spot for Bernard, but it proved to be inconvenient for the funeral procession. The hole opened too close to the iron fence, and a wooden gangplank had to be laid across it, between the tree and the fence. The plank would make it possible for monks to scuttle across the grave and lower the corpse with ropes from both sides.

Antoine went inside and washed. He put on a fresh habit for the funeral, then hurried to the sacristy to vest as an acolyte. The funeral Mass was simple and without sadness or emotional outpouring. The monks believed that Bernard had gone to heaven. After the closing prayer, the Abbot walked out of the church and into the graveyard wearing his mitre and carrying his crosier. The sky was gray. The air was cool but still. Six monks carried the catafalque. Aiming himself at the gangplank, the Abbot intended to conduct rituals from the far side. Antoine held his breath. The plank bent low like a stick ready to snap, but the Abbot made it across. Antoine followed. The thurifer went across. But next, when Brother Alphonse crossed, the plank snapped with a crack like a gunshot and he fell into the grave.

Everyone stood motionless, wondering what to do. Brother Camille tittered until the Abbot glanced at him. From down in the grave, Alphonse, jumping up and down, could not get a good hold on anything and looked distressed and angry. Several monks offered a hand, but the Abbot was afraid that more monks might fall in if they tried to pull Alphonse out. The Abbot sent Gennade and Roland to fetch a ladder.

While waiting, Antoine studied the waxen face of Brother Bernard; spread upon the catafalque, the corpse was clothed in the same white robe that each monk wore, the robe he was given upon making solemn profession. The hood was drawn up but the face was quite visible. He had no color, and his stretched lips gave him a ludicrous appearance. The twisted grin on the dead man was a farce, Antoine thought; it had no connection to heaven or hell.

Gennade and Roland returned with a wooden stepladder and lowered it into the grave near the hairy tendrils of an elm root. Brother Alphonse climbed out. While monks swatted dirt from his white cloak, the ladder was taken away and the Abbot incensed the grave. The corpse was brought over, taken off the catafalque, and placed on ropes. A prayer was said. Before Bernard was lowered into the hole, Father Jude placed a piece of cloth over the face, a clean white handkerchief of the sort that each of them had in his pocket. Antoine grabbed a rope as the Abbot sprinkled the grave with holy water and the body was lowered. When it reached the bottom, the ropes were pulled and the body moved, but it fell back into place as the ropes left it. Each monk took a handful of cold dirt and threw it on Bernard. Then, as the community walked away, Roland filled the hole, working with a shovel.

For many days after, as snow swirled beyond his window, Antoine noticed the pile of dirt heaped between the elm and the lilac. When he went through the snow to the cheese house he thought of Brother Bernard, his flesh as cold as frosted tombstones.

The morning Antoine pronounced vows, the sun was bright enough to melt the ice that hung from church eaves like translucent daggers. Relatives arrived. His eighty-six-year-old grandmother bubbled and spouted words of praise.

"Ma pitoune!" she shrieked, pinching his chin until it was red. "You little saint! You make up for everyone else in the family. *Mon Dieu*, if it weren't for you, I wouldn't get into heaven. None of my sons became priests. *C'est de valeur!* Nowadays, nobody is religious anymore. It's disgusting. All they do is watch television. In *my* day, we were on our knees praying the rosary."

Cousins arrived, along with Aunt Agnès of the Bon Secours sisters, who was not dressed like a nun except for her heavy black shoes. She wore a denim jumper and a pink blouse with a Mickey Mouse pattern running all over it. And René Lizotte was there wearing his orange parka, hugging people and saying over and over again, "Praise Jesus!"

For the ceremony Antoine's family sat in the back of the church behind an iron railing. The monks were in the nave, along with Father Pitt Colombe, the parish priest of St. Jean-Baptiste, who had arrived to assist at the altar. Dom Jacques

Bouvray and Brother Antoine stood in the sacristy waiting for the ceremony to begin.

"Are we ready?" the Abbot asked. He turned to Antoine. "You look a bit pale," he said. "Probably nerves. It happens to all of us. No need to worry. Once the ceremony begins, the adrenaline kicks in and everything flows smoothly. You'll see. And tomorrow morning you won't remember a thing."

Despite the reassurance, Antoine was afraid to move. Although none of the early warning signs of a migraine haunted him, anxiety made his knees lock. He wondered if his head would remain clear for the next hour and a half, when he especially needed to focus his attention.

The Abbot began the ceremony punctually and walked in procession down the nave aisle as bells began ringing at the top of the hour. When Antoine took his place in the transept, near the altar, he held himself straight.

A greeting was read, the community sang a *Glória* in plainchant, and the Abbot offered an opening prayer that thanked God for Antoine's vocation. Father Véran read the first lesson, Father Yves-Marie read from the gospel of Saint John, and the Abbot gave a short homily. After this, Antoine was formally questioned as to his readiness.

"Are you resolved," Dom Jacques read from a black-bound book, "to live this monastic life of chastity, obedience, and poverty, to strive for perfect love of God, to spend your whole life in generous service to your brothers in community?"

"I am resolved," Antoine answered. Something expanded inside his chest, and he thought he might be lifted off the floor like a balloon.

"Are you resolved to give yourself to God in common prayer, daily work, in silence and community living, in reflection on the Gospels and the Holy Rule?"

"I am resolved," Antoine said again. He felt no pain. His head was clear.

After he prostrated himself on the floor, monks began singing a litany of the saints. The linoleum felt cool. His skull rested squarely against the radius bone of his right forearm. He lifted his head slightly after a moment to see all the monks kneeling in prayer.

When the litany was over, Antoine rose and read aloud the formula of profession, written in his own hand. He promised with solemn vows to remain with his Cistercian community in stability, to be obedient according to the Rule of Saint Benedict, and to live each day in a manner appropriate to monastic conversion. He signed the document on the altar, and he was clothed in the voluminous white robe the Cistercians referred to as a cowl.

The canon of the Mass was calm. After an ancient and serene *Agnus Dei*, Antoine received communion first and stood behind the Abbot to watch each monk, in turn, take a sacred host in communion. *Behold how good it is and how pleasant, where brethren dwell as one.* He remembered these words of the psalm, sung every night at Compline. *It is as precious ointment upon the head. For the Lord has pronounced his blessing, life forever.*

Antoine marveled at how his greatest blessings had always come through others. Perhaps God dealt with saints directly, saving their souls in intimate and personal ways. But Antoine had been saved by others. His parents had loved and nurtured him. Catholicism was given as a legacy. His Cistercian community held him up and sustained his monastic vocation. He benefited by means of these souls who had received the spiritual life long ago and communicated it to him because they loved it.

When the Mass ended, Brother Antoine returned through the nave aisle with the Abbot to the sacristy. His family joined the monks in the basement of the church in a modest room called the *salle d'accueil.*

"A beautiful ceremony!" Madame Seneschal said, with tears in her eyes. "I stayed awake for the whole thing."

They drank coffee and ate cake and slices of the very cheese Antoine had washed and salted months before.

"As good as any Camembert," his grandmother pronounced, "but it is *très très innocent,* no?"

"Oh, but madame," Brother Sauveur said to her, "you hide the cheese in your cup at table, and in two or three weeks it becomes good."

The monks laughed. Antoine had joined them and stood next to his grandmother. "And then everyone in the house can smell it," he said. "It loses its innocence and becomes like Limburger."

The reception continued with a rousing birthday song to Madame Seneschal. She beamed. Antoine presented a jar of clover honey to her, and when she looked at him, tears rolled down her face.

"Oh my," she said. "I always thought it would be a phase, that you'd leave after being here in the abbey for a few years. But you won't, will you?" She pulled a sweet-smelling handkerchief from her purse and dabbed her eyes with it, almost dropping the jar of honey. "If I had had more sons," she said, "this wouldn't be so hard, *coconotte,* but you're the only one. You're my only child! And I will never be able to share this life with you. I don't know it. I understand marriage and children. If you had a wife and little babies, I could give you advice, but you won't, and I can't help you." Her lashes held big diamond drops. Smiling, she pinched his chin. "Ah, but if it makes you happy, *poutine,* then I will be happy too."

The reception continued for an hour, until the monks began withdrawing to sing Vespers. Madame Seneschal went looking for her husband. Omer had been parked all the while in the stairwell, talking to Brother Gennade about milk cows and oats. With large, eager eyes and a genuine smile, he appeared contented enough to join the abbey himself.

Antoine's relatives made ready to leave, pulling on coats, gloves, and hats. They pinched and hugged him.

"We'll be back," his mother said.

Left alone in the *salle d'accueil*, Antoine inspected the gifts. His relatives had left him with rosaries, a large crucifix, and several prayer books, as if the abbey might not have an abundance of these items already. But none of this mattered. He was overwhelmed with emotion. These people had been good to him.

He knew he was not responsible for the day; how could he accept credit for having come from a good French-Canadian family? And he knew that it was not for his intelligence or virtue that the Cistercian monks had taken him in. Even after he swallowed several times, his tears stubbornly flowed.

The emotion Antoine felt was broader than gratitude. He was appreciative, yes, but he also wanted to be better than he was: more virtuous, more sympathetic, more responsible to the world. He had an idea about what holiness meant — something the size and shape of Brother Bernard — and he struggled toward it. He wanted to make that shape his own somehow. He wanted to wish that shape upon the world.

8

The Color of Bones

Each spring, prairie snow melted into shallow draws. Flat land became green. Overnight, gurgling brooks appeared, moving toward the river through buffalo bulrush, marsh muhly, and tall reeds. Streams swelled. The Pembina, Roseau, Morris, Boyne, and LaSalle became swift-moving, chocolate rivers drowning the marsh marigold and yellow lady's slippers that bloomed on their banks. When the main artery choked, that mighty Red River of the North and all its tributaries backed up into long, snaking lakes. Not until the Winnipeg Floodway was opened did the waters safely skirt the city through a man-made channel to run on toward the north.

That spring, Brother Antoine watched the LaSalle rise over its banks and flood the abbey garden. Water touched the foundation of the pig barn and licked the steps of the seminary house before it receded, leaving tires, shoes, plastic soda bottles, rotted planks, and an occasional dead animal. This debris had to be carted off. When the mud dried, Antoine shared the work of making a dump look more like a vegetable garden. And soil was not always the richer because of flooding; oil and gasoline often contaminated some garden spots, along with concentrated amounts of ammonium nitrate or other leached fertilizers.

On a sunny day after the flood, Brother Roland hoisted a log on his shoulders and carried it off by himself. The small, gnome-like Father Jean-Marie found a tin of unopened condensed milk under a dead fish. He waved the tin at Antoine, then set it on the ground to use his hands.

"Still good, still good," he signed. Antoine was well aware of Jean-Marie's pride in discovering such useful items. Nearly every year he found an unopened tin. And with sign language he was good, too, able to communicate at length with his hands, more so than anyone else. "Same as last year," he managed to convey, first rubbing the sides of his forefingers together, then sweeping his right hand forward near his hip and striking his left shoulder with the edge of his hand. "Same as last year, when you speak final vows. I find milk tin that spring." Good memory for detail. Antoine would not have been in the least surprised if Jean-Marie knew how many aunts had attended his profession. He was not sure he could remember himself.

"Dirty," Jean-Marie signed, looking across the garden while rubbing his knuckles into his right temple. "Bad. Same every year. No good for vegetable. Dirty water. No good."

Jean-Marie continued making signs, inadvertently grunting for emphasis, but a tractor distracted Antoine. At the riverbank, Brother Roland was now pulling a mud-caked washing machine with the John Deere's three-point hitch and chains. All the garbage of the world seemed to have been left there, in front of him. Antoine had nothing against the LaSalle; flooding was natural with rivers. Nor did he have anything against the Floodway; before it was built, water came as high as the windows in the pig barn. What he could not understand was the rubbish. Where did all the debris come from? He wanted to ask Jean-Marie why so much stuff washed downriver. But with his limited skill, his signs actually meant, "Why people extra tools?"

Jean-Marie was confused. "Too much work?" he asked,

pounding his fists together, then drawing a line across his throat with the edge of his right hand while raising his shoulders in a question.

"No," Antoine signed. "Why this? Why so much stink around?"

Jean-Marie's eyebrows relaxed with some degree of comprehension, but he protested nonetheless. "Good stink," he signed. "Milk tin good luck. We are rich." And he walked away with his prize.

The cleanup lasted three days. A massive bonfire burned in the field near the grange house, an old building once used during the harvest. Back then, a threshing machine was pulled into the field by horses, and because the brothers worked late into the night, they stayed at the old house. Grange days were a kind of outing, a rare picnic holiday away from the abbey. But that was long ago, and as river garbage burned, the grange windows reflected no fire because they were empty of glass.

Smoke billowed high into the air. Antoine felt apprehensive about the flames, an absurd uneasiness, as if a skirmish had begun and the monks had unintentionally given their position away. The drama of the big fire fed his imagination. In reality, what did the world want with monks anyway?

After the garden was cleaned up, planting began in earnest. Carrot seeds required an ancient seeder. Designed by an old monk long since dead, the machine looked like a midget's bicycle with a small hopper instead of a seat. A long wooden handle ran up the back. Grain plates went below the hopper to spread the tiny seeds, and a grooved rear wheel covered these with dirt. Brother Roland normally planted a half mile of carrots. Green beans were planted by the acre, as were potatoes and corn.

None of this vegetable planting would have involved Antoine except that business in the cheese house had come to a standstill, and he had nothing else to do. For years, Father Casimir's meticulous and fussy approach to cheese making kept the government at bay. When the Canadian Food Inspection Agency demanded stainless steel countertops, these were installed. The CFIA demanded quarry tiles on the cement floor. These were also put in. They wanted stainless steel shelves to replace wood in the loft and in the cellar, and at great expense these too were set in place. But when the government demanded stainless steel doors at standard factory width, not even a miracle could make that possible. The abbey cheese house was simply too small for such doors. A new building would have been necessary to comply with CFIA stipulations.

As a result, cheese was no longer offered for sale. Casimir continued to make a small amount for the community, mainly to keep the mold alive, but Antoine was sent to the garden.

"Putting in seeds is okay for the time being," the Abbot said to him as he planted tomatoes in a long row, "but you need a permanent job." Bib overalls replaced Dom Jacques's habit. He wore a pair of cracked sunglasses and an ancient straw hat.

"Why not the barn?" Antoine said. "Send me back to the barn."

"Yes, I would, except that Brother Dominique is doing quite well there with Gennade and Théodore. Besides, what we really need is a cook."

Near the tomatoes, lamb's quarters and pigweed sprouted everywhere and Antoine's hands were full of it. "I don't know how to cook," he said.

"Oh, that shouldn't matter," the Abbot answered, waving gnats from his face. A small hole awaited a tomato plant where he knelt. "Around here, we don't ask a great deal of the cook. Boiled oatmeal and fried potatoes. That's the extent of it. Father Claude can't stay on his feet anymore, and we need someone else."

Dom Jacques was thinking aloud. Antoine wanted to know if the kitchen was a suggestion or an order. "Have you made up your mind?" he asked.

"Well, now, let me see," Dom Jacques said, leaning back on his heels. "I guess it has to be an order, since there's no one else I can spare just now. Don't worry. Boiling water and such. That's all it is."

Antoine raised his eyebrows. "And the garden?" he asked.

"Stay here until we get the bedding plants in."

That took all of three days. Thereafter, Antoine began duties in the kitchen, under the supervision of Father Claude Joly, with a view to taking over.

Claude was in most ways Casimir's opposite. Whereas Casimir was fanatical about cleanliness in the cheese house, Claude did not particularly care what objects fell into his bread pudding, or how done or undone the potatoes happened to be. The way he looked at it, he was seventy-eight; he had already done his share. Besides, Claude had better things to worry about than potatoes. Current issues of *l'Osservatore Romano* and *The Wanderer* awaited his attention. All the news he wanted to know of the world he picked up from these newspapers.

News and events gave him plenty to stew about. Once, he wrote a long letter of complaint to the archbishop about the unorthodoxy of allowing lay people to receive holy communion in the hand. And on the occasion when Mounted Police came onto abbey property, forming a barricade along the road, Claude spoke his mind to the commanding sergeant because he considered the action an invasion of privacy.

Kitchen matters, however, did not excite him. The entire community was aware of this. Food was bad. Even if a recipe could be found in the mess of his workplace, he lacked the patience to follow it. Oatmeal was scorched on a regular basis. Vegetables were boiled to pulp. But no one could be upset with the poor man. He had Parkinson's disease. His head wobbled like a wire-sprung doll in the rear window of a moving car.

The Abbot was eager to offer Claude full retirement. Of late, he had been getting slower. Meals were not on time. An abbey needed to run on schedule. Besides, a man in his seventies ought not be in charge of a kitchen unless he wanted to be, and Dom Jacques knew this.

Claude had not always been the cook. He joined the abbey at twenty, having been dismissed from a seminary in Québec. He had spoken his mind there and the rector had not appreciated what was in it. Claude never expected to be dismissed, and somewhat shell-shocked, he joined an order where no speaking was permitted. The superior sent him to work in the forge. There, he often lost his temper, yelling at the top of his voice because Brother Emery Terrien — who was only seventeen then — ruined rivets and misused the hydraulic press. As a punishment for screaming, Claude had to kiss Emery's feet in Chapter of Faults. Eventually, through the sharing and shifting of work schedules, Claude found himself in the kitchen, replacing Father Ignace. And for a while he liked the work.

Using pots and pans was easier for him than swaging red-hot iron like Vulcan. In fact, kitchen work did not even require a change of clothing. Claude merely placed an apron over his habit. Soon he discovered time-saving secrets, ingenious methods of throwing a meal together for thirty-five, leaving him the opportunity to do religious crossword puzzles and take naps behind the stove.

When Antoine was assigned to the kitchen, Claude had been cooking for twelve years. He was bored. A change would have been nice six years earlier, but the priest knew of no other job requiring less work. Besides, he had his routine, which he handed over in detail to Antoine.

The pattern was invariable. At four in the morning, immediately after the office of Vigils, the coffee urn was plugged in and cold toast set out that had been made the night before. Prior to Lauds, three gallons of water was set on a gas burner so that it might be boiling after prayer. Exactly fifty whole potatoes were rinsed and placed in a mesh bag for boiling during Mass. At eight o'clock, the burner was turned off. The potatoes were taken out of the water and green beans placed in a colander over the water to steam. A slow oven was switched on; the potatoes were dumped into a serving pan and placed inside the oven to keep warm. Three gallons of water was set on the burner for tea. Before ten o'clock, the green beans were removed to a serving pan and set in the oven with the potatoes. A cup each of cornstarch and chicken soup base were mixed with milk, enough to create a plasterlike paste, and stirred into the potato water. At eleven forty-five, the soup, green beans, and potatoes were served to the community for dinner. Tea was set out with the dinner. After the office of None, another three gallons of water was set to boil for oatmeal. Toast was made for the next day's breakfast. Twelve cups of oatmeal was stirred into the water and set in a slow oven before Vespers, and another three gallons of water placed on the back burner for tea. Oatmeal and tea were served for supper at six in the evening. Water and coffee were set in the urn before bedtime.

If Claude was off by ten minutes, everything was late that day. In Antoine he tolerated a certain amount of creativity: another vegetable might be served in place of green beans; lettuce might be set out in summer; and for feast days, a pudding could be stirred up, consisting of flour, butter, sugar, milk, and a little cinnamon. After all, the cook had little more than the main course to worry about. His responsibilities did not include setting out butter or bread, or filling milk pitchers or condiment containers;

the refectorian did that. Neither had the cook to bother about scrubbing pots and pans because the community washed them after every meal.

On Claude's last day, he signed "tired" to Antoine, dropping extended forearms to his sides. His eyes were focused upon the stove, but he was unable to stop his head from moving. The old priest waved good-bye to a piece of equipment he knew intimately. Without the least bit of hesitation, he walked away from the kitchen altogether.

Antoine had by then thoroughly shed all wariness about working in the kitchen. As cook, he did not intend to serve the same old food every day. Madame Seneschal sent cookbooks. He ordered things like rice and pasta. Potatoes were fried, mashed, baked, broiled, cubed, diced, parboiled, pan-broiled, French-fried, and stewed. Vegetables were recognizable again.

At first the community was taken aback by the variety and what seemed like a worldly concern for a balanced diet, but soon they grew accustomed to the food and even anticipated new dishes, particularly sugary desserts.

The kitchen suited Antoine. He discovered a special delight in feeding people. The monks, eating pasta with clam sauce, smacked their lips, and Antoine felt so proud that a sensual rush of goose bumps raised hair all over his body. He glowed, feeling responsible for their obvious pleasure. Or having spent an afternoon making berry pies, he indulged himself watching men smile, their mouths stained with purple juice.

He cooked everything except red meat. Chickens were roasted for the sick. Soups were sometimes flavored with wine or fresh chives from the garden. A variety of vegetables were stir-fried or sautéed. Fish was ordered from the grocer and poached for special occasions. As a test, he tried as many recipes as he could find for eggs and vegetables. A pancake was his favorite, made with shredded zucchini and carrots, chopped dill, grated onion, and eggs, mixed together and fried to a golden brown on both sides and served with a heavy dill cream sauce.

That first beautiful spring in the kitchen, Antoine cut fresh rhubarb for pies and carefully steamed asparagus so that deep green spears bowed tenderly when he lifted them from the colander, filling the refectory with an unmistakable beginning-of-season aroma. He was enjoying himself, and failed to notice signs of stress on the Abbot's face. Antoine was not prepared for the shocking announcement Dom Jacques had to make.

"I regret to inform you," he said to the community in the chapter room, "that we are being forced to move away from here."

The monks looked at one another with open mouths. Dom Jacques went on to explain that all the abbey's property had been absorbed into the city limits of Winnipeg. The community could no longer stay by the LaSalle River, where they had been for more than one hundred years, because their two thousand acres of land was now within the city's jurisdiction, and therefore taxable under new regulations.

Dom Jacques's voice trembled as he spoke. "We've also been informed that it's illegal to keep livestock within city limits. No cows. And if that's not bad enough, we must also use city water and disposal systems. Trenching pipes to the city system will cost us in the neighborhood of half a million dollars. So you see, our only alternative is to leave because we can't afford to stay."

Father Claude stood. "Well, where in hell are we supposed to go? They can't do this to us. And I won't stand here and take it. Give in to these damn bureaucrats? Never. I say we put up a fight. No one can shove us off our property!" His head wobbled as he spoke. He nearly fell into Father Marie-Nizier's lap while angrily swinging an arm.

"I appreciate your concern," Dom Jacques answered, "but

protests are too late. It's a *fait accompli*. We've already been swallowed up by the city. Now is the time, I think, to look for another place to live. Meanwhile, pray that the city gives us a grace period with taxes, water, and sewage. Pray that they allow us to keep the farm animals until we find them a new home."

Father Jean-Marie stood and used gestures instead of speaking, as if he were a deaf-mute. "Go where?" he asked, making a sweep outward with his right hand, then raising his shoulders with palms facing up.

Dom Jacques had a weary look. "I don't know," he answered. "But the Archbishop of Winnipeg and the Archbishop of St. Boniface have both expressed a desire that we remain in Manitoba. We've had good relations with people in this area."

Jean-Marie continued gesturing, something about the river.

"Oh, not me," Dom Jacques responded. "I won't miss the river at all." He was able to laugh. "In fact, that's one of the few good things about moving. I get nervous every spring, thinking about the water. In our hundred-year history we've seen several devastating floods, and even with the Winnipeg Floodway we seem to have a mess in the garden every year. Perhaps we can look upon our present circumstances as an act of Divine Providence moving us to higher ground."

The next few weeks were a puzzle to Antoine. None of the monks betrayed anxiety over the impending move. Monastic life went on as usual, as though the city, more than five miles away, had not swallowed up the life they knew. Outside, the temperature warmed, and under a baking sun the river began to smell of algae and humus. Shading his eyes, Antoine studied the blond bricks of the church and tried to imagine the building uprooted and moved to a new location, in lovely hills somewhere, or next to an ice-blue lake. But he could not think of the abbey anywhere except where it was. He knew, of course, that the buildings had to be left behind. The monks would likely purchase land not far away and build something new. For him, monastic life seemed unimaginable in any building other than the one in front of him.

He walked about as if in mourning, visiting his favorite haunts: barns, fences, particular trees, garden paths, bends in the river. He lingered and studied as if seeing them for the last time. But he really did not know when the move might take place. Six months? A year? Three years?

"One step at a time," Dom Jacques said. "Before the old place is left behind, a new place has to be found." And the Abbot spent considerable time on the road, searching for real estate.

Three possible sites were proposed: a five-hundred-acre potato farm near Morden, a two-thousand-acre horse ranch near Elm Creek, and an eight-hundred-fifty-acre mixed farm near Bruxelles. "I'll be sending some of you out to look at these places before we decide as a community what land to purchase," the Abbot said in chapter.

As he spoke, an idea came to Antoine. He might ask his parents to drive a car full of monks to Elm Creek or Bruxelles. The outing would be a wonderful opportunity. He could enjoy a picnic with his mother and father, the first since he joined the abbey, and share the occasion with a few brother-monks.

Immediately after the chapter meeting, Antoine went to the Abbot's office and put the idea before him.

"I realize," Antoine said, "that it's a peculiar request. We're usually not allowed outside the abbey to visit relatives. But these are extraordinary circumstances."

Dom Jacques Bouvray let out a sigh. "You're certainly correct about the extraordinary circumstances," he said. "I have a feeling we'll be bending many rules before the transfer of this abbey is completed." He gave his consent.

The following Wednesday the Seneschals arrived in their

Oldsmobile Delta. They had three picnic baskets in the trunk. Antoine prepared another two. The air was muggy and hot by the river and Madame Seneschal dabbed her brow with a perfumed handkerchief. She had spring fever and was ready for an excursion.

Brother Antoine sat in the front seat between his parents. In the back, Father Yves-Marie Morice, Brother Sauveur Conil, and Father Véran Michel crowded together. They had eagerly signed up to go. But now they were quiet, almost like strangers caught in an elevator together. During the two and a half hours to Bruxelles, they said nothing, but Madame Seneschal hardly noticed. She talked enough for all six of them in the car.

"Now, tell me again exactly why we're visiting this place. Because the city is pushing you out, I think you said? Well, let me tell you, as a mayor, *contresaintciboiriser!* To hell with those sons of bitches. It's the English against the French all over again. Omer, we've seen it happen before. You people have basic rights. Stick to your guns. Don't let them get the upper hand. You fight this thing out!" And on and on.

But her attitude changed when she saw the Bruxelles farm; it was east of the little town, on Highway 245, with a Victorian brick house hidden in the trees. She loved the fresh air and the pink coneflowers in the overgrown lawn.

The farm was in an area called the Tiger Hills, a place that seemed incongruent with the flat parkland of Manitoba. Level prairie was what they had seen the whole two hundred thirty kilometers from Winnipeg. These sudden hills seemed cut from Vermont; they rolled away in a complexity of distant stretching colors. Olive-green pastures emerged from russet groves and retired again, covering the slopes in a patchwork. In the distance, a field of blooming mustard shone egg-yellow. Wild finches sang in the trees. The air seemed less muggy at this higher elevation.

The farm was just off the highway. After some wet gravel on

the entry road, they found themselves in a yard protected by immense cottonwood trees. A garage stood before them to the west, stripped of its paint. Around it, a ragged lawn stretched from the base of a hill up to its summit, to the north, where an old barn sank into tall grass. A brief shower had coated everything with dew. Coneflowers waved in a pleasant breeze, and when the visitors climbed out of the car, they saw the abandoned house hidden by elms and overgrown lilac bushes.

"Well now," Madame Seneschal said after scrutinizing the pile, "that's quite a place! Nice brick. Not too run down to fix."

The old end-wall porch needed repair, but the house itself seemed solid. Its brick walls rose from a fieldstone foundation to a crown of gables and lunettes, and it was girdled with a cornice of Victorian ornaments. Each window was capped with a relieving arch.

"Omer, get those folding chairs out of the trunk of the car," Madame Seneschal said. "There's hot coffee in this Thermos and hot tea in that one." In short order, she had a domestic meal arranged on the porch. "You monks eat up that ham. Don't let that potato salad go to waste. Father Yves-Marie, you're looking thin. Brother Sauveur, there's lemonade, too, if you'd like it."

Delighted with Antoine's offerings, she helped herself to his picnic baskets. Biscuits and grapefruit-rosemary jelly, hot tomato-mint soup, pickled mushrooms, chunks of white cod in beer with raw vegetables and dill: these were some of his surprises. She wanted to know where he had learned to cook.

"You sent me books," he said. "I follow directions carefully and taste everything."

"It comes from me," she said to Omer.

The four monks had finally begun to talk, remarking on the clean air and good food. While Madame Seneschal was eating another biscuit, Brother Sauveur whispered a joke to her about two nuns and a donkey. She laughed until she turned red and nearly choked.

Meanwhile, Omer Seneschal looked about with large eyes while sipping on bottled beer. "This wouldn't be a bad place for monks. What do you think, Father Yves-Marie?"

"It's lovely," Yves-Marie said. The monks discussed the property for a while. Madame Seneschal had regained her composure and dabbed a paper napkin to her mouth.

"I would put the abbey right on the top of the hill," she said, "where the old barn is."

"Yes," the monks agreed. The barn looked like the highest spot on the property. They already knew that the farm belonged to a widower who had moved into a nursing home. His children were anxious to sell.

After finishing their lunch, they further explored the yard. An abandoned garden was discovered on the east side of the house, protected by thick evergreens. Rose bushes and potentillas grew there. They also walked down a long old path to a brook where Omer lost his shoe in the mud.

"Okay," Madame Seneschal said. "It's time to go when he loses his shoe."

By then, clouds had swallowed the sun, and the afternoon had taken on a chill. The little group climbed into the car and drank coffee while Brother Antoine drove. They decided to take their time on the way back, and stopped for pie and ice cream in the town of Starbuck. The monks had become quite talkative. They flattered Madame Seneschal by asking her questions about her job as mayor of St. Jean-Baptiste.

"Oh, it's nothing, really," she said. "If the garbage isn't picked up, I make a call with authority in my voice and I get results. Besides, I know everyone. It's like living in one big household, that town. And come to think of it, I learned all the diplomacy I know by keeping house. Being mayor *is* keeping house, on a slightly broader scale."

Brother Antoine drove through Winnipeg so that Brother Sauveur could see Golden Boy on top of the Provincial Parliament Building; Sauveur had never seen it. He was born and raised in Gravelbourg, Saskatchewan, and had never been off the abbey property in his six years since becoming a monk. The car headed south, through the city, to St. Norbert.

Antoine parked in front of the abbey gatehouse, and as the group climbed out of the car, Brother Henri appeared behind the big iron gate that blocked the road.

"Ah, Madame!" he said, waving. "Did you hear that we are being evicted?" She went over and talked with him through the gate, as though to a prisoner. *"Se faire organiser,"* he said quickly. "We are being taken by the city. Crooks, they are! They rob us of our land! They will drive us out for a nickel an acre."

"Ça parle au maudit!" Madame Seneschal exclaimed, and she continued in French. "I thought you were moving out of your own accord, because of city ordinances and taxes. I didn't think the city was grabbing your land!" She looked over to Antoine, who stuck out his tongue and whirled a finger around his temple.

"Don't believe a *word* he tells you," he said later, when they were alone in the gatehouse parlor. "The Abbot has had excellent offers for the land already, and he's being careful."

"Everything is all right, then," she said.

"Well, money-wise, yes. We'll get a whole lot more than five cents an acre."

"What, then?" she asked.

Antoine had tears in his eyes. "We're losing our home," he said. "Nothing will replace that."

★   ★   ★

Days went by, one after another, into later sunrises and cooler temperatures. Wild plums ripened with the corn. Along the river, ducks and marsh hens gorged themselves on grass seed, tubers, small fishes, mollusks, and insects, then left for warmer regions.

When leaves began to fall from the trees and ice formed in the river shallows, a British land-banking company purchased the abbey property. The monastic chapter was satisfied with the arrangement. The monks signed an agreement with Northstar Development to vacate the property in twenty-four months. Dom Jacques Bouvray had to have a decision from the monks about where to live.

Discussions were held in the chapter room. The monks could not agree on a property. Antoine had seen only the Bruxelles farm, and although he liked what he saw, the reports of the Morden potato farm and the Elm Creek horse ranch were favorable as well. Other sites were investigated, but nothing was as good as these three properties.

In the end, the cows made the decision. The Bruxelles farm was the only property suitable to them, and the monks voted unanimously to bring along the dairy herd. Morden was not large enough for cattle, and its land was rich, arable, and thus more appropriate to potato planting than pasture. Elm Creek was large, but its scrub pastures were more appropriate for horses or sheep. The Bruxelles property supported corn, barley, and oats and had a good record for hay production, besides having nearly four hundred acres of fenced pasture land. On the first of November, the monks offered prayers for their future and bought the Bruxelles farm.

"I can't believe it," Antoine said to the Abbot. "We're leaving. We're walking away from here. And everybody is so calm. I haven't seen a tear."

"Oh, you know they're playing tough," Dom Jacques replied.

"But this land, this property," Antoine said, "this is home! We're leaving everything we know. I feel awful. And I haven't spent sixty years here, like some others."

"Yes, yes, of course," Dom Jacques answered. "But you must know that it means more than they let on. We all regret leaving. I grew up less than ten miles from here, and this has been my home for thirty-five years." He shrugged. "There's not much we can do, though, is there? Moving will be a lesson in detachment."

If it was detachment Antoine learned, the lesson came in an odd way. Even before the architect presented blueprints for a new abbey, monks began clearing out attics and storerooms, places unopened for years. The things that came out of darkness were often peculiar. Why a birdcage, for instance? Or a stuffed lynx? And some of the items were so bizarre, Antoine did not even know what they were for: a wooden crate filled with knotted cords, bundles of them held together with cord handles. Father Jean-Marie's face lit up when he saw them. Having selected one from the mass, he reverently untangled it, almost as if it were a rosary; then, gripping the handle, he began whipping his back with it, swinging the knotted cords across each shoulder. It became clear to Antoine that these were grim instruments of penance, something that had been used years ago.

Books came out of the attic, more than seemed available even in the scriptorium, honorable titles such as Plato's *Republic, Beowulf* together with *Widsith and the Fight at Finnesburg,* Shakespeare's *Sonnets,* and Homer's *Odyssey.* They went into a fire out at the grange while books from the scriptorium were carefully boxed, copies of *Come Follow Me, The Joy of Serving God, The Spiritual Combat,* and *Introduction to the Devout Life.*

How was it decided, what to keep and what to throw away? To Antoine, there seemed to be no rhyme or reason. Apparently the monk responsible for the scriptorium kept or sent books to the fire, and the monk assigned to the forge kept or threw away tools and scrap metal. But who made the decision on things that came out of the attic? The stuffed lynx and the crate of penance cords went to the fire while the birdcage was saved. Antoine saw eight beveled trunks carried down the stairs, each with iron lacework and stuffed with old brown habits that the laybrothers used to wear. The trunks were like nothing he had ever seen, ornate wooden masterpieces from the Old world, perhaps brought by the monks from France. They were left near the chicken house for the fire, while laminated chairs were deemed somehow more useful and stacked on the landing for transport.

Not all things of a sacred nature were kept. For reasons unknown to Antoine, the apse altars and crucifixes — all of them carved from oak — were given away, while the large concrete crosses that marked the graves in the cemetery were loaded on a flatbed and hauled to the new property.

"The grave markers arc gone," he said to the Abbot. "How will the new owners know where the graves are?"

"The dead are coming with us," the Abbot replied. "That's stipulated in the contract of sale. This land will be used for residential development, and we can't leave behind a graveyard. Our entire community will go to the new place, dead or alive."

Just where the new cemetery would be located Antoine did not know, but he learned that the architectural blueprints did indeed put the new abbey at the top of the hill, where he remembered seeing an old barn. Up there, a patch of ground sixty feet square was selected to become the *préau*, the enclosed courtyard, and around it, the foundations of the church and monastery were to be excavated. The *préau* would be visible from a cloister walkway around it, through an unusual pattern of large and small windows. Sealed inside the *préau* as a sort of microcosm would be a dozen small paper birch trees and three boulders, in descending sizes, covered with lichen. Instead of grass, a dense Alaskan ground cover was planned, to make mowing unnecessary. Indeed, nothing needed to be touched. Around this terrarium of a *préau*, thermopane windows were to leave a beautiful pattern of sunlight upon the tiled cloister floor, reminiscent of ancient Cistercian abbeys of France: Sénanque, Le Thoronet, and Fontenay.

The architect wanted to build the new abbey out of Tyndall stone, a lovely gray material indigenous to Manitoba. But the monks could not afford it. The cost, even for one wing of the quadrangle in stone, would put them into debt, and Dom Jacques insisted that the entire move be made without liability. "We have barns yet to build," he explained.

"Yes, I suppose," the architect answered. "And the dairy barn will be bigger than the abbey, won't it?"

"Well," Dom Jacques said, "as a matter of fact, yes." To keep within affordability, new quarters for the monks had to shrink to half the size of the old, while the dairy cows absolutely needed their same floor space. The architect shook his head.

"Monks have changed since the Middle Ages," he said. "Nowadays, they build barns bigger than their churches."

Dom Jacques spoke freely about the blueprints in front of Antoine. "Your drawings make the new abbey look so boxy, so square," he complained. "Why don't you give it nice pitched roofs, lovely arched windows?"

The architect shook his head again. "The monastery you want is so small," he said, "that pitched roofs and arched windows will make it look like a miniature Fontenay. A dollhouse. What you're asking for is really nothing more than a large home."

Haggling over the project caused delays. When the LaSalle flooded again in the spring, monks were still in St. Norbert to pick up the debris. Ninety miles west, however, foundations were being poured for the new dairy, cheese house, and gatehouse, and brick walls for the abbey itself were rising. As soon as the gatehouse was finished, it became a temporary storage site, and moving began in earnest. Monks hauled furniture to the Bruxelles property in relays. Soon they were going back and forth with a U-Haul trailer twice daily, and the transmission on the farm truck went out. His hand forced, the Abbot bought a new farm truck and granted general permission for the monks to speak, so as to facilitate smoother operations.

"Things are disappearing around here," Antoine complained to Father Claude. They stood in the kitchen. The old priest was helping put kettles and pot covers in boxes, items Antoine did not regularly use and wanted to send on to Bruxelles. "I left a box of cracked and stained Tupperware for the burn pile, and it's gone."

"They took it already?" Claude asked.

"No. That's the mystery. Brother Roland promised to haul it away tomorrow, and when I told him it was already gone, he mentioned how many things are strangely disappearing."

"Anything valuable?"

"Only items meant for the burn pile. Someone is squirreling them away. Now, who on earth would want useless Tupperware?"

"Oh, I think I know," Claude replied.

"Who?"

The old priest was shoving a dented colander into a box. "Can't you guess? I haven't lived here all these years with my eyes shut."

"You mean one of the monks?"

"Of course I mean one of the monks."

"Well?" Antoine asked. "Which one?"

Claude frowned with impatience. "Who saves string and rubber bands by the bushel? Who collects glass jars? Who goes through all the garbage before it's carried away?"

"I have no idea."

"Oh, child," Claude exclaimed, "what else don't you know? Well then, let me ask you this. Which one of the monks takes great delight in the aftermath of the flood each year, poking around in that wet, muddy filth, always finding some treasure to carry off?"

"Jean-Marie?"

"Exactly. My hunch is that your Tupperware is in the old horse barn where he keeps the chickens. When it comes time to move chicken equipment, we're going to find garbage packed into every corner of that building."

Claude was right. The Tupperware was sitting in the horse barn on a pile of plastic bottles, jars, and bags. Another section of the barn was devoted to cans, another to glass. The loft looked as though chickens had been accidentally delivered to a recycling warehouse. They were in their laying cages at one end of the building, with broken furniture stashed next to them. Items thought to have been discarded long ago were lying everywhere. Brother Roland and Father Claude came with Antoine to see the junk. They were lucky to get in. Jean-Marie kept the barn locked whenever he was not there, "for good of chickens," he signed, rubbing his stomach, then scratching beneath the index knuckle of his left hand.

While in the loft, Antoine saw something that made him gasp. Roland and Claude turned to look. In a corner were the eight beveled trunks, the ones with iron lacework. Jean-Marie was standing in front of them.

"Left for fire," he signed, first crossing his forearms in front of his body and then blowing on a finger, "but still good. They are still good."

Antoine wanted to kiss the old pack rat. "May I look inside?" he asked.

Jean-Marie opened the trunks himself. With anxious little grunts, he began digging through tattered brown wool; the old laybrother habits had been eaten to ruin by moths. After a pile of wool had been heaped next to him in the straw, an oil painting was uncovered at the bottom of one of the trunks. He stood aside for the monks.

The painting was obviously old; its frame was of carved oak, with a black patina left by many greasy hands. Tiny veins like the crackle glaze of a potter ran through the paint, either from stress or a varnish or a *tenebroso* applied over the oil. The subject was Saint Francis in ecstasy. His hands were raised in prayer, showing the wounds of his stigmata: a quiet, mystic spirit. Colors were pure, indeed luminous, despite the *tenebroso*. This Francis was not iconographic, like saints done by Giotto and El Greco, but vivid in the down-to-earth and dignified style of Caravaggio. Antoine was spellbound.

"Where did you find this painting?" he asked.

"Inside," Jean-Marie signed. "In the trunk. Almost burned. Picture still good."

The Abbot was informed about the horse barn junk, and the next day he went out to see it. On his way back he stopped in the kitchen. Antoine had decided to use the broiler for the first time, to toast cheese sandwiches, but the gas switch did not seem to work.

"Amazing," the Abbot said to him, "how much rubbish there is in there. I had no idea! Jean-Marie is so protective of his chickens, I haven't been in there for years. And how will I ever get him to part with all that trash? We certainly can't take it with us."

"Did you see the painting, Reverend Father?"

"The painting?" he asked. "Oh yes, the Saint Francis. Well,

that thing isn't much good to us now, is it? We're not Franciscans."

"But Reverend Father, it's obviously old. Maybe it's valuable."

Dom Jacques scratched behind an ear. "Perhaps," he said. "And it's a pity there are no Franciscans in the neighborhood to take it away."

Antoine argued to keep the lovely painting when Brother Camille stuck his head inside the kitchen door.

"Visitors to see you, Reverend Father," the young monk said. "I left them in the graveyard."

The Abbot turned to leave. "I can't allow Jean-Marie to keep all that rubbish," he said on his way to the door. "If I let him have the painting, he'll want everything else. And we have nowhere to put tin cans and plastic bottles." He left the room.

Antoine was appalled. "I'm *glad* there are no Franciscans around here," he whispered. Checking underneath the broiler hood, he saw that the pilot light was out. "Give that masterpiece away? I can't believe he didn't like it." Matches were in the drawer with the paring knives. After turning off the gas, Antoine counted to ten. He was down near the hood, his nose nearly touching the oven knobs.

"Eight one thousand, nine one thousand, ten." He sniffed but could smell no gas. He lit a match.

Boom.

With a start, he discovered himself on the other side of the kitchen, sitting on his cookbook.

"What?" he asked aloud, completely startled. His nose throbbed. The possibility of burns entered his head, and with a racing pulse he lifted a hand to his face. Eyebrows came off on his fingers in black ashy smears.

Antoine limped out of the kitchen into the hallway and made for a flight of stairs. After reaching the third floor, he walked into Father Jude's dispensary, where he knew the infirmarian would be collecting medicines. Pills were distributed before the noon meal. He needed Jude to look at his face.

Antoine's nose felt like a grilled pepper, and moisture slowly ran from a sticky line on his forehead. Feeling hot and faint, he bent toward the dispensary window to cool himself in a current of air. Below was the graveyard.

The Abbot was in the midst of discussing a contract with five gravediggers down there. He spoke in a pleasant, even jocular, tone. Antoine dabbed his nose with a handkerchief and listened.

"*Mais ouí!*" the Abbot said. "They thought their traveling days were over, but the lucky devils get a field trip."

The gravediggers laughed while the Abbot smiled and rubbed his hands together. He spoke to them in French. "Can you have them out by next week?" he asked.

"*Certainement,*" a gravedigger said. "We can have half of them out today. We have our machine over there. But the iron fence must go, and I can't guarantee the safety of the trees and the shrubs." Each workman held a shovel, and a backhoe was parked next to the fence. The Abbot looked around at the graves.

"Some of these people I knew," he said, "and they were not thin. You might need a crane." The men hooted and slapped each other's backs.

"Maybe we're just in time," one of them said. "They'd be wanting some fresh air by now!" Their shoulders shook and they doubled over. They continued to laugh until they were wiping their eyes, and while they did this, the Abbot handed them a contract. They signed it right there in the cemetery. When the head gravedigger returned the Abbot's pen, Dom Jacques Bouvray spoke.

"Just a little detail," he said, folding his copy of the agreement and tucking it into his habit pocket. "Three graves over there by the fence have more than one body in them." He used the French-Canadian verb *paqueter* to describe how the dead laybrothers were packed into the grave as if into a telephone booth. The diggers howled, holding their sides. They thought it was a joke.

Antoine turned from the window to see Father Jude. The priest, with his nurse's composure, registered no surprise at Antoine's face. He merely squinted, the better to study the burns.

"What happened?" he asked. "Tossing together *un dessert flambé?* I wouldn't be surprised. You've been spoiling us. I've gained eight pounds since you took over as cook."

Antoine winced when Jude touched his nose. A mirror from a drawer showed him that his eyebrows and eyelashes were gone. He had open wounds on his nose and forehead. Even the stubble on top of his head had been singed. Jude dressed him with bandages. When the last strip of gauze had been taped down, Antoine examined himself again; he looked as if he had come from a battlefield.

"The gravediggers are here," he said while he touched the bandages. Jude grunted.

"They're in for a surprise."

Both of them went to the window. The men below had already opened a grave, and the digger on the west end scraped black gumbo off his shovel blade with a trowel. Father Jude shook his head.

"That's awful," he said. "They'll have to pick through mud for those bones. How did the Abbot get them to sign a contract?" Antoine was still touching his bandages.

"He neglected to mention details and they didn't ask. I'm sure they assume everyone is buried in a coffin. Is that Brother Eli's grave they're opening?"

"No, I think it's Brother Paul Sicard's."

Antoine left the window and went back to the kitchen. The monks had eaten the soup from the stove, but no one had thought to look under the broiler for sandwiches. They were all there, the white bread as dry as pumice. For the rest of the afternoon he peeled potatoes while looking at the wall. Somewhere he had read that the monks of Athos judge the dead by the color of bones. The dead are exhumed on that remote peninsula for want of burial space and removed to an ossuary. If ivory-colored bones are found, it is assumed that the monk went to heaven; if discolored or black bones are found, they went to purgatory, or even perhaps to hell.

Antoine wondered about black bones and white bones. Did the monks of Athos place the black bones in the same ossuary with the white? Or did they have a separate room marked HEAVEN for the white, and a room marked PURGATORY for the black? Or perhaps the black bones were put in a DAMNED room, and the discolored in a LIMBO. He had several hours to think about this as he prepared supper, and when he was finished, he carefully washed his hands and worked hand lotion into them.

Brother Camille came rushing into the kitchen. "Come look at the grave," he said with wide eyes. He paused, breathing hard, and stretched his neck toward Antoine. "What happened to you?" he asked.

Antoine turned away and uncovered a pot. "Nothing," he said. "I don't feel like looking at any open graves just now. I'm cooking." He was humiliated. Not knowing how to use a broiler was embarrassing. And his face still hurt.

"But you *must* come," Camille said. "It's Brother Bernard. They've uncovered him. He's incorrupt. Honestly! He looks as though he went into the ground an hour ago."

"An hour? He was buried three years ago."

"I know, I know. But he's incorrupt. The gravediggers had to telephone for a coffin because they can't put him in the metal box with the other bones. If you don't come and see, you'll regret it. He'll go back into the ground and you won't see him again. He's incorrupt. He must be a saint! It's so exciting."

Antoine removed his apron and went outside. The diggers were coated with mud. In just a few hours they had opened half the graves, and now they stood in various holes picking through mud and returning the monks' glances with animosity. If a bone was found, it was thrown out of the hole to be stored in a single metal container. Some of the graves were so old they had nothing left in them, and hardly any of the skeletons remained complete. Antoine saw that old Father Louis Rondel, buried three years ago, had already disintegrated into bone in a rotting monk's habit. What remained of his skeleton was ivory-colored, with a remnant of scalp clinging to the skull. Nothing remained of Gabriel's habit. Bits of black flesh clung here and there to the orange-colored bones, with a green chain and medal around what was once his neck. Antoine saw the remains of Brother Paul Sicard, killed by a Holstein bull, Father Ignace Lacan, who died in a fire, and Father Bertrand Fréchette, who passed away a month before Antoine entered the abbey. Their gray skeletons fell apart as they were lifted out of graves. Remains all went into the heap in the metal repository. Bernard, however, was another matter.

His body seemed not to have decayed at all. The gravediggers asked if he had been buried recently, confused because the soil above him had been hard and they remembered no break in the turf. They lifted the body out of the ground and left it to rest beside the open hole. His white choir robe was dirty but not muddy. His section of the cemetery had remained dry. While mud coated the bones of Louis, Gabriel, and the others, Bernard was clean. His body had been buried in sand. His flesh was not desiccated, and neither were his clothes rotted. Antoine knelt to touch the corpse; it was cold, but the plump flesh of Bernard's hand between the thumb and index finger felt fresh as a chicken thigh ready for the pan.

Monks and gravediggers gathered around Bernard's body. No

one spoke. They watched as the Abbot lifted the handkerchief, the same piece of cloth Father Jude had placed over Bernard's face three years before, and underneath was that odd expression.

"That's not his smile," someone said.

"No. Bernard had a beautiful smile."

"The funeral parlor must have done that."

"Yes, I remember that odd expression at the funeral," said Brother Alphonse. "Must have been the undertaker who did it. You know, they did the same thing to my aunt."

"He looks like he's drunk," Father Philippe said.

Antoine glanced at the Abbot, but Dom Jacques Bouvray was digging in his pocket and did not appear to be listening. Then Antoine turned to study the metal repository heaped with bones. Some of them were off-white, some partially black, and others a weak but grotesque orange. What did this mean? He looked again at Bernard, who seemed fresh and rested after three years in the ground. Perhaps the sandy soil preserved him, Antoine thought. Perhaps his physical chemistry had something to do with his condition. The weather might have been unusual on the day of his burial. Bernard might have taken some kind of medication during his years that somehow preserved his body.

The Abbot stooped and began snipping at Bernard's choir cloak with manicure scissors. Antoine was astonished. The Abbot wanted a relic. It seemed he had already concluded that Bernard was a saint, and that the body had been miraculously preserved by God as a sign of great holiness.

A sudden breeze cooled Antoine's bandaged face and rushed like a sigh through the leaves above him. For a moment he felt as though he would float away, as though his spirit might leave his body and travel away to where Bernard had gone. He wanted to disappear. But when he looked at the faces of the living monks around him, he knew he could not go. A chasm existed between the living and the dead, and he was not ready to cross it.

These odd faces he knew so well, men in search of God, no different from Saint Anthony or all the holy monks of old, these men had come to a remarkable place called the abbey, not connected to earth by geography. The holy desert. *We have come to find God here,* he thought, *and we are breathing God. The holy desert is full of God.*

How easy it had been, Antoine realized, these years in the cloister, to construct a sweet little program of the spiritual life. He had tried again and again to frame his spiritual growth within the safe boundaries of his own preferences and talents, his aptitudes and the means he had at hand. But the grand scheme brushes all human construction aside. If he had succeeded, if his scheme had worked, he would have led a pleasant, happy but small life, harmless and sunk in mediocrity. But it never came to pass. The abbey was being uprooted. His brothers were on the move. All along, the real monastic life of a greater scheme had forced him to practice more than he had thought possible. Detachment, self-denial, charity, all these things that make saints, these had come to him in unanticipated ways. The life of the cloister had overturned all his little plans and arrangements, as well as his opinion about others. The manner of death, the expression on a dead man's face, the color of bones: Antoine knew that none of these things made a difference. He knew, also, looking at the faces of his brothers, that they would become saints, each of them. Either willingly or by force, God would make them saints.

Brother Camille's voice broke Antoine's meditation. "This is an act of God," he said, "and I think we ought to put the body in a glass coffin."

"A what?" the Abbot asked, straightening his back. He had collected his relic and wrapped the tiny piece of cloth in a clean handkerchief.

"His body ought to be exposed for all to see," Camille said. "We could build a shrine."

"Oh no," Brother Alphonse said. "Not with a grin like that. Do you want a drunken saint in a glass box? How can we display him if he looks like he died drinking gin? I say we bury him again."

"Yes, bury him," someone said.

"That's the respectable thing to do," another said.

The monks, together with the gravediggers, slowly lifted the body into an oak coffin. The Abbot himself readjusted the white handkerchief over Bernard's face and closed the lid.

Two days after the transfer of the graves, Omer and Lucie Seneschal bought Saint Francis. They were not art collectors, but offered fifty dollars because their son was afraid the painting might vanish into the back end of a garbage truck, along with Jean-Marie's plastic bottles and glass.

"I'm not wild about the painting," Madame Seneschal said, "but I do like the trunk it's in."

When Antoine explained that there were seven more just like it, Madame squealed. She wanted them all. Omer offered a thousand dollars and the Abbot accepted.

"On condition," he said, "that we can pry them away from Jean-Marie."

But Jean-Marie did not fuss over the trunks at all. He was perfectly satisfied as long as someone made use of his articles, still good for wear. As a bonus, he threw in several tin cans, most of them without labels and none ever opened.

For Dom Jacques, the sale meant eight fewer items to move. Each day, flatbeds of farm machinery, lumber, and fence posts left the yard for Bruxelles. Truckloads of forge and carpentry equipment were readied for shipment. The new abbey now had glass windows. And even before rooms were painted or wall socket plates screwed in, furniture was moved from St. Norbert and left in hallways.

Tamarack boards taken from the old hayloft had been used as wainscoting in new abbey rooms. Thick pine pillars were also salvaged and used. These rose thirty feet from the floor of the new church to support a roof, and rough-hewn pine pilasters bolted into place crisscrossed within a clerestory to carry its well of light ten feet higher than the rest of the roof.

The new brick abbey was nothing like the old, and it was not what the monks had hoped for. Choosing to build small, the community wanted something functional, carefully designed to suggest silence and a connection with nature, a living space that was completely natural. Dutifully, the architect gave them their stand of paper birch and the three moss-covered boulders in the *préau*. This garth was at once traditional, like the *préaux* of European monasteries, and also natural, as a virtually untouched parcel of land around which the building was constructed. As for the rest, the architect gave them a whitewashed, sterile, and curiously fortresslike environment. It was all supposed to be like Le Thoronet or Sénanque, which the architect had seen in France, but it seemed merely boxy and white. As much as Antoine tried, he could find no resemblance between the photographs of Sénanque, with its graceful arches and clean patterns, and the cubic living container they were moving into. His brothers seemed out of place, unable to gain their bearings within the cracker-box hallways. Perhaps, he thought, the monks had asked for too small a place, too little room for moving around. Windows were like portholes to the wide-open countryside. He wished that more of the building had been glass, opening up walls and ceilings. He did not like the fortresslike protection, incongruous as it was, miles from any city.

Almost immediately Antoine found refuge in the new graveyard. A gentle slope had been chosen for the place overlooking a good stretch of pastureland to the southwest. On the north and east, the graveyard was hidden from view by ash trees. Solitude there reminded him of country roads outside of St. Jean-Baptiste where, as a boy, he escaped a busy household. The air was fresh. The same cow parsnips waved in the breeze. So did periwinkle-like blue lettuce blossoms, and tall, whorled-leaf lances of purple loosestrife, delicate yellow prairie buckbeans, sturdy black-eyed Susans, wide petaled gumbo lilies, and tiny bedstraw and vetch.

Brother Bernard's grave was there. The spot was marked with a modest tombstone of ashen granite that had a small vein of pink running through it. *Bernard Touzin 1896–1978* was engraved. Remains of the other deceased monks had gone beneath a single marker, a tall block of the same ashen stone with fifty-eight names on it, though bones of fewer than half had been found. On that slope, in that graveyard, the living community intended to bury their dead without coffins, as had been done in St. Norbert, and Antoine knew his body would one day be placed there. His bones would dissolve into that hillside.

He certainly did not consider himself a saint, like Bernard, if finding a body intact was indeed a sign of sanctity. Father Claude pointed out, on one of their frequent trips in the U-Haul to Bruxelles, that in the Orthodox Catholic tradition, finding a body intact was a sign of demonic possession.

"My goodness," Antoine had said. "Don't expect me to believe that Bernard was possessed by the devil!"

"I'm simply pointing out differences in cultures," Claude replied. "We're edified by a body that hasn't decomposed, but they're horrified. They don't know what to do with it, so they exorcise and rebury it. In other words, white for us is black to them. Which really means that signs are relative and we shouldn't take them too seriously."

Antoine shook his head. "I don't understand," he said. "Did anything evil come from Bernard? Did anything harmful come from finding him incorrupt? Then how could his body be anything other than a concrete proof of holiness?"

Claude said he never claimed to be an authority on holiness. "Hell, I don't know what it means," he said. "I've never been much interested in miracles anyway. The way I look at it, you believe in God or you don't. And when it comes to Bernard, either you liked him or you didn't. Any peculiar event, like finding his body fresh after three years, will only confirm what's already in your heart. If you liked him, it means he was a saint. If you didn't, I suppose it means he was possessed."

Antoine remembered these words. And now, standing on the slope of the cemetery enjoying a warm afternoon breeze, he knew what *he* preferred to think about Bernard and about miracles.

The air had a honey scent of wild clover. Purple and white flowers waved with grass that had already headed out with seed. Practically everything he knew was a miracle: a blessing, something that enlarged his life.

A miracle was at his feet. A small, dense patch of flowers there had an amazing color. He had seen them before, summers ago, and to see them again was an event, a reawakening to how perfect a flower can be. The blossoms formed a chain, one above the other, on a stem, and each blossom had a scarlet tongue, a yellow powdery mouth, and five petals that were candy-striped, rose and pink. The plant was known as striped coralroot; it grew on dead remains of other vegetation in the soil.

Not far away, another miracle bloomed: the rush skeleton-plant. Each of its small florets grew on a leafless stem two feet tall and waved in the breeze like a butterfly. Indians soaked the stems and gave the infusion to mothers to drink, because it increased milk flow.

If a flower was not a miracle, he thought, then perhaps incense was, or at least the effect incense had on him. Inside the church, smoke curled up from a live coal to create a sweet smell of clove and resin and something else, almost like fresh fruit vaporizing. When this smell reached his nostrils — this humble ingredient, smoke — it instilled in him wordless prayer.

Miracles were also moments in choir when voices moved in a smooth and elegant synchrony, unearned and certainly not common to men who habitually sang flat, hanging on to the rhythm in a flabby, inattentive fashion, yawning each day over the prospect of singing sacred verse. And then suddenly, unaccountably, and sometimes for only a single antiphon, everyone sang with one voice, like a heavenly choir.

A miracle was picking up a book — perhaps Julian of Norwich or Jean-Baptiste St.-Jure — and gaining a connection so real, over distances and centuries, that he felt the book read him more than he the book.

These things were extraordinary. But were they miraculous? In a sense, all of life swims and glitters. If a miracle was prodigious, something highly unlikely to occur in the natural course of events, then blossoms, incense, singing, and books were not supernatural. If miracles were the result of an incredible combination of natural factors providentially arranged, all of life was miraculous.

From his pocket Antoine retrieved the small stone he kept there, next to his rosary; it was glossy, smooth, black, and about the size of a golf ball. Every scratch and bump on it was familiar to him. When he was a postulant, an immaculate faith was what he wanted, something that never wavered. But nowadays he knew that such a faith only meant freedom from doubt, a place where decisions are no longer necessary. He had wanted to dwell in the light of a faith with clearly defined boundaries, where right and wrong were obvious, where certainty was comfort. But none of it had come to pass. Instead, he had felt drawn, again and again, from truism to surprise, from wonderment to faith —

if faith it was — a sort of faith that dwells in darkness. He lived in darkness. At night, however, every speck of light is prodigious. The sky sparkles. And a falling star may as well hit the nearby field as anywhere else.

He left the stone on Bernard's grave. He was leaving a treasure, something he loved. But he was finished with it now. He had seen more amazing things than a falling star.

The next day, Monsieur and Madame Seneschal arrived for a visit. Antoine's grandmother was with them. The old lady had turned ninety but walked with energy around the new abbey, looking behind doorways and poking into closets. Antoine showed them into a parlor, still unpainted, with a raw light bulb hanging from a fixture.

"*Mon pit,*" his grandmother said, pinching his cheeks. "You've filled out. Your face is rosy, now that you're a cook." She was right. Antoine had gained weight. "This place," she said, "it's a hole in the wall compared to the other one, eh? Are you all moved in now?"

"Oh no, Grand-mère. The cows haven't made the trip. Brother Gennade is still in St. Norbert milking every day. But we're moving them on Friday, and the Abbot will release me from kitchen work to be with the animals. Some of them remember me, from when I worked in the barn, and I want to help. They can't become too upset."

"*Ah non,*" she answered. "Otherwise they will dry up. Me, I milked, too, in my day. Tell me nothing. I know. Sometimes I was pulling on four teats while a *petit suisse* was sucking on my own."

"Momma!" Madame Seneschal protested.

"But it's true. Why not say exactly the truth?"

Madame Seneschal and Grand-mère pulled two tables together and dressed them with a paper tablecloth. They had carried in napkins, cups, doughnuts with pots of butter and jelly, and a gigantic Thermos of coffee.

"What's all this?" Antoine asked. "I could have fed you."

Madam Seneschal waved his words away. "We came only on some business," she said. "Omer, get your nose out of that newspaper and come sit down."

Antoine's father had been reading all the while. Obediently he folded the paper into a heap and sat at the table for a cup of coffee. Before long, doughnuts were being chewed. No one spoke, and Antoine grew nervous.

"It must be serious," he said, "this business."

"It's about the trunks," Omer answered. "The eight trunks I paid a thousand dollars for, which I didn't want but your mother wanted."

Madame Seneschal shook her head and waved both hands while she chewed. Swallowing at last, she placed a delicate hand on her throat, then took a breath. "Be quiet, Omer," she said. "You'll get it all wrong. Besides, we drove all the way out here for what? So *I* could tell it in person. Otherwise, I could have phoned him up."

The grandmother protested. "Let me tell it," she said. "If you want it right, let me tell it."

Madame shook her head and looked at the ceiling. "I should have left you both at home," she said. "Who is the one who wanted the trunks in the first place? The one who talked her husband into buying them? Who got Bruno Allard to go to the abbey and pick them up?"

"*Ah oui,*" Grand-mère said, "but the one who knew right away the trunks were valuable is me." And she whispered loudly to Antoine. "I knew exactly where to go for a good price," she said. "Because me, I knew what they were worth."

"So anyway," Madame said, "before I was interrupted, I

wanted to say that we sold the trunks. One I wanted to keep. But the buyer upped the price. We made a little money."

Grand-mère poked Antoine. "Which they will give back to you, my favorite grandson, because it's a sin to steal from the monks their money." She was beaming.

"Oh no," Antoine said. "You don't owe us money. You paid for the trunks."

Grand-mère poked him again. "They robbed you," she said in French. "For your information, they robbed an only son. How could I rest knowing that?"

Omer was writing a check. Madame Seneschal lit a cigarette and waved it in front of her mother. "The trunks belonged to the abbey, not to him," she said in English. "And to the abbey of course we would've given the money."

"But all of it?" Grand-mère asked, her eyebrows raised high. "There, you should be thankful," she said, turning back to Antoine, "that somebody else did not carry off these trunks."

"I'm thankful they were not burned," Antoine said.

The check went from Omer into Madame's hands, then from her to the grandmother, who scrutinized it carefully before handing it over to Antoine.

"It's made out to the abbey," he said. "That's good. But you have the zeros in the wrong place."

The grandmother grabbed the check again and looked at it. "*Exactement*," she said, handing it back.

Madame Seneschal blew smoke. "We quadrupled your money," she said proudly.

As for the painting — Francis in ecstasy — she explained that she hung it in her water closet. But Omer became annoyed by the presence of a saint whenever he had to do his business, and it was removed to a nail on the pantry door. Hanging there, absorbing flour dust, it was noticed by a Friday night bridge player who also happened to a member of the Ladies Auxiliary for the

Winnipeg Art Gallery. When she brought the painting in, with Madame's permission, it was identified as Spanish Baroque, somewhere perhaps between 1620 and 1640, certainly not a Velázquez, but very likely a contemporary of his by the name of Francisco de Zurbarán.

"What else could I do?" Madame Seneschal asked Antoine. "I left the painting at the gallery. Such a thing is valuable? They said if I loaned it to them for eight years, they'd verify it, whether or not it's genuine."

Antoine shrugged. "It's yours," he said. "You bought it."

His relatives looked at one another. Without a word, Madame Seneschal finished her cigarette, snuffed it inside an old compact case she used for an ashtray, and shoved the compact in her purse.

"I suppose we paid money for it," she said, "but there's no bill of sale. No proof of ownership."

Omer looked at his son. "It might be a good idea for Dom Jacques to check abbey records to find out where that painting comes from," he said. "Folks at the gallery say if the saint is genuine, it's worth somewheres around a quarter million dollars."

The grandmother poked Antoine in the ribs. "Did you hear that?" she asked.

On the day the cows were transported, Antoine said good-bye to the old abbey. Before sunrise, Brothers Gennade and Théodore had done their regular milking, and by the time the cows were customarily let out to pasture, two double-axle, single-unit truck trailers pulled into the yard. Antoine was right behind them, in the abbey's green 1973 Chevrolet.

The cows hesitated at the trailer gate with bulging eyes. Turning their heads to look behind them, they opened their mouths and lowed as if asking a question. The monks took their halters. One after the other, Claudine, Daphné, Françoise, Bernadette,

Josephine, Nadine, and the rest were guided into the trailer by the monks. Antoine slapped a rump here, a withers there, raising dust, and cows calmed, chewing again whatever it was they had eaten that morning.

The bulls misbehaved. No sooner had they been loaded into the second trailer than Julius rammed the gate. He escaped with Caesar and the calves. They ran through an empty garden to the cheese house, veered off, and nearly mounted the steps of the church before swerving to run around the empty abbey. They disappeared in the woods by the river.

The two truck drivers stationed themselves by the gatehouse. The big iron gate had already been removed to Bruxelles, and Gennade feared that the bulls might come out of the woods and run down the road toward St. Norbert. As soon as Théodore entered the woods, the bulls appeared again not far away, surrounded by the calves as if baby-sitting. Antoine took after them with a switch.

All the while, the cows, watching from their uncomfortable position in the trailer, began to bellow as a chorus, protesting their inability to join in. The calves responded instinctively, racing across the yard and down the farm road to their mothers. The bulls also registered interest. Ignoring Antoine's switch, they celebrated the female bellowing by jousting with each other, raising dust on the road and in the orchard, and raking up huge chunks of turf near the old seminary house. By the time Théodore reappeared, drenched in sweat and exhausted, the bulls trotted off to investigate the cows and stood attentively next to the truck trailers, sticking their tongues through the metal laths in an effort to reach them.

Because of a bent rod, the trailer gate had to be rigged, and this meant further delay. The bulls and the calves were ushered into their trailer once again. Equipment for repairs was in Bruxelles. Théodore, Gennade, and the two drivers argued back and forth about how to secure the gate, and when they could not agree Antoine asked if he might have one last look around.

"Fifteen minutes," Brother Gennade said. "That's all. The cows have a long ride ahead of them, and they don't need to wait for you." He and the truck drivers began threading wire through the trailer gate to keep it closed. "We should be finished here shortly. Théodore and I want to be in Bruxelles ahead of the trucks."

With so little time, Antoine walked quickly toward the church. He could have chosen the cheese house, or his favorite haunts near the river. Irène's bones still lay in the pasture, but he knew there was practically nothing of them left. Of all the places that had become a part of him — worn and familiar spots that made daily life a pleasure — he chose the church.

Pushing the front door open, he climbed the stairs to the balcony. The place was silent except for muted sounds of birds outside the windows. The wooden benches had been left behind. They were coated with dust. Antoine stood at the loft railing. The church reminded him of a high forest canopy, the way the nave arcade ran into the Romanesque vaulting. A faint sweet smell hung in the air like the remnant of a cedar fire, but the choir stalls below were empty.

He did not know, then, that the neglected church would soon catch fire because of vagrants cooking in the sanctuary, that flames would engulf the oak choir stalls, melt the windows, and cause the roof to collapse. The old abbey would soon be a ruin. And Antoine would never know that another Zurbarán, of the Holy Family, was destined to be lost forever, hidden as it was in the church attic above the cross vaults; it had been put there in 1904 by Brother Ovide — long since dead — who had been Henri de Courcelle de St.-Vannes, Comte de Boussac, before becoming a laybrother to do penance for his sins. He sold an estate in France to pay off the debts of the St. Norbert Cistercians, debt incurred by building that very church, and the only two items he kept were two paintings by Zurbarán. Ovide was horrified when the superior hung Saint Francis in the attic *vestiaire,* so he hid the other painting — the Holy Family — in the attic, neglecting to tell anyone about it before his death.

Antoine knew none of this. He knew only *his* story, and how he loved *this* place more than was perhaps good for him. A monk, after all, ought to be detached from the world and from everything in it, turning his eyes ceaselessly toward heaven.

The Monks

at the time of Brother Antoine's novitiate,
in order of seniority

Dom Jacques Bouvray, abbot, 50 years old
Fr. Anselme Rosier, prior, beekeeper, 60
Fr. Auguste Boillot, sub-prior, laundry, 48
Fr. Yves-Marie Morice, novice master, 45
Fr. Marie-Nizier Delorme, retired, 88
Fr. Cyprien Crey, wine cellar, 88
Fr. Louis Rondel, cobbler, 82
Br. Gabriel Eremasi, pig barn, 93
Br. Eli Baudrillard, retired, 80
Fr. Denys St.-Pieters, mailman, 78
Br. Bernard Touzin, scullery, 78
Br. Henri Artignan, gatekeeper, 75
Fr. Claude Joly, cook, 73
Fr. Ignace Lacan, retired, 71
Br. Norbert Gignoux, forge, 70
Fr. Aubert Pollard, confessor, sacristan, 68
Fr. Pierre Ollier, bursar, 65
Fr. Alcide Goupillard, retired, 63
Fr. Joseph Castinié, retired, 88
Br. Emery Terrien, forge, 63
Fr. Jude Sanders, infirmarian, 58
Fr. Jean-Marie Orève, poultry barn, 56
Br. Edouard Fouace, carpenter, 56
Fr. Philippe Fluet, forge, beef cattle, 56
Fr. Casimir Cochard, refectorian, cheese maker, 53
Br. Jules Rémy, farm, 53
Br. Gennade Couligner, dairy, 48
Fr. Théodore Levasseur, dairy, 45

Br. Roland Roy, garden, 45
Br. Alphonse Soubeyran, mechanic, 42
Fr. Véran Michel, library, 38
Br. François Luneau, music, outside errands, 35
Br. Martin Brown, baker, 32
Br. Paul Sicard, barber, dairy, 28
Br. Sauveur Conil, housekeeping, 28
Br. Camille André, organist, 26
Br. Simon Montmayeur, flowers and gardens, 23
Br. Antoine Seneschal, novice, 20
Br. Dominique Moulin, novice, 24
Charles Frémont, postulant, 23